Signs of Portents

Greystone Book One

Lou Paduano

Eleven Ten Publishing
BUFFALO, NEW YORK

Copyright © 2016 by Lou Paduano
All rights reserved. This book or any portion thereof may not be reproduced or used in any manner whatsoever without the express written permission of the publisher except for the use of brief quotations in a book review.

Eleven Ten Publishing
P.O. Box 1914
Buffalo, NY 14226

Publisher's note: This is a work of fiction. Names, characters, places, and incidents either are the product of the author's imagination or are used fictitiously. Any resemblance to actual events, locales, or persons, living or dead, is entirely coincidental.

Printed in the United States of America
Edited, formatted, and interior design by Kristen Corrects, Inc.
Cover art design by Kit Foster Design
First edition published 2016

Library of Congress Cataloguing in Publication Data
Paduano, Lou
Signs of Portents / Lou Paduano
p. cm.
LCCN: 2016946406
ISBN-13: 978-1-944965-00-6 (paperback)
ISBN-13: 978-1-944965-01-3 (eBook)

For Melinda

Always

PROLOGUE ONE
Eighteen Years Ago

There were freshly fallen leaves under her feet. The chill of autumn had entered the city quickly, giving no time for transition from the beach lovers to the nature lovers. Not that this was unusual by any means. It was the *sound* of the leaves that seemed uneasy to her ears. They did not crunch heavily or slide out from under her heel with the slickness of a mid-morning rainfall. They broke and cracked under her miniscule weight and the additional mass of the doll she carried by the hair in her left hand.

Blond. That was the color of the doll's hair she gripped so tightly. She had named her Lady of all names. Not terribly creative, but there was no doubt that it was cute for a four-year-old. The doll had been her companion through many seasons, taking the prerequisite beating that any toddler placed on their possessions. A missing eye, patchwork hair, and three busted seams made the doll unique, special, and no less important in the eyes of the child. The girl and her doll looked at each other, hearing the cracking sound of the leaves, hoping one of them would have the answer. Both, however, were silent.

A strong wind rushed through the air, brisk October weather that paved the way for the snowy November to come. The autumn leaves took to the skies, propelled by the gale, above the young girl. The leaves were dynamic, forming a myriad of colors above her. It made her smile, the colors that surrounded her. It would be a long time before she smiled again.

As the colors continued to brighten before her, as the leaves carried along by the wind swept around her, she realized the bright oranges and nuanced reds were not natural. They were not the autumn leaves that made up piles along the roads to jump in before the city workers could take them away. They did not crunch under her heels with each shift in position. No, these leaves were not meant to see the end of the season. Not meant to be admired for their beauty and color.

These leaves were charred.

The crackling sound overhead emanating from the leaves blowing in the wind was the sound of small flames still burning through each one. Lady was the first to realize this and the girl saw it through the glass eye that hung on to the doll's sewn face. If horror could have been written on her patchwork face, it would have, but still she smiled at her owner the same as she always had.

Behind her, a van continued to burn. The flames engulfed the tree it was wrapped around on the side of the large curve at the city limits of a place called Portents. The front half of the van was no more than a wall of fire and heavy smoke. The tree had suffered greatly, half of it gone in an instant, a giant matchstick helping spread the destruction.

The young girl stood twenty feet away, unsure of the ordeal, unaware of her role in it. It was the same way the emergency workers that surrounded the scene felt, roping off the area and attempting to clean up the accident as quickly as possible. Fire crews arrived late from the mid-morning traffic but worked quickly to put out the growing flames before they spread to the rest of the park that covered the eastern border of the city. Medics on scene found their role to be minimal, another set of witnesses and nothing more. Their only living patient was the young girl standing in the center of the road with her doll and not a scratch on her.

Attempts had been made to pull her away from the scene. After checking her vitals, everyone had taken a turn, offering quiet words of comfort and a hand to hold. No words were heard. No hands taken. The girl simply stood in place, Lady by her side, the van quietly burning behind her.

Words continued to be spoken between officers and EMTs who then mingled with the Fire and Rescue teams that arrived on the scene once traffic permitted. Most barely noticed the girl among the wreckage.

"She hasn't said a word. Doesn't even look at it like it's there," one of the EMTs said to his compatriot, a balding man with thin-rimmed glasses.

"You said her folks were in there?" the balding man replied, fixing his glasses to the bridge of his nose.

"Looks that way," said the first man. His voice was low and he turned away from the young girl. "Pulled two bodies out. They'll be lucky to pull dental records off of them though."

"Road isn't even slick." Another voice entered the fray, more distant than the others. "How fast were they going to do this?"

"What were they running from?"

The first man's response caught her ear but she did not turn. "She doesn't even know yet."

"Poor girl."

She heard those words clearly over the sounds of the sirens and the hoses and the chaos of the bend outside the city limits of Portents. They did not matter, however. None of them mattered. She was lost in the glowing air that sung sweetly along the autumn breeze, the leaves dancing before her, swirling in the air with a radiance she would never see again in her lifetime. One caught a second wind and raced back in the direction it came from.

She turned back to the accident for the first time. The van was unrecognizable from the midsection to the front, a charred memory that would never stick. The single leaf fell before her along the street, and her foot stopped its movement when something caught her eye under the singed shell of the van.

Slipping under the caution tape, through the overworked men and women on the scene, the girl moved like a wraith toward the wreck. No one saw her. No one tried to see her. The object was small, curled up tightly near the front wheels of the burning van that looked more like tar along the edge of the road. Something pulled her forward. She had to have the object. In that instant there was nothing else in her universe.

Lady slipped from her grasp in the excitement and found her final resting place among the charred leaves in the road—a third victim of the accident. Another piece of her life slipped away like the rest of her memory.

The young girl did not care. She raced faster toward the vehicle, crouching low beneath the flaming frame of the van. Her small hand grabbed the object and held it up so she could get a better look. It was cold to the touch, even among the flames that had surrounded it. She had never seen it before in her life. It was small and rounded with smooth, unmarked surfaces on all sides. As she

3

turned it over in her hands with wide eyes of wonderment, she thought for a split second that there was something written upon its face. She blinked deeply, passing it off to imagination. She held it before her once more.

A simple stone of grey.

PROLOGUE TWO
Four Years Ago

Greg Loren felt every dip and crack in the pavement through the worn-out soles of his Nikes, stepping out of the grocery store at Richmond Knoll. Down the Knoll, he saw the evening traffic coasting off the expressway into the Kings Lane district of the city, home to the second-floor apartment he rented. The names of streets, exits, and businesses flashed on signs, billboards, and taxicabs. The signs were the only way he could survive in the city. Even after living in Portents for the last six years, he still found himself turned around through the maze of downtown.

"It was designed that way," Beth always said with a smile at seeing his scruffy face round the corner, pouting at running late once again after taking the East End stop of the D line train instead of the East End stop of the A line. The city funneled into downtown like a garden maze, a myriad of dead-end turns and a dozen paths that flowed directly to the shining black tower that stood at the center of the city, never to Loren's destination of choice.

"Let's move there then," Loren said, jokingly. "We'd never get lost."

Beth never answered his jests. She tucked another set of maps into his bag or a handwritten note in the pack of smokes he swore would be his last.

He reached into the grocery bag when he passed the Kings Lane sign and pulled out the latest of the last packs of cigarettes. It fit nicely with the salad ingredients he stopped for earlier to surprise Beth with a healthy meal. He beat the unopened pack squarely against his palm three times then tore into the wrapper for a post-shift break from reality. It had been another long day at the precinct. The fourth in a row since what was dubbed the "Kindly Killings" struck the city. The case landed square at his feet even though he imagined it had been inserted somewhere completely inappropriate, because after four days of witness testimony and chasing his tail, Loren swore he walked with a waddle.

That was how it went in Portents. Murder and mayhem reigned supreme. Normality was cracking skulls and pounding pavement to find a way to stop it all from spinning completely out of control when everything around you said differently.

Thankfully, he had Beth.

Beth, whose smile rose with the sun and never faded even in the dead of night. This was her city and she saw it in a way he never understood. Hopeful. Proud. Where he saw madness and dreamed of running away, she saw people, places, and history. That was her gift to him. Hope. He had to marry her. There was never any question in his mind. From that first moment she made him smile, wearing a milkshake mustache and a sundress. Even though every instinct told him to escape the city, he stayed for her. Shadows seemed to lighten when she was around and he needed that every night he found himself walking the streets alone, searching for another indescribable beast to throw behind bars. She made it safer just by being with him. That was enough to keep him going.

Rubbing out the butt of his cigarette with his shoe, Loren felt a change in the air. As he bent down to lift the butt from the ground to toss it in the nearest corner receptacle, he had no doubt something had changed. Traffic had stalled down his street. Not a "Breaking News Update" by any means, but the fact that some had been vacated of passengers struck Loren as bizarre. Pedestrians had slowed to a crawl in their travels down Brockton Avenue, their eyes looking toward a four-story brick apartment building sandwiched between a deli and a Laundromat.

Loren's apartment building.

He rushed over to the mounting crowd of people as fast as his feet would carry him. Each footfall felt like a hundred yards. Each second that passed felt like an hour. Something had happened. Not to anyone else in the building. He knew, no matter how light the shadows had become since meeting her, he knew that something had happened to Beth.

"Excuse me," Loren said, shuffling through the crowd. He clutched firmly to the two bags of groceries to keep them from getting lost in the melee. He needed them to make dinner for Beth. He held onto that thought tighter than his grip on the thin plastic of the bags. "Please let me through. Police officer."

No one questioned this fact. They simply took a step to the right or left of him, their eyes never leaving the center of the crowd. Murmurs made their way through, whispers and rumors that Loren was afraid to hear.

"She just...she just fell," one woman said, pointing up toward the roof of the building.

Loren noticed the window to their apartment leading to the living room was open. Beth loved having it open to cool off the place and to hear the sounds of the city in the evening. *Portents never comes to life before sunset*, she'd say.

"Ambulance is on the way," a man said from Loren's right. Loren looked to the young boy beside him, holding him close. "I heard someone call but—"

"Not going to matter, I think," an older gentleman said, finishing his sentence.

Loren continued past him, his eyes catching the man's before slipping into the center of the crowd. After everything was said and done, when the crowd had dispersed and the day had ended, Loren saw those eyes in his sleep. Those sad eyes that had seen more than any man should in his lifetime. They were eyes that would never leave Loren.

A lone woman lay upon the sidewalk in the open circle, surrounded by onlookers. She stared up into the growing darkness of the Portents sky. Blood curled by her thin, pink lips and ran down to meet her blond hair that spread wide against the pavement. She wore an apron over what Loren knew to be a red sundress with rose print trim.

"Beth." The name escaped his lips. His groceries slipped from his hands. A romantic salad dinner that never had a chance to be made.

Loren fell to his knees beside her. He tried to lift her head, to hold her close, but felt nothing solid to grab onto under her stained blond hair. He could feel the tears stinging his cheeks, sirens blaring in the distance.

Too far away.

Too far gone.

Her hand grazed his cheek, pulling him back to her. Her dark blue eyes were oceans of calm staring up at him. She smiled through the blood. Her chest heaved under collapsed bones. Too shallow. Too slow.

He needed to know. His mouth opened once, then twice, all to ask the dozen questions that he would bring to the table at any other crime scene he investigated—but nothing came out. There were no words. Only tears.

His hand rested softly on her cheek. Her lips moved to speak and he bent closer. Beth continued to smile, her words lost behind the noise of the approaching sirens and the murmurs of the crowd. Lost behind the beating of his own heart in his ears.

All that remained was her smile when Beth's eyes closed for the last time.

Shadows darkened in the city of Portents as her smile carried her away from Detective Greg Loren forever.

CHAPTER ONE

Rain poured against the city of Portents, threatening to wash it clean. It beat against the tallest skyscrapers and the smallest row of houses along the East Side. It pitter-pattered on awnings and sewer grates alike, all of it flowing down and settling in a series of large puddles throughout the city. The warehouse district of the city felt it most, the band of clouds hanging around for hours after sunset. Where bright lights from the nearby club scene stemmed the tide against the torrent of raindrops, in the warehouse district of Portents where darkness was constant, rain meant clouds, which equaled more shadows.

Vladimir Luchik hated the rain. It was the way it chilled his bones, the way it slammed the top of his head like a jackhammer, and the way it never, ever could miss the opportunity to knock him further down when he could not possibly need the help. He could feel it in his sneakers. He could feel it soaked along his ripped jeans. He always hated the rain.

Tonight, however, he hated the shadows more.

Every corner he passed, every alleyway, was a threat. Shadows surrounded him, each step betraying his need for stealth. Water splashed under his heels, soaking his pants further. Still he pressed forward. His movements were slow, his feet sluggish and heavy. Sweat mixed with the raindrops. *How far had he come since it started?* He wondered but was afraid to look at the path he had traveled, afraid of the darkness that surrounded him on all sides. It was still coming for him. He could feel its breath on the back of his neck, could hear its eerie laughter over the sound of his heart pounding in his chest. He needed help and was in the worst place to find it.

The warehouse district was not known for being a hotspot of activity during the daylight hours. Most of the structures surrounding the small residential complexes near the rail yards had long since been shut down or abandoned. Some were reconditioned for office space, but none operated at night. Few people did in Portents; it was an unspoken instinctual rule of the city.

"Dammit," he cursed under his breath, then again for the pain that cut right through his abdomen. He reached into his pocket and found his cell phone. The damn cell phone. The reason he had been out in the first place. She was waiting for his call. *Anything for a girl*, he always said. He was looking to help her with a case, but found something else instead. Now he needed the help. Glaring down at the cracked screen, the rain pelting against it, he knew that help was not coming.

Something shattered the silence behind him and his heart stopped in his chest. He ducked into a nearby alley, whirling back toward the empty street. *Was it him? Could it even be called a him?* A large metal garbage can rolled along the sidewalk across the street, its displaced lid flopping along the pavement. The sound echoed down the large street but no one was near.

"Rats," he muttered. "Giant damn rats. Has to be." His left hand slipped from his abdomen for the first time since he started running. Instinctively he reached out to the nearby brick wall to brace his weatherworn body. He took the moment, letting his breathing slow and his heart calm from the pace. His head fell low, spit mixing with the rain running down the length of his chin. It flowed into the puddles beneath him. Puddles that were not clear, running deep and dark in swirls and spreading outward.

Blood.

His eyes shot to his left hand to see the same dark red substance dripping from his fingertips and down the brick wall.

His blood.

A streak of lightning cut the sky above, shining a thin light from the heavens so Vladimir could see the damage sustained. His attacker was quick but effective. Five thick gashes spread across his chest and abdomen, covered in the thick red blood that he then trailed along the ground down the city streets for anyone to follow. He hoped *anyone* meant that a Good Samaritan would rescue him from his plight and take him somewhere safe and warm. Maybe it would be a red-haired vixen with a penchant for bleeding men, wearing something slightly revealing and speaking with an accent.

Nothing too exotic. Maybe Irish. Of course, Vladimir knew better. His version of anyone following meant the beast tracking his every movement.

The garbage can clatter finally faded yet something still did not feel right to Vladimir. The shadows shifted across the street, deepening in darkness. As another bolt cut the sky, he swore he saw something swing back farther to go unseen. The bleeding man stepped deeper into the alley, leaving behind the large block letters that painted along the side of the building a single word. A name.

Evans.

At the far end of the alley, there was a large fire escape. Vladimir clutched tight to his wounds, hoping the rainwater would help keep them somewhat clean long enough for him to find cover for the night. Hope was elusive but it kept his feet from slipping along the pavement. It kept his hands from falling off the steep ladder of the fire escape while he climbed. It kept him sane.

At the first level of the fire escape was a large window, shattered like so many others that lined the streets. Broken glass lay within the thick frame and he was careful not to add any more wounds to his battered body. He felt weightless for a moment, his body hovering in the open air before he slammed against the wood flooring. Vladimir saw a wide, open space. A cavernous room stretched hundreds of feet. He had no idea what was once present in the room and the shattered glass had removed any foul odors that were once trapped within the building. Spiders were the prime residents of the warehouse from what Vladimir noted, trying to find his footing once more. He made his way slowly, each step echoing loudly against the floor.

Across the room a single staircase led to a row of second floor offices. Vladimir's eyes flitted back toward the broken window every time the lightning split the darkness, waiting for a chance to see his attacker, praying it would never come.

Nothing.

The uneasy feeling remained, even as he climbed the metal staircase. It creaked and moaned so loudly on the first step that Vladimir thought the whole structure might collapse. The second step was the same. Taking a deep breath, the young man calmed his shaking body. He lifted his foot slowly and let it slide along the next step. He ran his free hand along the rail and, using his upper body, lifted up his tired frame until his left foot joined his right.

There were no loud crashes this time. Vladimir breathed deeply, staring up at the dozen steps ahead, and pushed onward.

The largest office appeared to be the one farthest from the stairs. It was the perfect place to find cover for the night. The stairs alone would give enough warning; if not, the echoes reported each movement throughout the long-forgotten building. The office itself held all of its original furniture, unlike the main floor below. Dust-covered filing cabinets lined the right wall with a large desk pushed in front of them and out of the way. Across the room from the door, a row of shattered windows and broken shades stretched along the office. Vladimir closed the door behind him and entered the space, breathing easier.

He slipped out of his soaked shirt and wrung out the blood and rain on the wooden floorboards beneath him. The movement was agony for him but it needed to be done. He then took the shirt and wrapped it tightly around his abdomen, tying the sleeves into a knot. He screamed, feeling blood along his lips. The pain caused his knees to give way and his body fell with a loud crash. The agony continued for a long moment, a small smear of fresh blood filling the shirt. Still, Vladimir Luchik found the will to smile at having made it to safety.

The sentiment was fleeting.

It came along the cool, early summer wind. The smell of ashes and death. The smell of something old. Vladimir's eyes shot open, scanning the room while still tracking the scent. Shadows surrounded him. Shadows that did not seem so ominous moments earlier. In the darkness of the left-hand wall near the corner of the office, he saw them. Saw them and knew there was no more running in the cards for him. He saw two specks of light and knew the end had come for him. They were small and round, one of deep crimson and the other of sky blue.

Eyes.

"It's you, isn't it?" Vladimir called to the two mismatched lights surrounded by shadows. His voice carried out to the main floor of the building and echoed. "I can feel you. I can smell the death on you."

His knees shook as he struggled to rise once more. Defiantly, he shouted into the darkness. "You're there, aren't you?"

Lightning crashed outside, the thin light revealing a form in the shadows. The shadow answered Vladimir softly.

"Yes."

The bleeding man rubbed his temple. He tried to focus through the pain in his gut and the throbbing in his head. He looked around the room and saw everything clearly for the first time. There were fresh scuffmarks along the floor from where the desk had been initially positioned. They were smeared, however, by something else. Something, Vlad realized, surrounding him on all sides in red.

Blood red.

"You led me here," Vlad said to the darkness. He finally understood the merry chase he had been a part of was simply leading to this moment. His last moment. "You wanted this place."

"Yes."

His moment arrived. It came in the silence caught between them. It came without pomp and pageantry or the three-ring circus Vlad imagined pounding in every thought he carried. Vladimir Luchik saw his moment before him in the eyes of the creature that had hunted him all evening. He thought of his phone and the call he never had the chance to make. He thought of the woman at the other end of that call and of the strange grey stone she carried with her at all times, and how he would never see her again. He thought of missed opportunities and false hopes in a life never truly lived. Not the way it should have been. He thought of all of that in the shortest of seconds before screaming and charging at his attacker with every ounce of strength that remained within his tired, battered frame. He screamed the only question he wanted answered before the end.

"Who are you?"

He entered the shadows, his hands reaching into the dark for his assailant. They came back empty. The two eyes glowed deeper in the dark. With a single swipe and a bloodcurdling cry that echoed through the empty streets of the warehouse district on the east end of the city, Vladimir Luchik said no more.

"I am the end," answered the shadow that stood over his lifeless body. "And the beginning."

CHAPTER TWO

The apartment was packed months ago. The furniture sold, the mattress tossed. Every book, dish, and utensil boxed up and labeled. Life had vacated the second floor apartment in the Kings Lane district of Portents years earlier, the remnants of which waited until the lease finally inched toward expiration. Greg Loren stood among the wreckage of the life he once lived, the floorboards creaking under his shifting weight. He stared obsessively into the mirror that hung above the fireplace in the living room he once shared with his wife.

Who are you? It was a question he asked daily to the unshaven face. He used to clean up every day he could. It was ritual. It was important. For his life. For his job. For Beth. However, after she died, the rituals slipped away. Everything slipped away. Through the dark blond hair covering his chin and cheeks, Loren saw lines he had never seen previously. More lines than there used to be when he looked through old photo albums with Beth and laughed at the stupid poses they created for each one. The lines were deeper, thicker even. They belonged to an older man, not one shy of thirty-six.

Dirty blond hair hung low over his ears. Thin, brown eyes continued to stare blankly in the mirror, waiting for the answers to appear magically. Loren leaned heavily on the mantel of the fireplace, his shoulders slumped from the weight. Even through the dust covering the mirror he saw he needed to clean up and change. The riddled-with-holes Superman shirt hung well below his neckline and a few chest hairs joined the mix with his growing beard. It all added up to one thing in his mind.

It was time to leave.

The boxes surrounded him on all sides. Mementos of Beth and the life they had shared. Most were better left forgotten and were labeled for the garbage. Others—the dishes and utensils they used for meals on the couch and *Monk* marathons when they found they were afforded a weekend by their city jobs—were all headed to Goodwill for a loving family. He did not need them. He did not want them.

Some were labeled to make the trip with him. Books she had kept close to her—some for pleasure that still carried the scent of her soap in the pages, some for work as a local historian that contained her handwritten notes in the margins. They were her version of a diary and he refused to let them go. Those boxes and the few of his own possessions that failed to make the original trip east were the only items headed to his new home.

Chicago.

Funny to call it a new home when it was first for him. Born and raised Cubs fan. Home to his family and people he had not known as friends for a long time. Still, it felt good. It definitely was needed. There had been bright moments in the last three months since he departed Portents in the silence of the overnight train. A new job. A new apartment, thankfully keeping him from knocking on his sister's door with his head low. Work even overlooked the mistakes of his past, giving him the fresh start he needed to drown out the memories of Portents. Not everything was going right but that could be said of most people. The reminders were there at the periphery. It had only been three months. Still, the change felt incomplete. The door to Portents remained open, holding him back. Now that the final weeks of the lease were drawing to a close, he hoped the door would slam shut behind him.

He knew the likely culprit. It surrounded him on all sides but mostly it sat in the small duffel bag near the entrance to the apartment. He carried the file wherever he went. Beth's killer was still out there. In four years, there had been no break in the case. Half of that time was spent making sure the case was not filed as a suicide for the circumstances she was found in that evening. The other half was spent doing things Loren wanted more than anything to forget ever happened. Lines were crossed in the dark and he was lost for a long time.

That can never happen again, the stranger in the mirror reiterated back to the tired face of Greg Loren. *It's time to leave.*

Across the mantel, Loren's cell phone started to vibrate loudly. His hand was quick to snatch the small device before it fell to the floor but he hesitated to answer after looking to the display. It was a number he was hoping not to hear from until he had passed the city limits near the old charred tree on Olcott's Curve. He surrendered to the infernal vibrating device and hit the *Talk* button.

"Heard you were in town," the voice said immediately before Loren could greet the caller. Captain Alejo Ruiz's voice was cut thin by the sound of the wind, but Loren heard the smile creeping into his words. "I could use your help."

"Wish I could, Captain," Loren replied, watching the words flow from the lips in the mirror. "Pretty busy."

There was a slight pause on the line and Loren could hear metal clanging in the background before Ruiz returned to the call.

"Staring at your face in the mirror, wearing that rag that hasn't had the right to call itself a shirt in a decade? Definitely sound pretty busy to me."

Loren wheeled around. "Where the hell?"

It took him only a moment before he realized. Loren made a beeline for the window at the far end of the kitchen. He opened it up, letting the evening traffic sounds of the city fill the apartment. Crouching on the fire escape that led down to the side alley of the apartment was a middle aged, cocoa-skinned Hispanic with a grin spread across his face.

"I went to the trouble of climbing up here," Ruiz said. He closed his phone and slipped it back into his pocket. "May as well let me in."

CHAPTER THREE

Ruiz paced around the apartment. Loren stepped back, close to the mantel in the living room, watching his friend and colleague knowingly. Ruiz was methodical, never speaking, simply taking in the apartment. The boxes. The lack of furniture. When he looked at Loren, it was a quick glance, not wanting him to see the concern in his eyes though it was difficult to avoid.

Loren was studying his friend as well. Ruiz always wore the old dog look when he was deep in thought; it was not a new addition in his late forties. The graying hair, matted down on his head and slowly receding back and to the sides. Larger cheeks and a wider frame from a life of paperwork and politics in the captain's arena. Now, though, he seemed worse for wear even after only three months apart. Hair that once held tight to a thin black nature had surrendered completely to gray. The smile that he once carried through the workplace, the one that said, "When the dinner bell rings I'm going home to the greatest family on Earth, so who gives a crap about all of you and all this bull" was now sullen. However, it was the bags under his eyes that Loren had never seen before. Thick dark circles that swallowed his eyes unless the light shined directly on his face.

"No furniture?" Ruiz asked, lifting two books from the box closest to him. He put one back immediately but held tight to one of Beth's favorite works, one she helped put together about the history of the city, something Loren always promised to look at but never had time for in all their years together. *There is a level of understanding that comes from looking at the city from a different angle. The true angle and the true story of Portents.* He remembered those words from the foreword she wrote but that was where his reading ended. He found it to be the truest testament to the city surrounding him, truer than even his wife could know, and one of the many reasons Portents needed to fade behind him like a bad memory, though the book was making the trip to Chicago so he could keep the promise he had made to his late wife. None of that mattered to the stoic Ruiz, who promptly put the book back where he found it.

The act was not lost on Loren. He continued to watch the clever captain shift from box to box, slowly making his way to the front door of the apartment. He knew the question did not need answering. Ruiz put his cards out for him to see and Loren knew why. No matter how different their lives were—with Ruiz and his three daughters and a house in Venture Cove north of the city and Loren's empty life in his empty apartment—they were too similar for their own good. They were cops and nothing would ever change that. Still, Loren played the game the way Ruiz intended, knowing it would be for the last time. Chicago was his future.

"Sold all of the furniture to the thrift store down the block," Loren answered. "You came all this way to—"

"I could have helped," Ruiz interrupted. He opened up another box, this one closer to the door of the apartment. More books. He quickly closed it without pawing through the contents. Loren saw the realization on his face. It was all of Beth's things, not Loren's. It did not faze him, did not give the game pause. Ruiz continued toward the boxes by the front door. "Pack, I mean. One thing Michelle lets me handle when it comes to the annual Ruiz family vacation. I am well known for my packing abilities."

"No." It came out harsher than he intended.

"No, what? What no? All I'm saying…." Ruiz stopped at the duffel bag by the front door, slowly lifting the center flap. Resting on top was Beth's case file and a large spiral-bound notebook dogged by years of travel and scribblings. The past that refused to stay where it belonged. Loren moved away from the mantel, stepped beside the man he had called friend, and closed the bag once more.

"What you're saying and what you're doing are two different things, Captain." Loren reached past Ruiz and grabbed his coat off the hook to the left of the door. He dug his hand deep into the right pocket and removed the pack of gum he kept on him at all times. His last one, he continued to swear, even to the mystery man in the mirror. He hated the habit worse than smoking, but after Beth's death, after he stopped at the grocery store for that repetitive last pack instead of heading straight home to be with his wife, he knew it was time to change. The chewing gum crunched in his ear and everything tasted like layers of fruit whenever he felt the old need for one last drag. Damn, he missed smoking.

"You want to survey my mental state, just ask me like a normal person. You want to borrow a book, feel free. But this here? These boxes? This is me leaving."

"In a few days," Ruiz answered simply.

"No. Train leaves in a few hours, Ruiz. *Hours.*" Loren turned away, walking back to the mantel.

"I need your help, Greg," Ruiz said, his voice soft and his head low. When Loren packed his bags and returned to the city of his birth, it was not a choice made lightly. There was history in Portents. There were relationships and even a few remaining friends. And there was Beth. The decision was, however, the smart move. After ten years in Portents, after four years without Beth to keep him in the light, it was time for that change. He hated the idea of going back. Of coming back. He hated his own curiosity just as much at that moment.

"Not my beat anymore, Ruiz. It was never really my beat."

Loren's eyes flashed at Ruiz. The exhausted Hispanic was smiling again. "You know that's not true. Besides, don't you think I'm a little too busy to waste my time asking for your help?"

Ruiz opened the door. The smell of Mrs. Arbogast's stuffed shells was overpowering but it did not deter from his moment with Loren. The bearded former detective ran his fingers along his eyes to the bridge of his nose and nodded.

"Chicago," he said knowingly.

"My first call," Ruiz replied. Loren snapped his gum between his teeth loudly, catching a glare of disgust from Ruiz. "Lovely Captain Roberts, old friend as you know, cleared it immediately. And your sister was nice enough to let me know you were already in town. Come on. I even rescheduled your return trip for you. All on the city's dime."

Loren stopped in front of Ruiz, who held the door open for him. He blew a large bubble with the flat flavored stick of gum, then let it pop inches from Ruiz's face before continuing into the hallway for the stairs.

"You make a guy feel real special."

"Don't mention it," Ruiz said, closing the door to the apartment. He followed close behind Loren, shuffling down the stairs for the main entrance to the building. Mrs. Arbogast was only the most obvious neighbor to look out her door at the two officers, though Loren felt other stares through the small peepholes on the neighboring apartment doors. He kept his eyes on the bottom of the steps and the door beyond to avoid any awkward questions. As Loren reached for the door to step outside, Ruiz called out.

"Or the car. It's the wife's."

Loren stepped out into the city street and the cool evening air. Though summer was a warm front away from taking root in the city, the nights still struggled to be tolerable, much less comfortable. The grizzled detective spit his gum at the retaining wall next to the building's garden of dead or dying plants. He slipped his leather coat on, rubbing his brow deeply, and closed his eyes from the looming daylight surrounding him. He continued for the sidewalk, then backtracked. Two fingers reached for the sticky mass on the retaining wall to collect the gum. He tossed it in the trash receptacle on the sidewalk, wondering how many more times he would have to do that before he remembered to carry the wrapper. A parked vehicle sat in front of the building—a large, red minivan hugging the curb. A family bumper sticker clung proudly to the rear window of the vehicle, though it was one Loren had never seen. Four women surrounded a single stick figure man, all talking as the man ripped his hair out. Unique, but definitely Ruiz.

"Nice ride." Loren laughed. He tried to focus on the vehicle but his eyes wandered to the sidewalk in front of the building. Even after four years, he saw the chalk marks and the stains of blood.

Her eyes staring up into the darkness.

Beth.

He cleared his throat loudly. Shifting eyes and shifting hands came back with another stick of gum. *Filthy habit.*

"I said don't mention it," Ruiz huffed, heading to the driver's side.

"I know," Loren replied.

Ruiz reached in and grabbed the file from the passenger seat, tossing it softly on Loren's lap. Loren let it sit there, refusing to reach for it. Refusing to open it and the door back to Portents, one that wouldn't stay closed. It was Ruiz's turn to clear his throat. The driver's side door slammed shut to muffle it but Loren heard it even over his chewing. He stared out the window, looking back at the chalk mark long since removed from the sidewalk, yet always there in his mind.

"How bad?" Loren finally asked.

"Bad," Ruiz answered, shuffling for his keys. The ignition clicked for a moment and then the van whirred to life.

"Meaning no one else wanted it." Loren nodded, his gaze on the sidewalk in front of the apartment building. He didn't need Ruiz to confirm his statement. They both knew what Loren really meant. *No one else could understand it let alone solve it.* One of those cases that Ruiz kept out of the daily briefing so that there were no questions asked. One of those cases that ended with a brief statement but never an explanation. One of those cases that kept Loren going after Beth's death but eventually drove him away when he realized what they were doing to him. How they were taking over.

"Except Mathers," Ruiz replied.

"Christ," Loren muttered, thinking of Ruiz's opposite on the day shift. There were some things you can't run away from fast enough. "Sounds like old times."

The van shifted to drive and Ruiz pulled it away from the curb into traffic. Once settled on the straightaway leading from King's Lane east to the warehouse district, he turned to Loren.

"Welcome back to Portents."

CHAPTER FOUR

Darkness spread across the city like a blanket in the early hours of the evening. To the west, the sun did its best to continue to shine, fighting a battle it was destined to lose. Beneath the city streets, a shadow crept along an abandoned junction of the C line heading away from the center of the city for uptown's red light district. Her small, lithe frame was silent, stepping effortlessly beneath the people of Portents. She gazed through the neon lights that buzzed to life with the coming dark, watching closely while the citizens scurried from place to place.

They carried smiles she did not understand. They spoke of movies, books, sports, and more that she knew nothing about but wished she had. Her dark skin glistened in the trickling light under the city streets, never hesitating to get to her destination, though the temptations of the city called to her. Even after so many years in the dark, beneath the city, she still carried the dreams of being among them. That sense of wonder was not kept in her muscular frame that she had built over a lifetime of training. She hid it well with her small body, loose blouse, and torn jeans. It was not seen in the smirk that kept her light on her feet and light in her heart for the job she was meant to fulfill. The sense of wonder was in her eyes, the large brown eyes of a four-year-old girl watching the fiery leaves dance in the autumn wind.

She was no longer that girl, though. Her life ended that day and a new one began. With it a new name. With the stone tied to her hip, a new job. It took her months after the accident to speak, let alone attempt to remember the events of her life before that fateful day. Everything had been lost, including the faces of her family and the names they bore. Even her own. In the orphanage library, she found a book of names, and weeks of reading helped her locate the one that made her feel whole once more.

Soriya.

It was unique among the other girls, a plus for her need to stay separate from the group. Not that she ever shared it with them. They had their own names for her, names that made them feel more comfortable around her, superior to her. More than that, her newly chosen name derived from the Khmer word for "sun"—a sentiment she needed in the long, cold winter she endured within Saint Helena's Orphanage for Girls. Her surname was lost to faded memories but over time she was gifted with one by a man she would call Mentor, the first person to understand what happened to her, the first to help her understand there was more in the world. The surname also found origin in the stone she found the day her life was lost yet found in the same instance, the stone she held tight to every day since finding it among the wreckage of her former life.

Greystone.

Soriya Greystone.

She felt proud of the name—it made her feel almost normal, a feeling that was rare in her day-to-day life. Even now. Under the city streets, she still felt the distance between her world and the one everyone else knew. It was a necessary distance but one she found herself regretting more and more. She attempted to connect. Failed attempts for the most part, but attempts nonetheless. She wanted to be part of the world, their world, the one she had seen from the darkness for the last eighteen years of her life. The distance, however, was good for one thing: It protected her. It kept her safe to do what she was meant for.

Not that she cared. She wanted to be seen by the world. No matter what the consequences, no matter the pain that came with it or the joy, just for one moment she wanted to feel purely part of the city she inhabited. Mentor hated the thought of it. He hated the connections she made, what he saw to be distractions from the job put on their shoulders. Fatherly disapproval did nothing to assuage her desire.

Soriya reached her destination and grabbed hold of the sewer ladder. She held herself away from the grime that had collected along the metal bars, hoping to keep her clothes clean for the night's work. Slowly she climbed until she reached the manhole cover that slid open with ease under her soft yet strong hand. It was noisier than she intended, or maybe she had intended it to begin with, her desire to be heard and seen by the world sometimes making each action brash and unpredictable. It was a trait she knew would lead to nothing but trouble, yet still maintained, bringing a thin, wicked grin to her face.

The alley was empty and she vacated the sewer transportation system she tended to travel more and more. Passersby never flinched, continuing their gaze ahead to music pulsating the block from nightclubs and dive bars. Soriya wiped the grime away on a nearby piece of cardboard. She hung close to the wall of the alley. The sun was a memory and the night was taking its hold of the city. A chill settled in and she felt small bumps along her arms under the sleeves of her tight shirt. Reaching into her pocket, she retrieved her cell phone. The screen lit up before her.

Nothing.

No word from Vlad. He was supposed to call her the previous night after checking out the club scene. He was supposed to be more reliable. He was supposed to be many things, Soriya thought, looking across the street at the club Vlad was meant to be attending.

Night Owls.

Reports were filed for four women over the last two weeks, all of them having attended the hopping club close to the time of death. While no one from the bar was able to identify the women in question, Soriya had little doubt foul play was involved and that it started there. Patrols were stepped up, but even they had little effect, the last victim being three days prior. Newspapers failed to report it. City officials failed to identify it. Even Vlad failed to back her up. Strange, considering he brought the case to her in the first place, but not a stretch with their history. To Soriya it was the same old story.

It was her job and her job alone. The way Mentor wanted it to be.

Night Owls was packed already. The defiant youth, the lost, all those refusing to allow the night to dictate a curfew to their lives in the city. Soriya smiled at the sight of the bouncer working the door. He stood at seven feet tall, towering over the clientele even from the chair he sat on. The patrons of the club thought the light green hue of his skin and small horns that stuck through his thick black hair were a great addition to the club's atmosphere. Soriya knew they were not for theatrics or part of the club's act. They were part of the man she knew as Urg. His true face, hiding in plain sight. Still, he was able to be one of them, something Soriya had failed to be in all her years in the city. Another friend. Another distraction. At least she would not have to wait in line with everyone else, she thought.

Darkness settled over her. Soriya took a deep breath, stepping out into the city streets among the rest of the people. She was just one of the crowd. She tucked a single strand of hair back behind her ear, eyes never looking away from their objective.

"Time to get to work."

CHAPTER FIVE

There was always one thing everyone collectively knew when it came to a crime scene: keep your mouth shut and get the work done. Truly two things when spoken by most but after a few cocktails with the commissioner, Ruiz was sure they were one and the same. The edict held true as Ruiz ushered Loren into the scene, already cursing his curiosity. Where empty streets were the norm for the warehouse district of the city, news of the death had already spread and a cordon was put into place to keep the gathered press and onlookers well away from the scene. A line of crimson ran along the side of the building under the moniker that had been etched in the brick. *Evans*. Underneath, Loren saw the large stone masonry marking the construction of the building. *1896*. One of the earliest buildings in the city but still there was something odd that caught his eye. The nine had been obscured with red, different than the line that stretched across the brick. Almost deliberate in its defacement to the point where the nine was overwritten in red with the number seven.

Flashbulbs screamed. They lit up the darkening sky, following him and Ruiz into the warehouse. The grizzled man kept his head low, turning away from the parade of photographers and news crews. The last thing he wanted was his scruffy mug on the front page of the paper with the headline, *Bigfoot Found in Woods. Buys Clothes. Becomes Detective.*

Stranger things, Loren thought.

As far as smells went, Loren had been accustomed to much worse. The shattered glass of the warehouse allowed the rank mildew from forgotten machines and rotted floorboards to air out into the city streets naturally. The rain helped as well, with puddles throughout the outer ring of the main floor of the building. Along the center, in a straight line from the fire escape window to the single staircase that led to the second level, was a stream of dried blood. Forensics lined the thin patter of red for samples and photographs. Loren heard the echoes from his footfalls along the metal steps, climbing to the row of offices on the second level. Stares followed him, as well as a pair of glaring eyeballs from Ruiz who continued to edge him forward. There was a reason Loren needed Chicago but there was also a reason most in the Central Precinct were happy to see him leave for the Windy City. Already the whispers broke the crime scene rule, mutterings between the old guard to the new all watching curiously.

"Heard about him and Standish but never..."
"Wonder if he can still walk in a straight line..."
"Should have stayed away..."

Both heard the gossip threatening to tear the department apart. Both heard every whisper and rumor spread in the echoes of the large warehouse, never attempting to silence them. Not yet. Instead Ruiz continued to prod Loren forward to the large office at the far end of the level with the open door.

Spotlights were positioned in the far corners of the room but even with them, the scene was difficult to decipher. A few photos were taken while Loren stood in the doorway. He shifted to the right to let the last of the forensics team make room. From the bottom of the steps, one of the first responders called for Ruiz, leaving Loren as alone as he had been in his own apartment barely an hour earlier.

Behind the spotlights, Loren saw the sun fading in the distance. The night chill was waning but still bitter with the wind battering the broken shades along the far wall of the office. His jacket barely helped—not that anything would, with the body still present in the center of the room.

He was young. Even in the pale light offered by the spotlights, Loren could tell he was young. His neck had been snapped, the obvious cause of death. Wounds ran the length of his chest, long and thick. Five slashes, uneven in depth and width. The man's shirt was torn, filaments caught between his fingertips. *His own act then. Probably to stop the bleeding.* There was more. Much more that Loren needed to see all at once. Needed to but the want had long since left him. This was Portents through and through. There was little more to it than mayhem on most days, and upon the lucky few, the city threw murder into the mix to liven things up for its residents.

As Loren stepped into the room, his eyes on the broken frame of the young man and the disjointed arms lying across the center of the room, he felt something slide along his leg and scurry into the corner of the office. Loren stopped, leaning back to the door.

"Can I get some more light over here?" he yelled out to anyone within earshot. "I prefer to see the damn rats before I feel them."

Leaving the request to settle in the air, wondering what comments his rat statement would stir among his former colleagues, Loren moved deeper into the office, mindful of the floor before him and the crime scene. All of the furniture was tucked away into a single corner. Markings littered the floor leading to the large desk and bookcases that had been shifted to the side. They were brightly notched into the wood flooring. *Freshly put there.* He started for a closer look when a lanky, middle-aged uniform entered the room carrying two more spotlights. Even in the shadows of the room, Loren recognized the six-foot-four figure of Officer John Pratchett.

"Detective," Pratchett said, surprised at first at Loren's presence on the scene. His eyes brightened in recognition of his former colleague. Positioning the first spotlight along the outskirts of the room, Pratchett flipped it on, its battery-powered beam shining over the deceased like an angel's light. He shifted to the other side but Loren waved him off. Pratchett nodded. "This good then?"

Loren nodded, extending his hand. Pratchett accepted it with the same goofy grin he carried for everyone. "Pratchett. Still suffering under our lord and master out there?"

Pratchett chuckled, turning his head to verify Ruiz's absence from the room. John Pratchett may not have been the most ambitious man on the force, more than happy with his beat and his paycheck, but he knew who not to piss off if it was within his power. It was a lesson Loren struggled with more often than not. No, Pratchett was a career beat cop, content as long as he was holding the steering wheel of his patrol car. Satisfied at their solitude from prying ears, he leaned close to Loren. "He's gotten softer since you left. Like a teddy bear."

"I'm sure," Loren replied.

Pratchett's laughter faded, his eyes once more on the body before them. "It's definitely good to have you back, Detective."

"I'm not back," Loren shot back quickly—too quickly—and the words cut harsher than intended, drawing concern from the officer. Loren shook his head. "Never mind. Give me the room for a few."

Pratchett nodded, stepping for the door with the unused second spotlight tight in his grip. He shuffled past another uniform in the doorway. Loren caught the mixed cry of respect and fear that stuttered out of the officer's mouth. Ruiz had rejoined him.

"Not the whole room, I hope," the captain said. Small against the wide doorframe, his voice seemed far away, cut by the loud clamor of footsteps from the team on the first floor and those waiting at the base of the steps. The shadows of the room hid Ruiz's face from Loren, the deep bags swallowing the eyes they hung from like a black hole.

Loren crouched low over the body. He stopped looking at the man he called friend and returned to the job he wanted nothing to do with, but now wanted complete so he could put it in the rearview mirror of the bus back to Chicago.

"Tell me this is already over and make me a happy man," he said, half-jokingly. In Ruiz's hands were a number of files. Knowing the department as well as he did, Loren identified what each held. Witness statements were nil but preliminary reports needed reviewing immediately. Ruiz was in for a long night and he was looking for company.

Ruiz smiled at the statement. "The impossible task. Sorry. Out of wishes to grant."

"Run it down for me then," Loren said, still looking over the victim. There was a silver bracelet around his left wrist. The spotlight beamed off its surface. *Definitely not a robbery.*

"Squatter found him this morning. Got freaked and ran into a patrol," Ruiz started, looking down at the notes he had compiled over the course of the last few hours. "Lucky break for us, considering. Something like this usually stays buried for days until the smell hits the streets. This area of Portents? The way it's been? Probably a week."

The former Portents detective continued to look over the body. He stopped for a long moment at his face, turning away and then back again, remembering something.

"I know this guy," said Loren, finally breaking his silence. "Vlad. Vladimir something. I busted him once or twice. Small-time thug type. B & E. Possession. Nothing to warrant losing his guts, for sure."

"Maybe he took a shot at the big time," Ruiz replied. It had been a common theme in gang-related activity. Everyone wanted their piece of the pie but with only so many slices to dish out, eventually someone had to take one from someone else. Always turned bloody. Always meant more paperwork.

"Doesn't look like it worked out for him then," Loren muttered. He took out a pen from his pocket. He lifted up shirt fragments carefully. Most of the blood had dried and had become a permanent adhesive between the shredded shirt and Vladimir's torso. Loren managed to clear a small piece away from the gaping wound for a closer look. "These wounds—"

Ruiz interrupted quickly. "I'm going to have Hady take a closer look once she gets here but I'll be damned if I can figure the weapon that made them."

Loren's eyes shot up at the shadowed man, curiously. Ruiz used his paperwork as a shield. Loren smirked, an audible scoff escaping his lips.

"No weapon, Ruiz. This was done by hand."

Ruiz stopped cold. "I'm sorry, what?"

"You heard me," Loren said.

"A hand? Someone's hand did this."

Loren pointed to the wounds. Ruiz inched closer. Loren watched his friend's face flicker between spotlights, his words never matching his blank stare. "Look at the spacing. The depth changes with each swipe. This was an attack, not a delicate series of precision strokes with a penknife or any other kind of knife. This was by someone's bare hand."

"APB on Freddie Kruger?" Ruiz asked.

Loren stood and looked to the series of shattered windows along the far wall of the office. His hands rested on his hips, watching the rising darkness of the city. Always darkness. He closed his eyes. "As good a place to start as any."

"Hady can tell us more." Ruiz's voice was distant.

"She certainly can, Ruiz," Loren said, biting his lip. "And she already has told you more. *You*. You already knew about the wounds. I can smell that damn sanitizer that Hady uses to bathe herself in her tank every night. Judging by Pratchett's face, it was recently because it seems chewed out by the insomniac coroner."

"All right. Enough," Ruiz snapped.

Loren pointed to the body. "This isn't why you asked me here."

Ruiz hesitated for a long moment before responding. "No."

Behind them, Pratchett shuffled his feet into the doorway to make his presence known to the two men. They fell silent, both wanting to say more but glad for the respite.

"Are we good?" Pratchett asked, ironically.

Loren nodded, waving him into the room. He reached into his pocket and retrieved his pack of gum. Peach mango. He missed smoking. "Scene's yours, Pratchett. I have boxes to pack."

Loren stepped around the body, eyes on Ruiz the entire time. It was well past time to leave. After everything the two of them had seen over the years, he was the one person who should never be played. Ruiz never needed Loren. He needed the one person they never talked about in a crowded room. He needed the one person who never blinked when they were being told someone sliced someone else open with nothing but the whites of their fingernails. Wendigos, Sasquatches, Bigfoots. Myths and legends that people could grasp only when in the middle of a "three beasts walk into a bar" joke. However, she was the one person who knew they were real without a doubt. When things happened in Portents that could not be explained or understood, she was the one who handled it.

Ruiz knew it better than anyone else, even better than Loren, who at one time believed he was an essential part in solving crimes that landed on his desk with what was then referred to as "special circumstances." The last three months told him a different story. Still he played the game. Still he fought the need. Still he refused to reach out. Loren hated being the go-between. It had been his job for years until the time arose for him to leave the city behind. Yet he returned and was put back in the same situation all over again. Detective's badge be damned. Insights be damned. He was the mediator. Damn him for knowing it and for knowing how absolutely necessary it was to the job. They needed her.

They needed Soriya Greystone.

"She's not police, Greg," Ruiz called, stopping Loren at the door. The shaggy face of the blond-haired detective turned back. Ruiz stepped close, lowering his voice. "Simple fact."

"She can help. She chooses to help. Not for a paycheck or a pension. By choice."

"Captain," Pratchett called out from behind them.

"We can debate her motivations later," Ruiz continued. "I need this solved. Someone takes a chunk out of this guy with his fingernails as knives means I'm not playing in the sandbox with the rest of the department. I'm playing in yours. And, damn me for even saying it, hers."

"Detective," Pratchett called once more.

Ruiz's eyes looked behind Loren at the waiting forensics team, still gathering evidence along the stream of blood from the entry point into the warehouse. Other officers milled about, waiting for the shift to change or to keep the press at bay near the front doors. Loren watched his friend's eyes snap from person to person, checking to see if any were looking back his way.

"What aren't you telling me? What else happened to this kid?" Loren asked in little more than a whisper.

"Christ, Loren. The kid's heart," Ruiz managed to get out before covering his lips with his hand. His eyes remained low. "This sick bastard took the kid's heart. With nothing but his damn hands."

"What?" Loren hadn't seen the extent of the damage beyond the five slices across his abdomen. To manage something like that—the removal of the heart without eviscerating the entire torso—it was planned down to the moment it occurred. Methodical. Tempered. No rage at all behind it. Loren leaned close to Ruiz. "This is the last time you're not straight with me, Ruiz. Or I walk."

"Understood," Ruiz answered.

"HEY!" Pratchett yelled. The two men spun their attention over to the cringing officer. "Um…you might want to see this."

Ruiz nodded to Loren, who took the lead back to the body and the case they had before them. "What is it, Pratchett?"

"I don't know exactly," he replied, eyes following the contour of Vladimir's body. "Something under the body. The blood."

"The victim's blood. It's everywhere. We know," Ruiz slung back, annoyed.

"Wait, Ruiz," Loren said, waving him off. He took a step back to see the whole room. There *was* something under the body. Something he had not seen before. He nodded to Pratchett, a smirk on his face. "I see it. The spatter doesn't match. Victim was bleeding out long before making it to this room. But there's a pattern to it under him. Some of this is someone else's blood?"

Ruiz sidled up to Loren to see. Loren pointed out the long arcs that seemed to stem from the body. "It's an old factory. Could be from decades ago."

"This looks more like an office than a killing room floor. And I could have sworn somebody mentioned textiles as we were walking in." He smacked Pratchett lightly on the shoulder and pointed at the body. "Give me a hand."

"Loren."

"Hady had her chance to take the body. Get her up here in a minute so she doesn't breathe too much fire out of those nostrils of hers, all right?" Pratchett laughed at the joke. Loren took care to grab Vladimir's ankles gently to prevent any additional bruising. Pratchett did the same under the young man's shoulders and they lifted him aside.

"What are you two seeing?"

In the center of the room in dried blood was a marking none of them had ever seen. It arched up and cut back like two crossing scythes.

"Like a tattoo or something," Pratchett stammered out, confused.

"Any ideas?" Ruiz asked.

"None."

"Some kind of message?"

"No clue, Captain," Loren answered plainly. "Some kind of sign."

Ruiz turned to Pratchett. "Get Hady up here for the body. And get forensics too. I need pictures and samples. I want to know if this guy bled just to send us a message."

Pratchett nodded reluctantly. Loren smiled to him, knowing that Hady Ronne had no problem killing messengers with her glares. Dead people were the important ones in her eyes. Loren crouched down over the sign. Dried blood older than the victim's. The murder was planned for this spot. Was it about Vladimir or something else? Loren cursed his own questions. He wanted out but the more he stared at the sign before him, the more he was being pulled into it all again. Just as Ruiz planned. Still, he hated the feeling, the one that gnawed at him that this was more than he could handle. More than anyone with a badge and a uniform could handle. Ruiz hated it too, standing over him, staring blankly at the sign sprawled along the floor for them.

"I have fifty-two open cases I can't solve using standard methods. I have a sign that makes me think this is bigger than all of them put together. I haven't made heads or tails of any of it since you left."

"Apology accepted." Loren extended his hand and Ruiz took it. They shook once hard. Some said it was easy for them to let the little things slide because they were men, but it was more than that. They were soldiers on the front lines of Portents. Fighting back the darkness, piece by piece, yet never truly accomplishing their goal. They were brothers in arms, stronger than any gender bound them. Stronger than blood in most cases as well.

"She can help?" Ruiz's question was cold.

Without looking to his friend, Loren nodded. "I hope so. I have a feeling we'll need it."

CHAPTER SIX

As the bar roared around her, Eileen Mayfield felt alive for the first time in years. Cassie and Steph had asked her dozens of times to join them out at Night Owls and Eileen never took the opportunity. They were friends for years, been through the best and worst of times. Eileen's wedding. Steph's divorce. Kids. Deaths in the family. Everything. Still, with the growing concerns of the home, two kids and a husband who seemed to need more attention than the little ones, Eileen found free time to exist only in the form of six hours of sleep every night. It was not a complaint, not on her end. It never was, only a simple state of fact, she told Cassie and Steph time and time again. Life in the dim lights of a club, surrounded by strangers, not caring where the night went was a thing of the past for Eileen.

Until tonight.

She needed it. She needed it bad. Chuck was working double shifts, the first at work and the second on the couch never lifting a finger. Eileen never complained but as her three-year-old wrote gibberish on the living room walls in his favorite blue crayon under his father's watchful eye, she knew it was time to escape. Luckily for her, this was a regular event for Cassie, whose need for companionship was only outweighed by her need to drink her face off as often as possible. Why was a mystery to Eileen but she was glad to have her friends that night.

Music blared from speakers mounted to the ceiling in every corner. Steph put dollar bill after dollar bill into the jukebox to control the blend of 80s hair band rock screaming through the air around them. Eileen sipped her beer—nothing fancy, and only two or the whole night would turn into a blur. That was her rule. It didn't matter, though, and she let her hips sway under the spell of

Poison. Cassie sang along with a group of frat boys that had been wooed over with the promise of a free round from the young redhaired woman.

Eileen watched in wonder at her friend's gift with the opposite sex. Chuck had been her one and only. A smart, charming boy she met in college that grew into a respectable man then stopped growing at some point. Never a complaint, she said, never an issue. She always thought there was more though and, as one of the fraternity hunks ripped off his shirt at the height of the chorus with the other four boys cheering him on, she was happy to see that there wasn't.

Laughter poured out of her. It had been a long time and it startled all three of the women. Cassie smiled, lifting her drink before Eileen, and the two toasted as more dollar bills jammed their way into the jukebox from Steph. The smile refused to fade from Eileen's face. Her drink dripped along her lips and down her chin. She immediately put the glass down on the table beside her, reaching for the roll of paper towels that had accompanied their food. The towel tore free of the roll and she cleaned her face.

That was when she saw him.

The sea of people that separated them parted, allowing Eileen to see a man watching her from across the club. He wore a loose fitting V-neck but she could see his biceps hugging the fabric. His jeans aided in her focusing on his lean physique. A defined face and thin scruff made him appear ruggedly handsome. There was more but none of it compared to his eyes. Beyond deep, beyond wide, there was something in them as if light beamed from them and poured into her. As if his very look filled her with something she had not felt in her lifetime. She wanted more of that feeling and his look said the same.

Cassie bumped her accidentally, holding tight to her shoulder to keep from drunkenly falling to the floor. Eileen's eyes broke from the man across the room for a brief moment. The heat from their connection was palpable. She felt sweat rising on her skin. She was dizzy from it all, reaching for her glass. She downed the remainder of her beer in an instant, hoping it would cool her down but as her eyes wandered back to the man the heat rose considerably.

He was closer. Slowly, he stepped toward her, his eyes never falling and hers never leaving for an instant. She never felt this way about Chuck—hell, even for her children there was love...but if that was love, what was this?

Eileen no longer remembered Chuck's middle name. Remembering what she made the kids for dinner the previous night disappeared from her memory as well. Even why she loved a lazy man like Chuck faded from her thoughts. Her hand slipped into her pocket and worked the wedding band from her finger. It fell silently to the base of her pocket among the lint and random loose change.

What are you doing? Her conscience demanded an answer but none was forthcoming. Everything blurred before her. Lights, sounds, even her friends as they danced and laughed without a care in the world. Couldn't they see what was happening? Couldn't they see him coming to take her from the waste her life had been for so long?

He was closer than ever, a smile flowing freely along his face. The heat was unbearable and she unbuttoned the top of her blouse. It did not help in the least nor did she care. She wanted him like no other. Nothing else mattered.

Then he was gone.

Eileen felt her heart stop. Someone had stepped between them—a woman, cutting them from the night of pure bliss she had formed in every thought since his arrival in her periphery. As she caught her breath, she felt a cool chill cut through her and she quickly fastened the undone button. Steph turned from the jukebox for the first time in over an hour and saw Eileen's pale face.

"Everything all right, sweetie?" she asked, concerned.

"I don't know. I don't think I feel well all of a sudden." Her hand rested on her forehead, cold sweat greeting it.

"Where's your wedding ring?" Steph asked, her eyes scurrying to the floor in a panic.

"Oh." Eileen reached deep within her pocket and found the piece of gold that had only previously been removed for its quarterly cleaning. She slipped it back on, her world of kids and marriage bearing down on her like a freight train. Her gaze fell upon the woman once more. She held out a shot to her companion and the man offered a smile that had once only been for Eileen.

"I have to go," Eileen said. Cassie and Steph immediately attempted to stop her egress but Eileen pressed forward. "I'm sorry. I need to leave."

Passing the man of her dreams and the brown-skinned harlot of her nightmares, she heard the woman utter the words she had planned to say before fate intervened.

"Care to join me?"

CHAPTER SEVEN

It did not take long for Soriya Greystone to find who she was seeking. As everyone in the club jammed in close in tight corners, there was a significant distance surrounding a single individual, a man wearing a V-neck shirt and jeans. A protective barrier encircled him, though no one seemed to notice. Soriya watched the man's movements across the room from her stool at the bar and with two small glasses nestled between her fingers. He walked with confidence, if walking was even the correct term. The way his feet slid through the air, he appeared to glide across the room more than walk. When she noticed his eyes fixed on the young redheaded woman near the jukebox, Soriya stood.

Time to go to work.

The focus of his attentions was doing her best to draw him in all the way. *She has no idea what she's getting into*, Soriya thought. Seamlessly moving between patrons, her eyes never left her target. The drinks in her hands never shook unsteadily, never spilled from the constant shifting of weight from one foot to the other. A smile spread across the man's face as she neared. The woman's top button slipped undone. Soriya was amazed at the unnoticed foreplay occurring among so many people. She was also amazed at the man's talent. He loved this part. That much was obvious. He loved the thrill of it. The game.

The hunt.

Soriya stepped in front of him, shattering their connection. She smiled coyly, playing the game he needed to play. She held the two shot glasses up. Johnny Walker. Red Label. *Nothing but top shelf for him*, she thought.

"Care to join me?" she asked, confidently.

The man paused. His eyes, light enough to be mirrors rather than windows, looked her over. Every inch of her was catalogued in quick fashion and summarized for his pleasure. His look suggested confusion, a small joy she took from their encounter. It had taken her hours to prepare, dousing her body in subtle perfumes. A multitude of scents that complimented her but at the same time drowned his ability to get a true reading on an emotional level.

His lust-o-meter, she called it. Or, as the young redhead raced out of the club, eyes down on her wedding ring and nothing else, Soriya knew it better as his *barometer-o-skankiness*.

Satisfied with her presence, the man took one of the glasses. He raised it before her and she followed suit. Their eyes remained connected, refusing to break the stare. Around them, the night moved in quick order with the blasting of loud, obnoxious songs that Soriya knew were written long before her birth, but in their small protective circle on the floor of the club, time was barely in existence. There was only the two of them—exactly what each of them wanted in their own way. Though the man was careful and prudent, his gaze continually searching for some sign from Soriya and coming up short, he was arrogant. He tapped her glass with his and downed the drink in an instant. Soriya did the same. As the stinging liquid went down, she ran her tongue over her lips, lapping up the remains of the drink. The man's smile grew wider. He took the glasses and placed them on the bar.

Soriya grabbed his arm. "Let's get out of here."

He stopped her, his hand pulling hers off slowly. His fingers melted into her own, grazing down her palm.

"So soon," he said. His voice was deep. Even over the speakers and the buzzing of the crowd, each word cut through her ears clearly. Something came alive in his voice, something that mirrored the look in his eyes. Soriya understood what the redhead felt in that moment, heat rising from her chest.

"Why wait?" she said. Her smile remained.

"I don't even know your name," he said, coyly.

She leaned in close, lifting her small frame on her toes so that her lips were scant centimeters from his left ear. "Will it matter after tonight?"

She fell back on her heels, taking his hand.

"How true," he replied.

As soon as they vacated the club, Soriya's companion took back the lead. Passing the line of people waiting for admission into the club, she felt the cold stares from the bouncer. He was concerned, had every right to be concerned but there was no time to discuss the situation with the brooding bouncer named Urg. Soriya easily dismissed him with a small wave and thin smile. They continued down the street, leaving behind the stares and the crowds. The man in the V-neck with the mirror eyes caught her straying gaze but she was quick to return it to him with an added bonus. Away from the crowds, she leaned in close. Her lips met his in a long kiss that startled even his confident grin. Any suspicion he held in that moment faded behind the deep pink of her lips. They parted and slowly moved back toward his ear, this time on the right side.

"My place isn't far," she whispered and felt his skin chill at the notion.

Taking his hand once more, she met resistance. Looking back, her eyes betrayed the smile still plastered in place. The man had stopped cold. She pointed down the block, in the shadows of the city.

"Here will be fine," he said, standing within the mouth of the alley separating Night Owls from the two dive bars that made up the rest of the block. Darkness echoed the words. Nothing was visible in the deep night embedded in the alley. Soriya hesitated, quickly realizing the error in that judgment. Hoping to win him back, she stepped into the alley, letting her hair out of the ponytail so that it flowed against her shoulders.

"If you say so," she replied. Kicking off her heels against the closest wall, she scanned the area. No exits. No witnesses. No help. "I was just thinking about some drinks and a nice couch or a bed or—"

His hand slammed against her shoulder and spun her around. In the blink of an eye, his other hand wrapped around her neck, lifting her against the wall of the alley. Even in the darkness, Soriya saw the change. The young man in the V-neck and jeans was gone. Where perfect skin and dimpled cheeks once lay across his face there was nothing but a cracked golden hue and black lips. The glow of his eyes, once magical and enticing, was nothing more than glassed-over orbs of gray light in the shadows. They showed nothing but rage, pure wrath spewing from his every word. She knew she had found her man, a term that did not relate to the beast that stood before her. No, *god* was more on point when it came down to it. His name screamed in her thoughts, her lungs fighting for air.

Anteros.

"No more talking," he said, squeezing tighter. "It spoils my fun."

CHAPTER EIGHT

"Love. You don't even know what it can truly be," Anteros spat. Soriya Greystone dangled by her throat, pressed against the wall of the alley, clawing at the man's wrists for some leverage. Where there had been cracked skin moments before, of which flakes flew in the night air around them, a golden hue under the surface was revealed. Even the decayed, black lips of her attacker had changed to match the bronzed shell, hardening and shining in the dark. Where most cities dealt with wife beaters and deranged killers, Portents catered to a higher class of psychopath—that of the gods themselves.

She knew Anteros the way she knew most of his kind and any other deity. She read a lot of books. Anteros, brother to Eros, was the god of requited love. He was born to love Eros. The fancies of a lonely god. But loved in return? That wasn't on the menu for Anteros. Hence the anger.

"Poor, deluded humanity and your concept of love," he said. "You fornicate, cheat, and lie then call it love. But you do not know its meaning."

With a scream, Anteros tossed her aside as if she weighed as little as the air around them. Soriya's body slammed against the cement hard, rolling deeper into the alley. Her lungs filled with air that never tasted sweeter, even among the garbage piles and dumpsters. Holding her body up with her hands, she breathed deep, calming every inch. Anteros moved for her quickly.

"I was born out of love. Born to love but never loved. Denied for me for all eternity. Just as I will deny you that love."

Anteros lifted her up by the neck once more, his eyes wide with anticipation. They, however, failed to see the thin, pink ribbon snaking down Soriya's left arm and out of the sleeve of her blouse. Or the vengeful grin spread across her cheeks.

"Not this time, Anteros," she spat back. The pink ribbons shot out of her sleeve, wrapping tight against Anteros' wrist. The ribbons, a gift from the Hindu Death Goddess Kali, acted with a mind of their own but always listened to the situation. As they tightened against the golden flesh of the Greek god, Anteros saw smoke rise from his arm. He screamed over the sound of his flesh burning from the ribbons, and dropped Soriya to the ground. She landed on her feet, glad to have removed her heels upon their arrival. The ribbon retracted and she let it hang down her left side, ready for anything.

"You bitch!" Anteros screamed. His fist swung through the air but made no connection. Taking the opportunity, Soriya waited for her opening and unleashed an uppercut to his chin. He staggered back and she continued, slamming her fist against his face.

"Now, that's no way to talk to a lady, Anteros," she replied with a grin. "Anteros, right? The lost, little brother of Eros. Couldn't make it as an angel like him, couldn't cut it as a demon like the rest of the siblings. Poor Anteros. Created to be a pet. The family cat no one really needs except for five minutes a day to remind them how much better off they are in comparison. How their lives mattered compared to yours."

His blood ran along her fists, more added with each blow pummeling deeper into the alley. Lost in the moment, she failed to notice the small pile of debris and refuse that had collected near her left foot. She tripped forward, Anteros sidestepping her blow and allowing her to fall before him. Her hands braced for it and she quickly spun to face him once more but it was too late. He grabbed tight to her black hair and pulled her toward him.

"I was born of love, you peasant," he spat. "I was a child of Zeus!"

Soriya pushed off the ground, her whole body airborne. Her right foot snapped out, slamming into Anteros' left knee. Any normal knee would have shattered from the blow but the god felt nothing more than a sting. Her left foot finished the combination, however, hitting his chin. Anteros flew backward from the blow, deeper into the alley. Soriya casually completed her flip in the air, landing catlike with a smile. The small pouch on her right side opened and she pulled out the item she had carried with her since she was four years old.

The stone of grey—or as she was more likely to call it since taking it as her namesake, the Greystone. It was the same as it had always been, cold to the touch on the hottest of days and warm on the coldest. It fit squarely in a single palm now, and she held it before her, facing her attacker one last time.

"Daddy left you a present." Her words were hardly audible over the crackling sounds ripping through the air above them. The Greystone, after a long moment of appearing little more than what it seemed, lit up before the unsuspecting Anteros. The bright light wiped away all shadows within the alley, then receded to form a single symbol upon the stone's surface. A rune.

ᚺ

"What are you...?" Anteros did not know its meaning, only knew that it was meant for him. The crackling air around him kicked into a gale force wind. The symbol was one Soriya learned at a young age and it always brought joy to her face upon seeing its impact. Hagalaz was the name of the rune. As its meaning was becoming more and more clear to Anteros, it symbolized the wrath of nature. Symbolized, and through the power of the stone, summoned it forth.

"Say goodnight, Anty," yelled the young woman over the wind.

The night remained clear. There was not a single cloud in the sky, or the chance of a dribble of rain. Out of that clear sky, a bolt of lightning ripped from the heavens. It shot with a clear purpose and target. Soriya saw Anteros' glass eyes close at its advance. She heard his screams for mercy.

Too late.

The lightning bolt crashed into him and Anteros was no more.

Soriya lowered the stone, the rune of the Elder Futhark fading from its surface. The wind died down around her and she felt the ribbons of Kali sliding up her left arm. She placed the stone back into the small, cloth pouch attached to her right hip.

Where once a golden Greek God stood, now there was nothing but ashes, remnants of his body to be swept away with the rest of the trash in the Portents alley. Soriya towered over them, her hand rubbing gently along her neck from her fight. The wound stung but she gladly bore it compared to Anteros' fate. Four women were dead by his hand. He forfeited his future with those actions. Soriya hoped that wherever and whenever Anteros ended up, it was truly over. Somehow, she doubted it. The crazy ones always managed to find their way back after a time.

Footfalls inched into the alley. She spun to greet them, hand reaching once more for the cloth pouch and the profound weapon it contained. The shadows shifted at the mouth of the alley and a lone figure stepped out of the dim light. He sported a thin, white beard on his cheeks to match his thick hair. Down his left temple, there was a single scar streaking toward his ear. She did not need to see him to know who it was. She did not need to see the thin slits where his eyes stared down upon her or the pursed lips always ready to debate. She did not need to see the dark, green overcoat he wore over his hunched frame or the worn-out sneakers on his feet. She knew who it was the second his voice ripped through the shadows. The second she heard the cold gravel of his words digging into her.

"Took you long enough," said the man called Mentor.

CHAPTER NINE

There was a time when Soriya saw only darkness. In the days that turned to weeks that stretched to months after the accident, Soriya knew only the shadows of her life and never the light. She was a girl of four without name or origin. She was a mystery to all, even her own thoughts. Those days, those weeks, those months were difficult ones. Many lessons were learned during that time from many teachers, children and adult alike. Still, there was no light in her world. Until he came for her.

Until Mentor showed her the sun.

"You're welcome," Soriya exclaimed, standing over the ashes of her assailant. The Greystone worked its miracles in secret under her wing, its origins as mysterious as her own. She asked Mentor from time to time but the answers always returned the same. Answers were not his to share but hers to discover. Lessons were the only parenting tool he commanded and he commanded them well over the years. The stone was cool against her hip, surprisingly so considering the justice it had unleashed on the unsuspecting Anteros moments earlier. The pride of the moment, the feeling of accomplishment melted with a look to Mentor, his eyes glowering down upon her.

It was the look only a father gave, but he refused the title. He never wanted it though she mistakenly took him as one in the early years together. He was a simple teacher in need of a student, and she was nothing if not eager to know something. If not about her own life, her own beginnings, then she would know that of everything else there was in the world if she was able.

"This was a mistake," Mentor replied, stepping further into the alley away from the neon lights of the clubs and the stray glances of passersby curious about a random lightning strike on a clear night.

None were curious enough to remain for more than the flicker of a moment before remembering their own destinations, plans, and dreams.

Soriya's chest rose and fell heavy, still slowing from the fight. Her smile refused to fade. Mentor discouraged such raw emotion during the job. It was a distraction. *Everything was a distraction*, Soriya always shot back in a tone that harkened back to days of teenage angst better left forgotten. It was true, however, but secretly he smirked at the youthful exuberance she put into the task they shared. Always when he believed he was alone, away from her watchful eye.

"You should not have put yourself in this situation," he continued. Soriya turned away when he neared, heading for the brick wall. She retrieved her heels and placed them back on her feet, then rested with her back to the wall. "He could have—"

"It was the best way to draw him out," she cut him off. The same fears were not theirs to share. While the rest of the world did what they could to forget their own mortality, she needed it to do the job.

"No." His voice was low. Calm. It infuriated her. "It was the most reckless. That's why you chose it."

It was the same lesson she sat through with the Harpy the previous year and the So'la the year before that. It was the same argument but the results remained the same.

"Four women, Mentor," she answered. "Four women that won't be home with their families. Four was enough."

Mentor fell silent, pausing. He nodded. "I don't disagree with the sentiment."

"Says the hermit from the sewers." Her eyes fell down to her feet, her cheeks turning slightly red from the outburst.

"To the kettle. Yes." His grin matched her own, but quickly faded at the sight of the small pile of ashes in the center of the alley. "Four was too many. But you almost became five. Do you know why?"

Her hand slammed back against the wall. Her knuckles continued to sting from her pummeling of the golden-skinned god and she immediately regretted the action. She turned away from Mentor, detesting the sentiment of his words. Years she spent learning from him, years spent in the dark beneath the city, waiting for the day she could walk among the rest of Portents. Twenty-two years old and she remained separated from the city she protected. His choice, never her own.

"This stopped being fun years ago. These lessons."

"Because you choose to ignore them," Mentor replied, his voice pleading to be heard. He moved closer to her but she continued to step away from his comforting hand. "Because you feel you know better. Because—"

"Because I did it on my own. Without you." Her voice echoed through the alley in anger. "The answer to your question. But I wasn't alone. Not here. Not anywhere in this city."

Neither of them spoke. Neither of them knew if this was a compliment or a condemnation for Mentor's actions over the years. Neither wanted to figure it out any further. There was more to it, though. The shared feeling that his presence would end, or had already done so. It was something she had wrestled with since his arrival in her life at the orphanage. It remained every moment of every day, that feeling that their time together would end. The feeling of darkness returning to her life. It stemmed from the aches running the length of his right leg to his lower back. He was getting old and there was still so much she needed to know, so much to be shared between them. He moved in close, his hands resting on her shoulders. Still she looked away but his words needed to be said, if not heard.

"You are the Greystone, Soriya. In more than name." He smirked, beaming pride upon her, though she failed to notice in her anger. "You have a responsibility to more than your own needs. Your own desires. That is not what we—"

"I know," she replied, pulling away slightly. She gazed up at him with large brown eyes—the eyes of that four-year-old girl still hidden within the brown orbs. "I know all of it. I am trying to be more. To be what you want me to be."

Mentor crouched over the remnants of the god, gritting his teeth at the creaking in his knees. "It shouldn't have happened. None of it," he said.

Soriya stepped closer to him. It was the one point where they could both agree. Escapes were rare but when they occurred, they turned bad. The problem was that they should never occur. Anteros was not meant to be in the city, was not meant to be anywhere near the earthly plane of existence, but somehow swooped in under the radar, taking the lives of four women before they were able to act.

Mentor spoke of the same thoughts that ran through Soriya's mind. "Anteros should not have been able to cross the Bypass on his own. The balance has tipped."

It always came down to balance. Darkness and light. Right and wrong. Balance was the center of Mentor's universe so it was the center of Soriya's as well. Everything made sense when balance was taken into account. Everything followed rules.

Except when it didn't. Then everything went straight to hell. Real quick.

"Something has changed," both said at the same moment.

They were both aware of the dull hum of an engine at the mouth of the alley. They both heard the slight slam of the passenger side door and the sound of sneakers sliding against the pavement. Neither knew how much was overheard but both turned at the voice that called out to them. The voice of Detective Greg Loren.

"You could say that."

CHAPTER TEN
Three Months Earlier

Few people roamed the halls of the station the night of Loren's last shift. Even fewer said goodbye. Not that it mattered. All that could have been said had been long before the moment Loren closed his office door for the last time. Well wishes were plentiful for months after Beth's death. Food prepared. Friends visited. Eventually it all faded away. Calls were no longer answered. Greetings no longer exchanged. The sandy brown hue of his eyes darkened to the world for a long time.

Then the bottom dropped. Friends turned to colleagues turned to strangers. His obsession clouded his work. His anger took him the rest of the way. Ruiz finally pulled him aside. Then Loren realized he needed more. He needed to leave.

With Beth's case file, a parting gift from Ruiz, tucked securely under his arm, Loren felt the handle click as the door closed shut. He twisted it twice to make sure it stuck. He swore there was someone always leaving it open when he arrived in the morning yet he continued to double check his own handiwork. Not that it mattered any longer. He slipped the key off his chain and let it slide back into the lock. He left it there, his gun and badge secure within the desk drawer at the center of the office. He did not want to see Ruiz. He wanted to slip away without saying goodbye to his one true friend.

They said their piece months earlier. Loren was lost in another case, another murder, another something to take his mind off what remained of his life. He closed it, hoping it would help. It failed. He followed up on it, only to learn the perp had walked. Lost evidence. Misplaced reports. An error on his part, one he would never make. Without call, without approval, Loren found the colleague working against him. A man the department had censured and demoted on more than one occasion. Standish. He could have turned it over to Ruiz at that point.

He didn't.

Standish ended up with a broken arm and a concussion.

That was the end for Loren, pushing the rest of the department out of his corner. While justified, the downright inhumanity he displayed on a daily basis was enough to warrant Ruiz's interference. It was enough for Loren too. Time off, a couple different therapy groups and Loren started to remember a time that life didn't hurt as much. Where there wasn't as much anger in the world. He needed it again. To see the light away from the darkness. Seeing Ruiz only added to the plain and simple fact that he couldn't do that in Portents. He couldn't do that around Ruiz.

Pratchett stepped out of the elevator at the far end of the hall on the second floor. He poked and prodded a young man into the hall toward the holding cells. The young man's hands were secured behind his back. He scurried along the hallway, his body continually threatening to topple forward in a face plant with the tile floor below due to his pants wrapped tightly around his ankles. The polka dot boxer briefs concealed his unmentionables. Loren was grateful.

The tall officer snickered, nudging the punk along the hall. He towered over the man who looked more like a boy the closer he came into Loren's view. No older than twenty. Tattoos lined his right arm. Loren recognized the spider dangling from its web adorned on his bicep from a gang that had infected the north of the city.

"Friend of yours, Pratchett?" Loren asked when they passed. Near the stable at the center of the floor, heads were slowly rising from desks at the sight of the young man.

Pratchett smiled, the same childlike grin he always shared with Loren's sense of humor. "Found him tied to the post outside the stoop. Freaking note around his neck like a present from Santa."

Pratchett handed Loren the note. A single line was scrawled on a small piece of cardboard with a string attached to the top to fit around the man's neck. The marker lines were thick and black. It read: *Felt like parking my stolen cars here for a while. No room in the garage.*

Loren smiled. Not the cleverest of messages but the point was clear. He handed the note back to Pratchett. "I'd ask Santa for something else next year."

Pratchett laughed. "No kidding."

Loren gave a nod and made his way down the hall. He stepped past the elevators for the stairwell adjacent and knocked the door open. Even with his back to him, Loren felt Pratchett's curious stare at his turn toward the parking garage. The towering officer, however, made no comment and no movement to inquire further, leaving the departing detective in peace.

The parking garage was vacant except for the glistening vehicles shining in the moonlight. Loren slipped his hands into the pockets of his jacket and held it tight against his body. Through the leather he could feel the small pack of gum he kept in the right breast pocket. He fought the urge to retrieve a stick, not wanting to hear the soft clicking to match his shoes on the concrete. Winter was passing quickly, and though it had been mild in terms of snowfall, the cold chill of night was bitter against his skin. Echoes followed his every step for the ledge overlooking Evans Avenue and the downtown district. The Rath Building, named after the founder of the city William Rath. He had settled the area with hundreds of wayward souls in the early 1890s—or so the plaque under his statue in front of the building read. The Rath, or "Wrath" as it was called, was the office of the Central Precinct for the Portents Police Department. The city was made up of twelve districts with twelve precincts but Central oversaw them all. Most knew it as "lucky thirteen" when it came to precincts but still it remained the envy of most officers. Ruiz believed it was the idea of being able to work within the same building as the commissioner, a man rarely seen and heard fewer and fewer times each year. For Loren it was never about the politics. For him, the draw of working at the Central Precinct was the view.

The ledge of the parking garage was only feet from ground level. It was the only type of ledge Loren felt comfortable near since Beth's fall. It was peaceful at the spot he always picked, a long view of Evans Avenue and Heaven's Gate Park. A row of streetlamps shone on the snowy remnants of winter, no longer quite white in color. The look was deceiving and he knew it.

It was time to leave. Long past time. It still felt right, even with the beauty of the city stretched before him. This was never his city.

It was hers. It belonged to Beth. Not him. He merely survived it, though he rarely saw the last four years that way. They were empty moments filled with more regrets than his entire life held. Regrets and mistakes.

The quiet of the garage settled over him for a long time though he knew he was not alone. Even in the darkness, he felt her watching over him, waiting to make her presence known. When he was tired of his own thoughts, he ended the quiet, his eyes still watching the dim lights of streetlamps in the park.

"You need to stop beating people up and leaving them on our doorstep," he said to the darkness.

Soriya Greystone stepped out of the shadows. "Tell them to stop stealing cars from old ladies and I'll be glad to stop. Not your doorstop anymore anyway."

She sat on the ledge beside him, looking him over. She wore a light cape coat that matched her skin over the same blouse and jean combination he had seen her wear dozens of times before, though every time it seemed unique where his own wardrobe seemed drab and uninspired. It was the confidence behind the clothes or the uncaring attitude that said, *Who gives a damn what I'm wearing.* Her hair lay flat upon her shoulders and upper back, her legs dangling from the ledge. She looked so young even in the shadows that covered most of her small frame. Too young for the life she had led. Her eyes were wide but he refused to meet them.

"Don't," he said, still looking out into the city.

"Don't what?" she asked, her voice rising. "Don't talk you out of it? Don't try to get you to stay? I wouldn't know how. She died, Loren. You didn't have to follow her."

"I tried. I tried real hard to believe I could move on. That I could get up in the morning, put on the badge, and do the job. Hell, to do your job too or whatever the hell it is you call it. But I couldn't. I couldn't see that guy in the mirror anymore. The one that saw hope, that saw light, because there isn't any. Not anymore. That guy died with her."

They fell silent, looking away from each other. The experiences they shared, the losses they carried, bound them in a way no one else could have possibly understood. Loss was all they felt when together. Loren needed to feel something else. Anything else.

A small smile broke across Soriya's face. "Do you remember the first time we did this?" she asked.

He nodded. "You mean the first time you dropped off a present at the precinct to get my attention? Yeah. I remember."

It was right after Beth's death. The Kindly Killings proceeded while Loren lost his way in grief. Days turned into weeks. For a time Loren thought the two were connected, that maybe he came closer than he realized to solving the case. The smile on Beth's lips. Her joy at taking the image of Loren's face with her when she passed seemed to line up with the killer's methods. Ruiz didn't see it that way. No one did. They were busy trying to catch a killer and console a friend, though they were unsuccessful at both.

Then Soriya intervened.

On a night much warmer, Loren stepped out of the precinct to go home to an empty apartment only to find a man hogtied on the front steps of the building. His mouth was stretched into a smile with a note pinned into his chest, not his shirt since he wore nothing other than a pair of socks and some stretched out underwear. Little droplets of blood stuck to where the pin met flesh but still the man did not whimper in pain. The note read: *I smile at killing nice people. Please lock me away and throw away the key. Sincerely, Mr. Kindly, AKA Douchebag Scum.*

The handwriting was the same used on the man Pratchett found. The knots on his bindings were a match. It wasn't until he took the man to holding that a call came in directing him to the parking garage.

Soriya was more elaborate back in the day, doing her best to make a first impression on him.

When he finally made it to the parking garage to meet her, after dozens of questions from everyone he saw in the halls of the Rath Building, she simply smiled from the shadows. There was no discussion. No requests were made that night. Nothing but a quiet nod of understanding. A new and true friend watching his back.

They shared that moment whenever they could. Loren needed it, a little notch in the "win" column. Soriya solved the case that lorded over him for months. The Kindly Killer was nothing more than a greeter at a local department store chain. He handed out coupons and smiled at the rude customers. Those he took offense to, he followed closely after his shift and ended their lives. Rudeness was their sin. Loren definitely needed the win.

The two of them relived the moment the same as they had relived so many others. The start of their time together, a time that turned out to be one of the few highlights of Loren's final years in Portents. It just wasn't enough to keep him from leaving.

"When?" Soriya asked after a long silence.

"Train leaves tomorrow," replied Loren, solemnly. "I'll come back for my things once everything settles down."

Soriya hopped off the ledge and moved away from Loren. His eyes followed her.

"Greg," she said, turning back. She never used his first name. Not even in anger. "It won't bring her back."

"I know," he answered.

Her eyes pleaded. "Then why go? Why now?"

Loren knew the answer. He knew it the moment he reached the decision to leave. He looked to his friend and partner of the last four years with hope in his eyes.

"I'm hoping it brings me back."

Loren stood at the mouth of the alleyway. Behind him, the patrol car's engine whirred. Pratchett sat in the driver's seat listening to the loose belt whipping under the hood. He was Loren's babysitter and chauffeur for the night. His eyes looked back and forth at the street in front of him, glancing from time to time at Loren out of concern.

"Loren?" Soriya called to him. There was disbelief in her voice, as if there was a chance he wasn't standing before her. He smirked at hearing her voice, causing her own bloodied lips to spread wide. Mentor stepped between them.

"Detective," the old man said coldly.

Loren ventured deeper into the alley. Mentor moved aside, letting the detective look over the area. His eyes caught Mentor's deep grays. Soriya did her best to keep the two of them apart, the reason becoming clear every time they met.

"Always a pleasure, Mentor," Loren said. He noticed the small pile of ashes in the center of the alley. "Do I want to know about the ashes? No. I'll go ahead and answer that myself. No, I do not want to know about the ashes."

He turned to Soriya and mouthed a hello to her. His gaze rose to the deep black of the sky and then back down on the young woman leaning against the wall of the alley.

"I told Ruiz. Follow the lightning on a clear night in Portents and find trouble. And trouble's off-putting uncle."

Soriya stepped over to him, holding back the urge to reach out and touch his arm to confirm his existence. "You came back."

"It wasn't exactly by choice." His words stung and he regretted them. Soriya watched Mentor's disapproving glances from the far side of the alley.

"Oh."

"We have work to do, Detective." Mentor started for the mouth of the alley, motioning for his ward to follow. "If you'll—"

"You're going to want to see what I have to show you," Loren called after them. He moved for the car and opened the back passenger door. Mentor held back but Soriya looked with curiosity. She moved for the car without hesitation. As she ducked in, her eyes washed over Loren. She was inspecting him, searching for answers he didn't have and probably never would. Was he different? He didn't know. Neither of them did. But something had changed. Loren waited a long moment after she was seated in the back then called out to the skeptical old man. He refused to join them until Loren spoke once more, each word proving his sincerity.

"It's bad, Mentor. She's going to need you."

CHAPTER ELEVEN

When birth rates dropped at the turn of the century in the city of Portents, the need for the Westmore Elementary School diminished greatly and the school was shut down. Seeing an opportunity to use the school rather than let it fall into disarray, a graffiti paradise for the local population, the mayor's office recommended it put to a better use as the new coroner's office and the largest morgue in the state. The large L-shape configuration of the building offered plenty of space for administration, equipment storage as well as areas to continue internship programs from city-based universities. It was a windfall for everyone involved, including those at the Central Precinct of the Portents Police Department who were happy to see Hady Ronne and her staff depart the Rath Building for greener pastures. Distance made the heart grow fonder and the elevator less odorous.

From the entrance, the building split with the majority of the training and lab work completed on one end, while offices and the viewing rooms were at the other. Former classrooms worked perfectly for viewings, as some were small and compact enough for privacy and others large enough to fit the occasional influx. On the opposite side of the floor were the administrative offices, including that of Head Coroner Hady Ronne, or the "Waddling Dead" as Loren called her, among other choice names that were also on point when it came to the rotund woman.

Two sweeping double doors led to the main room at the end of the hall. Three bodies lay on tables in its center. Charts containing scrawls of notes and drops of unmentionable fluid were clipped to the base of the tables. The summary of three lives. All were covered when Loren led Soriya and Mentor into the room. The clock hanging on the wall announced the new day, though the darkness of the midnight hour reminded them that it was simply a continuation of the old. The lights flickered on and off, a continual problem that creeped Loren out to no end. An electrical problem that stemmed from construction work on the school was always the official word but Loren knew Hady was involved somehow, though he never said it aloud for fear of reprisal. He had no doubt the ghoul of a coroner preferred the darkness for her work.

The car ride over offered nothing but silence. No one wanted to speak, though Pratchett attempted with his usual weather-related banter and other miscellaneous anecdotes that sounded rehearsed. When more silence answered him, he looked to Loren, who simply nodded. There was no more chatter after that though Loren took the moment to glance back at his two companions. Mentor was lost in thought, staring out at the city at the blur of light and traffic. Soriya remained fixed on Loren, her large brown eyes begging him to say something. They were still locked on him.

"Whoever this person is, they've been busy. Three victims in five days. At least if Hady's estimation of time of death is correct on the previous victims," Loren said. He stopped before the two bodies positioned side by side. Above them, a thin florescent light beamed off the white cloth. Loren's eyes fell on the shrouds, never looking at the notes he held tight in his grip. He may have needed them earlier that evening but no longer. Everything was wrapped up in his mind. "Abigail Fortune was found in her home. Old-style ranch, as old as Portents from the looks of it. No signs of forced entry. Martin Decker was found at the end of a dark bar down near the docks. He was still propped on his stool. No one noticed."

"The Town Hall?" Mentor asked from his position in the corner of the room. He remained in the shadows as much as he could, refusing to let the overhead lights reveal too much of his presence.

"Pardon?" Loren asked in return, taken off guard by the question.

"The name of the bar. Was it the Town Hall?"

"Yeah," replied the curious cop. "How did you know?"

Mentor hesitated a moment. "I knew Decker a long time ago. Please. Continue."

"Right," Loren said slowly. There was something in Mentor's voice. Something knowing. Something that frightened him even though his face remained in darkness. Loren turned to the third body in the center of the room. He pulled the sheet back so it covered the majority of his frame but his face was visible once Loren shifted to the side of the table. "Vladimir Luchik, here, came next."

Soriya's eyes widened. She reached into her pocket and Loren saw her thumb her cell phone for a brief moment before letting her hand fall away. The young woman moved near Loren to take a closer look at the man on the table. Loren ambled aside to give her room.

"This one was more brutal," he continued. Soriya's hands clasped the side of the cold table that was Vlad's resting place. "Vlad fought. But this guy…. It looks like Vlad was led to the spot of his murder. We found a trail from the street to the warehouse office where it ended. It had to happen there for some reason. Ritual, maybe. At least that's how it appears because of this."

The photo slipped free of his notes and landed between his fingers. Loren held it out and waited for the hand of Mentor to reach out and grab it. He did not wait long. Soriya remained fixed on the body before her as her guardian peered over the photo of Vlad in the center of the office atop an image. The bottom half revealed the image in full. Even in the darkness, Loren saw the old man's eyes flare.

"This is how it looked? Nothing was changed?" Mentor asked hastily. His need immediate.

"Nothing's changed." Loren's brow furrowed. "Why? Does it mean anything to you?"

Mentor fell silent once again, stepping back into the corner of the room. Loren wanted to press the issue. There was something he knew, something that would break the case wide open or at the very least have the whole affair make a semblance of sense. He knew Mentor's games. He played them, reluctantly, for years when the old man jumped into the middle of his investigations with Soriya. They had been hard lessons for Loren to learn but even after every false lead or untold clue from the man with only a title for a name, he continued to trust Mentor. It was a mistake, he knew, but one he counted on in the long haul to pay off for the better. *Hope*, Beth would say. It always came back to hope. And to Beth.

Loren, however, was unable to continue his questioning of Mentor. The doors to the room slammed open and a short, plump woman with long black tendrils for hair stepped into the large lab. She held a clipboard low. Her eyes never left it. Looking downward at the stack of notes clasped to it, the bags under her eyes were still quite visible. They bounded up like bowling balls above her cheeks. Loren moved away from the center of the room, giving a wide berth to Doctor Hady Ronne.

She stopped a few feet into the room, her eyes still glued to her notes. "Please tell me I can get back to my body before the sun comes up, Loren. And tell me that unauthorized personnel are not touching my bodies."

Loren faked a smile. "Hady."

"Doctor Ronne, former Detective." Her words chilled the room. "Now let's pretend for a minute that this isn't the best place to bring a date for cheap and maybe let me help catch a killer."

Loren stepped over to the stumpy woman, looking down at her. "Still charming the pants off dead people," he said as calmly as possible. "Five minutes."

"Loren."

"Five minutes," he insisted. Slipping his hand into his pocket, he slipped out a slice of peach mango gum. He held it out with the nod of his head. A peace offering.

She paused a moment then replied coldly, "Be gone by then."

Hady slowly vacated the room, the double doors swinging back and forth from her movements. Loren could still hear her sighing before she slammed the door to her office just outside the room. He instinctively gripped his cell phone, waiting for a call from Ruiz then let it fall away. Old habits. Old politics. One of the nice things about only consulting on the case. None of them mattered to him anymore. When he felt the calm return to the room, his focus shifted back to his companions. He slipped the stick of gum into his mouth and felt his teeth crunch into its cool, hardened shell. Mentor studied the image still caught in his grip. Loren was more concerned about Soriya, whose gaze looked softly at the deceased Vlad and never flinched from him.

"You knew him," Loren said.

She nodded slightly. In their time together, there were things Loren had seen that could never be explained to the layman on the street. Monsters in the dark that would force people to run for the hills or curl up next to mommy in bed and never again sleep with the lights off. He had seen Soriya handle them all without blinking.

She was stalwart, exuberant, and brash. She loved what she did. Her joy never faded. Loren never, not in all of those years, saw her grief stricken. He never wanted to see it again.

"He was supposed to call me earlier," said Soriya. Her eyes remained on the young man's broken frame. She pulled back the sheet more until the wound became visible and she stopped. "We were working on something together. I waited. Figured he was blowing me off. Flaking out like he does. Never thought it could be this."

Loren stepped closer then backed away. Mentor's eyes were on him and he didn't care for the looks heading in his direction. "There was no way you could have known. The victims of this guy are random from what we've been able to determine."

Soriya and Mentor's heads turned at the same moment before Loren finished his sentiment. Their eyes shifted to each other slowly then away, never toward Loren. The former detective ran his tongue across his top teeth, nodding at the knowledge they were keeping from him. He cleared his throat audibly. Mentor nodded to Soriya.

"Show him."

"Show me what?" Loren asked, impatiently.

"The victims aren't random, Loren," Soriya said, pulling the cloth away from Vlad's left arm. Around his wrist was the silver bracelet Loren had noted at the crime scene. Markings were etched along its surface. Markings Loren had never seen before. Slowly, with tender fingers running along Vladimir Luchik's cold pale arm, Soriya unclasped the bracelet. Instantly, the young man's body changed. Where once there was the tattooed, skinny white frame of a man on the metal table; instead, there was a hair-infested mongrel of a beast. Dark brown hair covered his body from head to toe.

Loren had read fiction his entire life. He loved movies and worlds unimagined. After four years knowing Soriya, he realized imagination couldn't hold a candle to what was waiting in the darkness of Portents. When Loren saw his first werewolf, the descriptions of the beasts that he read about as a kid now made perfect sense. The sight caused him to fall back on his heels before moving in for a closer look.

"How the hell...?" he started.

Soriya held the bracelet before him. "It's a glamour. It maintains his human image."

"So he's actually always like this."

The corner of her lip rose. "Cute, right?"

Loren bit his tongue. Bizarre was more like it. "And what you're both saying about contestants one and two over there is—"

"Someone knew about them. Yes."

"Abigail and Martin had lives they hid from the rest of the city—just as this young man did," Mentor reiterated, bringing the point home for Loren. There was a pattern. Beyond the sign that had been left at the scenes. Now there was a new pattern behind the victims.

"You're going to want to tell us about the trophies taken now," Mentor continued. Loren's head shot over to him, feeling that fleeting moment where he had the upper hand slip from his pocket as easily as loose change at a strip club. The old man pointed to the exposed chest wound on Vlad. "The boy's heart for starters. What did Abigail and Martin surrender to our killer?"

"Her eye. His hand," Loren reluctantly replied. "What does it mean?"

Neither of them answered.

"Someone tell me." He felt his anger rising.

Finally, Mentor stepped for the double doors. He held one open and motioned for Loren to follow. "A word, Detective."

"Great," Loren muttered under his breath. He turned to the woman beside him. Her eyes were still locked on Vlad. "Soriya?"

"I'll be fine." Her voice was small. "I just need a minute."

Loren's nod went unobserved. Taking a deep breath, he moved for the hall slowly like a kid heading to the principal's office. At the double doors, he turned to see her lean close over her fallen friend's body. Her lips tapped the young man's forehead as she said goodbye to Vladimir Luchik.

CHAPTER TWELVE

The hallway overhead lights flickered dimly, running the full length of the hall that led toward the entrance at the opposite end. A dull hum rang through Loren's ears from the fluorescents. He imagined it was a perfect lullaby for the employees serving under Hady Ronne, anything to keep them from having to listen to the venom she spewed. Through the glass positioned on the top half of her office door he saw the hunched-over frame of the stumpy woman leaning over her desk. He heard mutterings, low and guttural, but Loren could only imagine what curses was placing upon him at the moment. Not that he cared, but when Mentor stopped before her office, Loren pointed farther down. The two men walked side by side, Mentor's staggered steps forcing Loren to slow his pace. The detective knew about the leg pain the older man suffered on his right side but never mentioned it. Neither of them did. Slowly the two walked down the hall, away from the eyes and ears of the few people that inhabited the building at such a late hour.

Loren didn't give Mentor the chance to speak. "I don't want to hear it."

"What?" Mentor asked. Standing so close to each other, Loren was surprised at how small the old man seemed. How tired. No longer completely in shadow, Mentor's presence shrank, the thin light of the overhead bulbs illuminating every crag and nook in his worn skin. He was no longer the imposing figure in the corner waiting to strike him down at a moment's notice. The playing field leveled out between them.

"The line," Loren continued. "The same one you always give when you're about to cut me out of a case for my own protection. A case I came to you with despite all good reason."

"Besides being ill-equipped for it," Mentor interjected. Loren gritted his teeth. Mentor spun his finger in a circle for the man to continue.

"A case you know more about than you're willing to share, or did you forget about the sign and what it means? And don't pretend you were about to say anything different."

"You're right." The old man's eyes flared. "But I'm not the only one holding back details, am I?"

Loren remembered the missing tokens taken from each victim, the detail the police had been able to keep out of the hands of every member of the press corps and even out of the gossip that spread across the station. Loren stroked his prickly beard, wondering if he had meant to leave that out or if he was lost in the moment with the two people he had not seen in months.

"At least tell me about those then," Loren said, whispering. "The eyes, the hands and the heart. Why?"

"I don't know."

"Come on, Mentor. Give me something," Loren's voice carried and he slowed down to keep from bringing everyone in the building over to listen. "Tell me Abigail Fortune had laser eyes or x-ray vision. Tell me Decker was the greatest massage therapist on the planet. Something to explain the trophies."

"X-ray vision?"

"Heat vision. Microscopic vision. She came from Krypton. Something!"

"She saw the world clearer than anyone I knew and Decker's hands could master any tool or weapon. As for the boy's heart, I can only imagine living as a wolf his heart gave him a unique edge. The real question, the one you don't want to ask, is what the killer is doing with these trophies."

"You're right. I don't want to ask. But I have to, don't I?"

"So do I," replied Mentor, sharing his lack of knowledge. "There is more, isn't there? Even still, you're holding back."

Loren remembered the feeling walking into the warehouse, the feeling of something more hidden beneath the surface. It began simply with the sign out front, the bloody smear running along the stone changing the date of its construction. A simple change from a nine to a seven, as if it was meant to be there instead. It was probably just a fluke but it stuck out in Loren's mind, unwilling to fade. Much like the symbols etched in Vlad's bracelet, the city was covered in writings that Loren never thought twice about or even noticed. However, to be at that scene, the office that served as the final resting place of Vladimir Luchik and carry that feeling toward some conclusion was something else. It *was* something Loren was keeping from Mentor. Hell, he was even keeping it from Ruiz. Why, he couldn't rightly say, but he felt it was too soon to share. There was more to it. He needed more information. He needed more time with it. Something so that the pieces would start to fit into place.

"I know" was all the detective said in response. He looked to the wide doors to the main room at the end of the hall and then to his watch. "Our five minutes are up."

Mentor nodded. Loren turned to join Soriya, the old man calling him back. "You should walk away, Loren. Take the opportunity. Put this behind you. You wanted to leave this place. Leave this business. You wanted to leave her."

"Soriya?" Loren asked, confused. "It had nothing to do with her."

"You're a distraction, Detective." Mentor moved close to Loren, his glare piercing. "You are a connection you should have kept severed for yourself as well as for her."

Loren refused to back down or look away. Then he saw it. "You're worried about her. More than usual. This isn't the standard overly protective father routine. This is different. Why?"

The door slammed behind them and a short, stocky student bounded into the hallway. His papers fell from his sweaty grip, a failed attempt to juggle them while fixing his glasses and reattach his access card onto his belt in one less-than-fluid motion. At the sight of the two arguing men he stopped, a dumbfounded stare spreading across his face. Mentor sneered at the boy. His eyes widened in fear, then dropped to the floor. He quickly gathered his materials and flew down the hall as if giant flames were giving chase. Once again, silence filled the hall. Mentor leaned close to Loren.

"Something is here, Loren," he said, quietly. His words were carefully chosen but Loren could hear what was behind them. Concern. Even fear. Things he never heard from either of his two companions before that evening. "It is no coincidence a god like Anteros was brazen enough to take to the streets at this exact moment. Someone's here. Three murders and we knew nothing of them. Someone is playing a quiet game. And a deadly one. She is not ready. Soriya. She is not ready for what is coming. Especially now."

Loren peered back to the double doors then back to Mentor. "She was closer to Vlad than she said, wasn't she?"

"Another connection. I've tried to keep her from them."

Loren mockingly let out a laugh. "Keep her isolated, you mean. Keep her safe from pain and loss. True grief. Great decision."

"Her responsibility outweighs needs," Mentor shot back. "It is about more than our lives. She will learn that much in time."

"When you deem it appropriate to learn, of course. She isn't your kid."

"She isn't yours either."

The words sat out there though neither wanted to hear them. There was enough for one night. Three murders. Plenty to digest and ruminate without further antagonizing allies. Mentor held out the image of the sign scrawled on the floor of the warehouse office where Vladimir Luchik was found. Loren waved it back.

"Keep it. Plenty of copies sitting back at the station."

Mentor nodded and started to back away.

"Before you do your creepy fading into shadows thing just level with me, Mentor. Do you know what this is? How she can stop it? How we can stop it?"

"No." It hurt to hear but Loren sensed the honesty behind it. "Not yet. But I will."

Loren turned and Mentor was gone. He called out to the darkness that seemed thicker in the hallway.

"And I get to what? Wait for you?"

"No," a distant voice replied through the dark.

"Then what?" Loren yelled.

The sound was barely audible but Loren heard the message loud and clear. The fear behind each word was palpable and it said more about the threat than Loren thought Mentor meant to share. It said it was going to get worse long before the end. All with three simple words whispered in the dark.

"Keep her safe."

CHAPTER THIRTEEN

The night dragged on, with people lost in revelry or home in their beds. There were no malicious thoughts that clouded their minds, no malicious intents but one. In a darkened apartment living room he stood, a shadow among shadows. His hands delicately ran along the south wall of the room. His fingertips were dipped in blood and deep reds covered the standard off-white paint throughout the small domicile. His thoughts were racing but he kept his motions slow and deliberate, afraid of his hands outpacing his intentions.

His time was near.

Three had fallen. His fingers reminded him of that every moment. While his left hand remained mangled with crooked fingers and missing nails, his right glimmered in the darkness. They were the fingers of a painter and he used them well in his own style. However, they were not his own fingers. They were a gift of the man in the bar. The man with an aura around him that called out to be taken. In the right place at the exact moment he needed him. The pieces were lining up, placed perfectly for him as if by some grand design. Three pieces in place and the fourth an inevitability.

Another must die.

A low groan escaped him. Eyes, one not his own, peered from under the black overcoat that shrouded his withered frame. Underneath, muscle and sinew were all that covered him and small streams of blood carried along capillaries spilled out among them. He was not whole yet. More was needed before the end. However, it was not yet time for the final piece so another had to be taken. Another sacrifice to save the city he held so dear.

He took a small capillary from his side and squeezed. It burst open and another stream of blood ran free. His mangled hand caught it, painting his fingers in crimson, the only color the shadow knew. His makeshift brush continued the large circle upon the edifice of the apartment until it reached the base in a large sweeping motion. His adopted fingers joined his own in the center to finish the image. Already the blood dried, hardening against the thin layer of plaster and paint. From crimson, it ran darker, as if it was decaying before his eyes.

It was done.

The shadow admired his creation with a vision not completely his own. Perfection stretched before him, a masterpiece ready to unlock the secrets of the city. It was only part of the equation. The sacrifice was the other.

So he waited.

The time was fast approaching. His time.

Standing across from the door of the apartment, the shadow that was once a man waited in the darkness for his sacrifice. There was nothing to stop him. There was no one who could. Every piece stretched out before his eyes like a perfect symphony. The darkness was his ally and their enemy. He used it like a musical instrument to play his song across the blood-filled streets of the city. As he bled for the city so long ago, now the citizens of Portents would follow.

A lipless smile stretched across his face. The tearing and rending of muscle caused more blood to flow freely down his cheeks, but he did not care. Time was on his side although he wanted his prize so desperately. He felt it in the air, he heard it in the noise that ran through the city streets. Surrounding him were looming towers and speeding cars, and none of them saw—truly saw—what he was creating for them. For himself. He wanted them to see, to witness his return and the greatness it foretold. He wanted it now.

A slow breath silenced the rage of thoughts. He was patient. Standing in the darkness, he waited for the sacrifice, the smile never fading. He knew how the story ended. He wrote the final chapter centuries ago.

CHAPTER FOURTEEN

Keep her safe.

Mentor's words rang strongly through Loren's thoughts as he pushed the large double doors to the main viewing room of the morgue. The look in the old man's eyes, the despair he hid so well with every word, frightened Loren. There were always times of shaken confidence, of doubt, but never with Mentor. Never with Soriya either, for that matter, but her slumped shoulders remained when he entered the room.

Loren stood in silence. He remembered when Beth was taken from him, remembered when he saw her body lying on a slab of metal much like Vlad. He spent the night beside her, despite Hady's declarations. Grief triumphed. A shuffling of feet reminded him of their five-minute deadline. The last thing he wanted was another bout with Hady. Something about that woman scared the hell out of him, which he appreciated telling her every chance he had.

"Soriya," he began, tossing his not-so-long-lasting flavored stick of gum into the garbage near the entrance. Her hand rose from the side of Vlad's table. Slowly, she placed a small metallic object down next to Hady's other instruments that lined the side of the slab. Loren squinted in the darkness to see what it was but could not make it out. Surrounding her were deeper shadows and it took her spinning around on her heels and briskly stepping toward the door to realize they were not shadows at all. It was not darkness in the room surrounding the tables.

It was hair.

"We can go now," Soriya said, quickly. She held a small, triumphant smile upon her face and the thin silver bracelet in her right hand.

"All right, but if you...." Loren's vision shifted from the passing Soriya back to the room. Vlad's body lay completely exposed, hairless. Stammering, Loren continued. "You're more than okay staying if you...did you...?"

She stopped before him. With her thumb as their guide, she pointed to the door at the far end of the hall. "We should go now."

The door to Doctor Hady Ronne's office opened. Loren looked back into the room, nodded in agreement, and the two moved for the door quickly. The coroner stepped into the hall and when they passed, her eyebrow rose.

"All yours, Hady," Loren called back, refusing to make eye contact with the stumpy coroner. "Pleasure, as always. Get some sleep, though. Does wonders for bedside manner."

No response came, and none was wanted by the former Portents detective. He looked to Soriya and a fiendish grin passed between them. They heard the double doors push open and the heavy footfalls of Hady enter the room. As they reached the exit, the cantankerous coroner's words echoed down the long cement hall.

"Where did all this hair come from?"

Outside, the night was brisk, a stiff wind falling low then rising up into them when their feet fell upon the paved walkway. Surrounding the premises of the morgue, a large field of green stretched out to the street. Centered within the field was a large gated fence and within it a playground, a holdover from the Westmore Elementary days. The city attempted to remove it to keep the children away from the death that resided in the former school, but the residents who grew up in the area and raised families to enjoy the playground petitioned against the action so it remained. Fences were erected and all signage pertaining to the occupants of the school were removed to keep curiosities curbed as much as possible. Children from all around were heard laughing and playing while the dead were examined and identified less than a hundred feet away.

No children occupied the large, plastic clubhouse nor the swing sets that surrounded it. Few cars passed them. Soriya hopped the small fence and fell gracefully into the nearest swing. They were alone. Neither spoke, both quietly smirking at the thoughts that must be rummaging through Hady's head at the sight of a body's worth of hair. Loren unclasped the gate and stepped within the confines of the playground. He watched the grief fade behind Soriya's smile. There was still sadness in her eyes, distant and looking out to the city streets that roped around the large field, spreading like vines into and out of downtown. Sadness brought them together at all turns, Loren remembered.

When he spoke, he was leaning along the side of the fence near the swing, Soriya floating back and forth on the small plastic bench. His words were low, the look of contentment he once carried gone. "I am sorry for your friend."

"Thanks," she said, plainly. She looked down at her friend and continued to swing through the night air. "Is that what people say to that? Thanks?"

"I never know either," Loren replied. "I guess they say what they want to say. What they have to say and nothing else."

She hopped off the swing and joined Loren at the fence. The two rested their palms on the metal bar that ran along the top of the fence.

"We had some laughs. Mentor hated him, or at least the idea of him, so that was a bonus. It felt...." She trailed off, her eyes catching sight of an unseen memory that Loren had no part of, nor did he need to pry. Her lip curled at the fading reflection of days past. "I don't know. Bottom line, it felt and I needed to feel."

Loren understood perfectly. After Beth, there was nothing inside, a large cavernous space where his heart had once resided. He filled it as best as he could over the last four years. There was work. There was always work. However, other than the cases that paired him with Soriya, work was as empty as he had become. Crime never ended, it never abated. The futility of it, the scenes filled with more and more Beth's drowned what remained of his life so that there truly was nothing. Until he found something else. It didn't matter at first. Booze was easiest but did little for him. Rage worked more often than not. Rage at criminals that earned his ire, rage at colleagues who walked the fine line between patron of the city and the soul suckers who took what they wanted because they wore a badge. Rage helped quite a bit, until the adrenaline passed or the day ended or there was no release. Until it exploded out of him. Until Standish and the fallout. Suspension. Therapy.

And then it was Chicago.

Until Soriya had her something else, her Chicago, to grab onto and never let go, Loren knew there was always the rage to fall back on, though he refused to allow her to follow the path he had fought so hard to change. The case would be release enough. It had to be. He owed it to her for being his small glimmer of light in a sea of shadows over the last four years.

"Something did this to him, Soriya."

She nodded. "Whoever did this had some serious muscle. He may have barked at the moon in nothing but the fur his mother gave him, but Vlad was good in a fight."

Loren recalled the five long gashes through the abdomen of Vladimir Luchik. The handprint staring him right in the face, daring the weary detective to find its owner. Where the struggle had begun, Loren had no idea, but where it ended and how quickly the killing stroke came was clear from the images tucked under his right arm in the case file. Although it was clear the weapon used was nothing more than a hand, Loren still doubted the humanity behind the attacker. Something neither Mentor nor Soriya seemed to have in doubt.

"Whoever." The thought escaped his lips. "Mentor said someone as well. You're both so sure it's a person."

Soriya's hair shined in the moonlight, her brown eyes glistening. "You've always been limited by definitions of humanity, Loren. One thing that should never surprise you is that boiled down to its essence, violence stems from man."

"Not a very healthy outlook," he replied, plainly.

"But an accurate one." She tucked a single strand of hair behind her ear only to have the breeze whip it back in front of her face. Her words were matter-of-fact, so sure of the notions behind them that Loren trusted her instincts completely though he could never believe in them fully. Violence may have solved the world's problems for centuries, but so did diplomacy and leadership. Over the years, Loren lost sight of that in the dim haze created by the loss of Beth, but not any longer. After the rage, he knew there was more. Compassion trumped cruelty and he wouldn't flounder again. He smiled, staring out at the city streets.

"I missed this."

"Is that why you came back?"

Loren shook his head. "Ruiz called. And I was here."

"Packing," she answered coldly. No matter what else could be said about Soriya, it was that when a connection was made, no matter how few and far between they were, it was there for life.

Strong connections held tight and the idea that Loren could simply leave it behind was tough even for him to see. The sharp words, the distant glares, and their last night in the parking garage helped make it clearer for the dim detective.

"It's the right move," he said, trying to sound sure of himself, completely confident that every decision he had made relating to his leaving was sound. Every judgment. Every justification. He knew he fell short of the mark. "Chicago. It's the right move. I have family there. A new job. I can put it behind me."

"Can you?"

His head lowered. "No. But I have to try. Don't I? I didn't leave you, Soriya. Just this city. What it is."

"Meaning you're the same as Ruiz. As the rest. Unwilling to see the city, to know what really goes on in Portents," she said quietly. Her eyes burned through him. When they met four years earlier she opened his eyes to what she saw plain as day, every day. The true city. The world inside the world. When he stepped through that door, everything changed. There was no going back. The idea that he could turn his back on that stung deeper than any betrayal. It was the acceptance of ignorance.

Loren replied, simply, "Who would be okay knowing that truth?"

"You were."

He nodded. "For a time, sure. When I thought there was something out there to hunt. To catch for what he or she or it had done to Beth."

"But you left instead."

"And did you find it?" Loren shot back, angrily. His words were sharp, bitter against the cold wind that blew through the rag he called a shirt. He was tired of defending his decisions. Tired of feeling his justifications failing him with each accusation. Soriya's eyes fell away at the question. She knew there was no answer she could give him to satisfy the pain that came with the night Beth fell. Loren nodded at the silence. "Then we don't need to talk about it anymore."

Soriya licked her top lip, deep in thought. "You're right. You're right. I have a friend who might be able to help us. Muscle we might need."

Finally, Loren thought. Something to help the case so he could return to the new life he was attempting to carve for himself.

Something to move things forward. He slowly reached for his pocket and the cell phone inside.

"Good. I'll call Ruiz. Get a car to take us...."

Emptiness replaced the small, lithe frame of Soriya Greystone. Loren called out her name, knowing the futility of the act. The same act as her teacher. Standing alone in the shadow of the morgue, Loren felt like Commissioner Gordon after being handed a lead by Batman. *Used.* A puppet in a game controlled by anyone and everyone else.

A small fluttering sound beat against the fence rail. Loren reached for it and found a piece of paper with a note scrawled on it in black marker, the same handwriting that accompanied many criminals delivered handily to the Central Precinct. Across the piece of paper, torn from paperwork found within the viewing room of the morgue, was an address.

1252 Glenview. Apartment 12C.

He wanted to turn around and go home. He wanted to call Ruiz and cancel the whole deal. Let him handle it. Let anyone handle it. Mentor and Soriya were more than capable. Hell, Pratchett could probably stumble on a clue or two without even looking. Just not him. Not anymore. Portents stared down at him in the moonlight. He heard the call of the city in every car that raced down the street and in the flicker of every lamp that lined the field. He felt the city in the wind, brisk against the coming summer days. It surrounded him. It challenged his every thought. In that instant, Loren blinked. *Keep her safe.* He snatched the piece of paper from the fence and tucked it into his pocket.

"Yeah," he said defiantly to the city surrounding him on all sides. "It's great to be back."

CHAPTER FIFTEEN

Patterns. Everyone lived by them, even Soriya Greystone. When her parents and the entirety of her previous life vanished in the blink of an eye, she guarded herself to the future. She built a wall, separating herself from the pack of orphans surrounding her. Then Mentor came. The wall teetered. He built it back up, showing her how to live apart and serve a higher calling.

Then Vlad showed up, opening up another world to her. Friendship. And more. Sure, she wasn't close any longer with the young wolfen male, not in the way they had once been. He offered her a hand with legwork on occasion, but the former feelings remained, buried but present.

There was also Loren. The other side of the equation. The normal side of the city. Their time together was some of the best she ever experienced. They were partners, colleagues, and though Loren would be hard pressed to admit it, friends. The city surrounded her on all sides and as much as she loved the thought of the disconnected path encouraged by her teacher, the city overwhelmed her judgment.

Connections were everywhere. From the street vendor with a penchant for taking in strays to the barista that sold her weapons from the back of his shop. She laughed at the idea of a life without connections. She wanted it.

But she also wanted to be what Mentor asked her to be more and more each day. She believed she was becoming that person. Trying to become that person. For Mentor. Then her associations came back to haunt her. Loren's return. Vlad's death. She was better off leaving Loren behind. She was better off tackling this threat solo, solving the mystery behind three murders. The "smart play," as Mentor would see it.

Her choice instead? To ask another connection for help.
Patterns.

The neon sign over the side of the apartment complex buzzed loudly. Soriya approached the building from the rear, not wanting to smile for the cameras that lined the lobby. The blinking red lights of the EVANS LUXURY APARTMENTS sign forced her to tuck in closer to the building, making her way to the small walkway that served as the emergency exit. She had discovered the faulty handle on the door during one of her visits to the complex. Though it seemed to click into place, the lock never caught, making admission to the building easy.

Climbing the steps to the third floor of the building, more doubts crept through her thoughts. Three were dead already. Though she knew of Mentor and Decker's previous relationship, when Mentor still allowed for interaction on a professional level, she knew very little of Abigail Fortune. The loss of the woman's eye made it clear, however, that her gift came from a unique perception of the world. Why the killer would strip her of this after death was the question. Vlad's heart as well. What good would it do the killer? Sustenance? Ritual beyond the symbol lining the floor? Like Loren, Soriya hated the mystery of the work. Her strengths came in the physical arena. She needed to feel flesh and bone against her knuckles or the cold heat of the Greystone in her grasp when she took care of a threat. Explanations were Mentor's strong suit and another in the long list of complaints against her own methodology. She needed to take care of this one on her own, meaning with anyone and anything other than Mentor.

Which brought her to Urg. The bouncer at Night Owls was one of the first "people" Soriya met during her early days in the city. She was only seven, walking side by side with Mentor during a bad rainstorm. The gray clouds rolled in and she hugged close to Mentor's waist to share the umbrella he carried. That was when she saw him. He stood as tall as a mountain to the young girl, his horns cut short atop his temples. Light green skin marked his cheeks, flowing seamlessly to a deeper shade down his neck. He made no movement in the rain, simply staring up at the approaching night. His mouth opened wide and Soriya could see sharp fangs of white on the upper and lower sets of incisors. Droplets of rain crashed upon the white teeth, running along his gray lips and down his face. He seemed at peace with his role in the world. As she passed, Urg looked down at her and waved. She met his smile with one of her own and waved back. Mentor never noticed the exchange and she never mentioned it, but after that day, thoughts of the 400-pound orc never strayed too far from her mind.

Down the hall from apartment 12C, Soriya stopped. It was time to turn around. Time to walk away. Time to leave Urg to his latenight television and his ice cream topped with pig's blood. She could handle the darkness of the city. It was her responsibility and hers alone. She knew next to nothing about the killer haunting Portents. Nothing except the strength he displayed when he slaughtered Vlad.

The image of his torn body and broken limbs snapped her back to the reality of the situation. Her need for Urg outweighed her fear of involving him. Whoever killed Vlad had muscle behind the fingers that made the killing blow. Muscle that was beyond her own. Having an orc in her corner was too appealing to pass up.

The door to the apartment was ajar and the dim light of the television flickered along the shadows on the wall inside. Again, Soriya stopped. Her left eyebrow rose. A mistake? After the night she'd had, there was little doubt that it was no accident.

"Urg," she said, her hand resting on the doorframe. Slowly she pushed the door open. "I was hoping you were home but if I walk in and there are naked celebrity orc fights on Pay-Per-View again, I'm—"

Lying in the center of the room was Urg. A large red stain streamed from his body in a single line toward the door of the apartment. The television blared background noise over the sound of whimpers still emanating from the gray lips of the large orc. The beast's chest heaved and more blood oozed into the stream, but Soriya failed to follow its path. She was stuck on the figure kneeling over her bleeding friend.

The killer.

At the sound of the door opening, the shadow of a man spun around. Mismatched eyes, one of sky blue and the other of deep crimson, met Soriya's. His frame remained in shadow, tucked beneath a large trench coat. It was in tatters, probably a result of the struggle with Vlad the previous night. In the dim light of the television, Soriya saw a grin widen on the shadow's lipless face. The shadow took off for the large window at the far end of the living room. Something large, like a giant banner, waved in his right hand, his feet carrying steps of blood across the carpet for his escape.

"Don't even…" Soriya yelled, giving chase. A gasp from the center of the room stopped her. Urg's chest stopped heaving. She shook her head and kept running for the window.

The shadow slammed into the glass, shattering the window outward. Shards chimed, crashing to the alley that separated the building from its neighbor. The thick wood frame disintegrated from the force of the impact, collapsing outward against the side of the complex, its momentum bouncing it back and forth with the wind.

Soriya reached the window in time to see the shadow land on the rooftop of the neighboring building twenty feet away. Her eyes widened at the distance, her legs ready to attempt the jaunt. Soriya stopped herself from making a move, rational thought winning out over adrenaline and rage. In the blink of an eye, the killer was gone, lost among a city of shadows.

All that remained was Urg. Soriya ran to his side, knowing it was too late. She was always too late, it seemed. The giant creature's chest failed to move. His eyes were fixed on the ceiling above, locked in fear. There was too much blood to see the wound that ended her friend, not that it would have mattered, as tears stung her eyes, clouding her vision. She fell to her knees beside her friend.

"Come on. Come on, Urg," she muttered in the dim light of the television in vain.

Urg was dead. Another victim. Another friend lost. Her watery eyes looked up at the back wall of the living room. In a wide arc on the beige paint that covered all of the walls in the apartment was another sign.

O

Another calling card of the maniac on the loose in the city of Portents. Lost in a haze of grief and rage, Soriya pulled the cell phone out of her pocket. She knew the cost of the call she was considering, knew the risks involved in bringing in help.

Nevertheless, she needed him; she needed someone, and knowing Mentor's reaction left only one person.

She needed Loren.

Patterns.

CHAPTER SIXTEEN

Loren sat on a park bench across the street from the Central Precinct as the bell tower behind him chimed in a new early morning hour. From his position, the statue of William Rath stood before him. The building's namesake towered over Loren, a fifteen-foot monument to the city's founder though the contemplative detective believed the legend would be disappointed with the praise. The statue was cracked and worn from age. There were a number of imperfections in the face and hands as if changed after the fact. The dedication plaque held the same issues with dates overwritten and marred, either by age or man Loren could not say for certain, but the date *1893* read false when compared to the rest of the writing that adorned the stone surface of the commemoration. It reminded him of the change on the date marking the warehouse where the body of Vladimir Luchik was found.

Focusing on the statue and the plaque was the fourth distraction Loren had created to keep from leaving the cold metal bars of the bench. Anything to keep him from heading into the stationhouse and the waiting Captain Ruiz. Ruiz wanted to go over the case, the same way they always had in the past. A pot of coffee split between them and a piece or three of kuchen from the captain's wife, Michelle. Ruiz wanted everything to be the same, the way it had worked between them for so long. Loren wanted anything but that. Things had changed. Hadn't they? Change was good. Change was needed. Change meant growth; it meant movement, be it forward or backward. It was movement and Loren needed to keep moving.

It took three rings before Loren realized his phone was going off in the left-hand pocket of his leather coat. It took another two for him to work his hand around the thin device, scan the caller ID, and make the decision to accept the call. There were certain people who expected calls after midnight. Loren was not one of them. Family, however, trumped the late hour the same way it did almost everything else. At least, that was what Loren wanted to believe, holding the phone to his ear.

"Hello?" he said over the wind. He turned away from the night chill that crackled into the phone, letting it fall on his back instead.

"Greg?" the voice on the other end asked. A deep sigh of relief blew into the line. "Oh, thank God."

"Meri?" Loren rechecked the caller ID. It was definitely his sister. "What time is it?"

Meriwether Atkins, formerly Meriwether Loren, guffawed into Loren's ear loudly. Loren used to enjoy the sound of his sister's laughter when they were kids but since she had started a family of her own, he realized that her laughter typically meant something else entirely different than joy.

"What time is it?" she repeated. "About three hours past your train's arrival. You know, that train I stayed up to meet so I could drive your ass home?"

Dammit. He had meant to call. Meant to text. Something to let her know about Ruiz's rescheduling but it slipped his mind as if Chicago and his life there no longer existed. There was only the mystery before him, just like it had always been. Just the way Ruiz wanted it.

"Oh." It was all he could mutter against the wind. He never should have asked in the first place but their relationship had been so strained, even with his return to Chicago. Part of him wanted to connect, or at least make the attempt he had been putting off for the last three months.

"Yeah. Oh," Meri replied. "Anytime you want to make with the explanations and the apologies, I'm all ears. And don't for a second start chewing in my ear with whatever nonsense flavor you're craving today."

Loren looked to his left hand that had retrieved a pack of gum from his pocket. He quickly tucked it back inside. *Sisters. When they know you, they know you.*

"Ruiz called me in." Loren looked to the Rath Building and the dim light from the second floor office of the waiting captain. He felt the eyes of the statue of William Rath burning into him as fiercely as Meri's undoubtedly did from the other end of the call.

"Of course he did," she muttered. There was no surprise in her tone but Loren heard the disappointment. "He knows that's the last thing you need, right?"

"He does."

"But there you are." There were things older siblings should never teach younger ones, Loren realized, hearing the biting sarcasm that filtered through every word his sister spoke.

"Here I am." He joined her tone.

"Stop it."

"What now, Mer?"

"Stop pretending to listen with your repeating answers and actually listen." She took a deep, audible breath. Loren waited patiently on the bench that overlooked the front of the stationhouse of the Central Precinct. He snapped open the package of gum, slipping a stick into his palm. He let it rest there rather than incur more wrath from the responsible Loren. He knew there was enough coming his way as it was.

"That place almost destroyed you. You know this. You chose to come home, so come home. It might not be what you were hoping for, and God knows we can be just as screwed up as anyone, but family is family, Greg."

He heard her every word. He had said them to the cracked and weary face in the mirror more times than he cared to recall. There was a time when family was king of the hill and everything else in the world was sitting at the bottom of the pile of priorities. That was how the world was supposed to be. Beth became that family to him in Portents. When Chicago no longer felt like home, she took that place. Even in her absence, she held that place while he spent every waking moment looking for who or whatever took her from him. Meri was right—he had come home, and it wasn't the way it was supposed to be. *Family was family though, right?*

"How is she?" he asked quietly, his eyes shifting up to the night sky.

"You should call her and ask her."

"Meri..."

"She's...she's okay, Greg." There was a sadness in her tone. "Tired from watching my kids all day but okay."

"Good."

"Greg. How are you?"

The question always surprised him. He didn't have an answer. He never really knew how he was doing. Not really. Between being back in Portents with Ruiz and Soriya, and now with the case laid in his lap, there was too much to consider to answer the question neatly.

"Craving the stick of peach mango I unwrapped."

A deep sigh was Meri's reply. It was clear she knew the question would never be answered. "Go, Greg. Go to Ruiz and your work. I'll be here to pick up the pieces."

"I'm fine, Mer."

"I know."

She was already gone from the conversation. He pushed her away as easily as he had when he first left Chicago to make a fresh start. "I'm sorry about the train hiccup."

"Took you long enough to get there."

"I am an idiot sometimes."

"Sometimes?"

"I'll be home soon." The words slipped out and he tried to retrieve them by clearing his throat loudly. "I'll call. Tell Mom—"

"You tell her," Meri replied quickly. The phone clicked and Loren was alone once more. He let the phone hang by his ear, wondering if he would ever again feel like he could be there for his family as much as Meri had been there for him when he really needed her. There was a divide separating them, one he had put into place long ago. It was more than his work, though, which was what drove him away in the first place. That, and what his father put them through over the years. Loren couldn't stay in Chicago and watch his family crumble. At the time, he wasn't strong enough to stop it, the abuse both verbal and physical. His strength came later, with Beth, but by then the split was complete. And remained complete, even after so much water under and over every bridge separating the Loren family.

He tucked the phone away. Dry, cracked fingers ran through his uncombed hair, massaging his scalp to wake him up. Loren had barely slipped the stick of gum between his lips when the phone lit up once more. He clicked the accept button, the first burst of peach mango hitting his tongue.

Her words were sparse, long pauses cutting through them that were not from reception issues, though Loren swore his phone knew when to crackle and fade with each and every call received. Soriya Greystone was distant on the other line, her mind somewhere else while she spoke.

"The apartment. Now." Three words summed it up. Then she was gone.

Loren placed the phone back in his front coat pocket. It was the last thing he wanted. When she left him in the park next to the morgue with the address, Loren considered tossing the scrap and walking away. Soriya and Mentor ran their own tracks, investigated in ways Loren never could and rarely would. He wanted to sleep, but even after everything, he returned to the one place he escaped three months earlier.

Before that, there was Ruiz's call at his apartment to explain. Why answer any of them? Why agree to this case? Loyalty to a friend? Curiosity? Loren no longer knew the reason. All he had was three dead bodies that needed justice or whatever the Portents equivalent ended up being. For the moment, it was enough.

The door to the apartment was open, the light of the television filling the room with a strobe effect. The carpet beneath his feet sunk in when he stepped inside. Looking down, he lifted his torn sneaker and watched the dribble of blood pool back to the floor. The small stream led to the center of the living room. With her back to Loren, Soriya knelt before a large body. Her head was low, her hands before her on the chest of the large man.

"Soriya," Loren called out in a whisper. She nodded, acknowledging his arrival but never turned away from the lifeless husk in front of her. "Is he…?"

He knew the answer before he asked. The amount of blood. The blank stare of the man's eyes toward the ceiling of the apartment's living room. There was more but he let the observations slide into the background, joining the syncopated rhythm of the broken window frame beating against the side of the building.

"I'll call it in," he said. He slid his shoe off to avoid trailing more blood. In his pocket, he removed a large plastic bag he carried from the warehouse crime scene and placed the shoe inside. "We won't have much time before they arrive, but once we let Ruiz know, he can have units patrolling the area within the hour."

"They won't find him," she said in a raspy voice, faded against the backdrop of the television. Loren found the remote on the couch and muted it, making sure his hand was covered to leave the scene as undisturbed as possible. The room fell into darkness except for a single light that beamed in from the street lamps that lined the side of the apartment complex. An orange hue shone across the ceiling. Soriya knelt close to the victim in the center of the living room, hands covered in blood.

"Probably not," he replied. While Soriya blocked most of the light, Loren was able to see the blood dripping from the man's gray lips. His torso was covered in red, making any distinctive wound indecipherable for the investigator, but enough little gashes and blows indicated it had not gone well for the man. "This was your friend? The one you—"

"Urg," Soriya interrupted. "His name was Urg. An orc."

When she lifted her head, Loren saw the dried tears on her cheeks. Another friend lost. As her hands left the body, blood trickled from her fingertips. Loren stood quickly and moved for the kitchen off the side of the room. He found a dishtowel wrapped in front of the stove and snatched it. Returning to the living room, he held it out to her. She slowly reached for it, rubbing her hands deeply along the microfiber cloth, knowing the stain would never truly be removed.

"Your friend, the orc," Loren finally said. He took the dishtowel and placed it in the bag with his shoe. Her eyes narrowed at him.

"He was one of the good guys, Loren."

The sadness in her face made his cheeks fall and his eyes lower. "Yeah. I can see that."

Loren took a step back, looking around the room. Near the front of the living room where the apartment door remained ajar, there were a series of bookshelves. Each was packed with books except for the middle shelf on each unit. Instead of books, there were a series of keepsakes. Loren leaned close for a better look, his eyes narrowing to cut through the darkness of the room. Bowling trophies. Family photos. The large orc, complete with shortened horns and pale green skin, posed in several photos that were made into a collage to celebrate his birthday. The life of an orc that made Loren's existence seem much emptier. Images of Urg riding on his motorcycle. A baseball signed by the 1961 Yankees. Loren wondered if he was at the game back then or if he spent his evenings cruising around eBay like everyone else.

The computer desk was positioned adjacent to the shelves of books and knickknacks. Tucked beneath the keyboard was a handwritten list of names and positions. Football players for a fantasy football team. Loren chuckled audibly then stopped from any further reaction. Though the notion was ludicrous to the exhausted detective, there was still the little thing of the man, or orc, or whatever lying dead in the center of the room.

Looking back, his grin fading, he saw the scrawl on the far wall. It seemed darker in the orange hue from the streetlights. Loren recognized the same paint strokes from the previous image. Just as before, some of the markings were lighter than the rest. Urg's blood mixing with the killer's. Some of the pattern remained. However, the image itself was a mystery to Loren.

"Another sign." Soriya's words cut through the silence of Loren's musings. He stepped into the center of the room for a full look at the symbol.

O

"It's different than the other. All unique from the rest." Loren took out a small notepad and drew the image of the large O with the twin markings at the peak and base of the letter. "Any ideas?"

"Languages," Soriya replied. She pointed to the large letter. "Dead and forgotten languages. This one is Cyrillic. But what it means beyond the letter it represents in the written language, I have no idea. Mentor would know. He would see it immediately."

"So we go ask him," he said. She shook her head against the idea. Whether it was matter of pride or the fear of a disapproving father being right, Loren was unsure. Not that it mattered at the moment. Now the only concern Loren had was catching a killer. Pride be damned. "He didn't lose someone close to him tonight. Two someones. If he can help, we should—"

"Why Urg?" she asked, cutting him off. Soriya leaned on the couch, staring down at the body. "Why here?"

Loren knew the moment was gone. Each player was set on their own path, just as it always happened when letting Soriya and

Mentor choose the game. Loren stopped caring long ago about it. He needed their expertise more than they needed his resources. Or his skills. The whole deal left him cold, knowing he would need all of his energy to figure out the killer's motivations and pattern on his own. Soriya's questions were near the top of his list, as was the choice of trophy. Trophies. It brought him back to the body serving as an area rug. What was taken? The light made it difficult to decipher. Nothing seemed to be missing, no appendages lopped off.

Something caught his eye in the periphery. It came from the window, causing a slight break in the rhythmic beating of the frame of the shattered window against the building. Curious, he moved for a closer look, the orange-hued light of the streetlamps shining in his face. Looking out along the side, careful not to lean on the base of the frame where shards of glass remained from the killer's flight from the apartment, Loren saw something large caught in the frame. It looked like a giant flag waving in the night breeze.

"I think…" he started, leaning out of the window into the cool, night air. Carefully, he pulled the window frame closer and grabbed hold of it in his hand. "I think I might have an answer…but it only brings me more questions."

"What is it?" Soriya asked.

Loren pulled loose the giant banner-like cloth and immediately realized what he was holding. It felt thin and hard with a layer of film lathered along its surface. It was a green he had seen before—in the photos that adorned the entire apartment. The small hairs that covered the item in Loren's hand brought it the rest of the way and the mortified man dropped it on the living room floor. It spread wide between the two of them like a blanket. It was not a flag blowing in the wind.

It was skin.

Urg's skin.

"I think our killer was looking for a new suit."

CHAPTER SEVENTEEN

Deep in the heart of the city, under the shine of skyscraper and monument, there was a wellspring of light. Below the streets and the morning roar of humanity there was a place where humanity sang. It was a secret place, those held most treasured by the city of Portents, but unlike most that took shelter in the open spaces, tucked outside of view by being on full display for the public, this place remained hidden from all.

Taking the C line at Evans Station in the heart of downtown, there was a junction, unused since the earliest days of the city. Few knew, even fewer cared, as most passengers of the subway waited for the train in silence, their eyes locked on the music players and the mobile devices they toyed with endlessly. It was a junction off the far line, one rarely used, as it led to the warehouse district that was for the most part vacant. The junction remained bolted up and forgotten over the decades.

Forgotten by most, that is to say.

The access door was large and red, though the lack of light beyond the emergency bulbs that ran the length of the track every fifty feet made it easy to miss when viewing the metal-plated entrance to the junction. It was heavy as well, its handle rusted from age, its track worn down over time. No spider webs lined the door, though, as evidenced on many of the forgotten junctions throughout the city. This junction saw use, greater than anyone could possibly imagine.

Beyond the door to the abandoned junction was a large stairwell. Wrapped in darkness, the stairs journeyed deep beneath the sound of footsteps and the screams of humanity. No tracks of light lit the path along the thin, creaking steps, but at the very bottom of the stairwell, a soft, green glow greeted visitors to the room.

The base of the stairwell opened to a large cavern, its ceiling over forty feet high. Four large marble columns supported the structure. Adorning each of the pillars was a unique language carved in the stone, all sharing the same quality as the room itself. They were forgotten languages of the world. The carved letters strung together, from floor to ceiling, around each pillar.

To the right of the entrance was a series of smaller rooms. None of them sported the same gravitas as the large cavern, though each maintained a ten-foot high ceiling. Two bedrooms, one restroom, and one common room made up the small domicile in the corner of the larger structure.

All of these details, every nuance from the marble of the pillars to the languages upon them, paled in comparison to what lay directly in the center of the four columns. It floated a few feet off the ground, guarded on each side by the columns. To the layman, it was a glowing orb of green light. To the man who stood before it, it was the gateway to knowledge. The man known only as Mentor knew it as the Bypass.

Skating along its surface were small slivers of darkness, mixing and flowing with the green light that filled the room. Looking deeply within the floating orb, one could see cityscapes in the distance, coliseums and capitols. Places not seen for centuries. Within the Bypass, they all existed as one. It stood as a crossroads to every place and every time. All heavens and all hells. It was the final destination of all.

Mentor knew all of this, standing before the glowing green light. For hours he waited, preparing to face the orb. Hours spent deep in thought, swearing off all food and water for the journey ahead. He knew what secrets the Bypass held, what answers could be told and what questions must be asked. Knowledge was power—and within the Bypass, the knowledge of eternity itself. Any question could be answered. All mysteries solved. If he chose to ask the question, the answer would present itself, though not simply in most cases. He could ask anything. He could know everything. Knowledge, while powerful, was as corruptible a force as greed and lust if asked for the wrong reasons. It was the choice, the responsibility Mentor carried for decades, an honor he had attempted to pass to Soriya over the years though there were times it seemed to be the impossible task.

That morning, as the sun rose over the city, Mentor stood before the light of the Bypass with a single question. A single task. Three people were dead and a killer was loose in his city. He had done all he could on his own, poring over the extensive collection of books and notes he had accumulated over the years. Loren's work had helped as well in this regard, though Mentor would never verbalize that amount of praise on the officer of the law. He even had an inkling about the information the grizzled detective failed to share. Information that seemed to be central to the case. There were ideas brimming to the surface, thoughts and notions about the who and what of it that needed confirmation. Mentor stood before the growing green light of all knowledge looking for a very simple answer.

A single name.

Mentor knelt before the floating orb. He took a long, deep, cleansing breath with his eyes closed. Exhaling, he felt the world around him fall silent until there was only him and the whole of eternity locked away within the Bypass. He opened his eyes, truly seeing the worlds held below the surface of the green light. His words were whispers carried on the wind throughout the room.

"Let's begin."

CHAPTER EIGHTEEN

Everything was black.

"Greg…"

A voice called out of the darkness but Loren was unable to see the face behind the sound. The name was breathless, lost in the abyss that surrounded him. Loren blinked hard several times to clear the image. His eyes refused to adjust. His mouth moved to respond to the voice in the thick black but no sound escaped. Mute, lost, and increasingly terrified, the detective realized his hands were unable to move to shovel away some of the darkness or to act as a guide through the black pool. His legs followed suit. He was immobile.

"Greg…"

The smell of lilac infected the air around him, filling his senses. The black that surrounded his eyes started to fade to dim gray, yet everything remained obscure. There was nothing to indicate time and place. How he arrived was also a question he failed to ask until that moment. The lilacs overpowered his senses. It had been a long time since he had smelled such a potent variety. It had been the last spring before Beth's passing. She planted them in the window box off the front of the living room that looked over the sidewalk where she met her end. It wasn't until the pungent odor of lavender lotion entered the equation that Loren realized what surrounded him.

"Greg."

His eyes opened to the rooftop of the apartment building. He had only been up there half a dozen times in the two years he shared the apartment with Beth after their wedding, but he recognized it immediately. The sun was coming up over the rise and Loren shielded his eyes from the sudden brightness. Squinting through his fingers, he realized the brightness was not due to the sun's intensity but to the sheer size of the orb rising before him. It was three times its normal size, filling the sky in front of him. The enlarged globe burned in a deep orange red instead of the normal early morning yellow. Loren's eyes screamed from the glare, but he fought to see the small shadow near the edge of the rooftop. Everything spun until he found one item to focus on.

Beth.

She wore a red sundress with yellow lilies along the trim. Hair flowed down on her shoulders, not a single strand out of place. Her blue eyes were wells of sadness that stared through him. A small tear dripped down her pale cheek. She stepped back to the ledge, her bare feet running along the edge of the building.

"No more sunrises, Greg."

She fell, tumbling over the edge while her words hung in the air. Loren screamed her name but the sound failed to escape once again. His body, no longer immobile and confined to the darkness, raced for the edge of the building. Greg looked down to the street to see Beth's body continue its plummet. Rather than waiting to embrace her, the street, completely in shadow, reached out to her. Shadows encased her pale skin, blue eyes begging for help, for mercy, for some kind of action on Loren's part. All he could do was watch the darkness swallow her whole.

"Beth," he screamed, jolting awake. The office was empty but Loren heard the footsteps of officers in the hallway. The precinct was in full swing, but for Loren the day was in its infancy. Crime scene photographs surrounded his makeshift bed on the floor. His coat served as an adequate pillow but he could feel the tightness in his back from the tile mattress. The case files pertaining to the three murders sat beside the photos, but none of that interested Loren. He scrambled for a spiral notebook that sat on the corner of the desk in the center of the room. As he pulled it down, it crashed to the floor and the pen that sat within shot out, rolling across the tile until his hand snatched it up. Loren opened up the notebook to a half empty sheet. His lips were muttering the same phrase repeatedly as he wrote.

"No more sunrises. No more sunrises."

He felt sweat on his brow from the dream and the accelerated heartbeat in his chest. As soon as the note was in place, he let the pen fall back to the floor. He stared at the three words he had scrawled on the page. They were accompanied by a myriad of half sentences, half thoughts, and musings. Sights. Smells. People. Faces. Impressions in the dark. Every detail was important. Every remembrance a key to that night.

"No more sunrises."

He heard the words once more, reading each one on the page. *What did it mean? Was it what she said in that last moment? Why would she? Why would she smile when she said that of all things?* Too many questions plagued the exhausted detective. Too much guesswork and zero police work, but that was all he was left with in the end—guesses.

He tossed the notebook aside and turned to the window. Gray clouds hung over the city, leaving the morning light dimmed and the skyline in a thick haze that would last throughout the day. His dreams were right. They always were. No matter what else could be said about the message his deceased wife brought him while he slept, one thing was true: There would be no more sunrises for him. Not without Beth.

And not in Portents.

CHAPTER NINETEEN

"Greg."

When Loren finally woke up to face the day, Ruiz stood in the doorway to the office. He stirred at the sound of the name, waiting for Beth to visit him once more with another message. Anything to help make sense of the last four years and the four minutes he spent with her at the end. Instead, the thin gray eyes of Ruiz met him when he stirred. Sweat dripped down Loren's hair from the interrupted sleep. He watched the captain's eyes scan the room systematically, looking over the open case files strewn about the tile floor to the spiral notebook and the pen marks throughout the open pages. Loren supported his weight with his hands, shifting his body back so that he leaned against the wall of the office. He was still exhausted. He knew it. So did Ruiz.

"Go home, Greg," Ruiz said, taking a slow sip of coffee, forcing it down. It was office coffee and most assuredly cold.

Loren rubbed his eyes deeply. He used his sleeve to mop up the small beads of sweat. "I'm fine."

"Yeah. You're the picture of mental health."

"And you're Dr. Oz," Loren snapped. "Is he still a thing? It's too early for snappy pop culture references." He shuffled the paperwork back into their respective case files and piled them next to him. "I was just resting my eyes."

Ruiz lifted a book from his desk. It was thick and a large number of the pages were earmarked for later reference. Loren tried to grab it but Ruiz pulled back, pacing the room. He quietly flipped through it, stopping at the pen marks throughout, marks much like the notebook at his feet. The title read, *The Secrets Kept in Dreams*. Both knew the author, Mr. Arnold Finney, well.

"Don't give me that look," Loren said, catching Ruiz's look of disapproval. Ruiz let the book fall in a loud thump against the tile.

"Then explain it to me."

"Title says it all, doesn't it?" he replied, refusing to give anything more than the prerequisite sarcasm.

"Finney is in prison for murder and you're reading his book. He claimed he could commune with spirits through dreams and they made him kill for them."

Loren sighed. "I remember. I locked him up."

"*You are reading his book.*"

Loren gathered the files, the book, and his notes. He placed them all on the desk in a single pile then went back and collected his coat. He needed a shower and a shave. Hell, he needed another twelve hours of shuteye, but that was out of the question as well.

Ruiz still stared him down. Loren could feel the thin eyes cutting into him. He held out a small hope that Ruiz would simply remove him from the case and send him packing but he knew that was less likely to happen than the twelve hours of beauty rest he dreamed of in his waking life.

"If I start killing people, we'll know why then, won't we?" Loren said. He opened the desk drawer and found a pack of Styrofoam cups. Officers always kept an extra stash of supplies wherever they could, in case they were holed up for a double shift or simply forgot to clean out their mug for the last month and the mold finally won out. Cup in hand, he moved for the door with Ruiz in close pursuit.

"Very funny." Ruiz was not laughing, following Loren down the hallway to the break room.

The station was dizzy with people. A large board hung in the center of the second floor with names written down one column and case numbers along the top row. Red and black were the standard colors throughout the board to signify the status of the case. Everyone hated the sight of red on the board, hence the flutter of movement throughout the halls. The detective bureau held tight to the second floor of the Rath Building; most of the other departments were located on the first and third with administrative, and higher political offices took up the top three floors. Loren was sure everyone that could be in the building at that moment was located on the second floor.

He scuttled past a series of conversations he wanted nothing to do with, hearing the tonal shift when former colleagues caught a glimpse of him. Boisterous gossiping and timely jokes turned to quiet whispers and murmurs. Loren wasn't surprised by the glares that served as his welcome back party to those who had been unaware of his arrival in the city. He never claimed to be the friendliest person on the planet, though there was a time when hitting the bar after a long shift to grab a beer after closing a tough case sounded like a great idea. With close colleagues on either side, Loren had plenty of laughs over the years under the dim haze of a local tavern or three. Those days disappeared with everything else in his life. So did the friends.

"How long did I sleep?" he asked over the drone of a dozen conversations. He grabbed the handle to the break room door and stepped inside.

"All day," Ruiz answered, closing the door behind him. Loren heard the click of the lock over the sound of the coffee slipping into his cup. His eyes rolled and he shook his head. "Sun is already fading. Now, let's finish talking for real."

"Dammit, Ruiz," Loren replied. He remembered waking up earlier in the day, making his notes, but not falling back asleep. To lose the whole day was a mistake, but to make it worse, the sleep failed to make him any more awake than he was before his eyes closed. Ruiz waited for an answer about the Finney book, not caring about any of the thoughts racing through Loren's mind. The tired detective sighed. "It's an interesting take on what our subconscious stores that we never consciously remember. Finney was a damn nut but he knew his stuff when it came to dreams. Three doctorates attested to that, at least."

"I'm waiting for the why of it."

Loren downed the cool coffee and poured another cup. "There are details, little things, I can't remember about that night. The people in the crowd. In the windows. Shadows. Just a lot of shadows. And something about sunrises. She was trying to tell me something but all I can remember is something about sunrises."

Ruiz stepped away from the door, leaving it locked for the time being. He stood before the window, looking out at the city. He nodded, lost to the pink and purple hue of the fading light of day. "Not too many of those anymore. I always make those promises to Angel. We'll get up early and see it rise. But there are always clouds blocking our view. Or I'm here."

Loren joined him by the window. It had been awhile since he heard Ruiz speak about his daughter, his family, or anything normal. It had been awhile since anything in Portents seemed normal. Ruiz was always there to show the city that it could be done. That the mundane, the simple life, was possible.

"Beth was a health nut," Loren started. He took a small sip of his second cup. The taste was worse than the first but he let it slide down his throat before taking another. He blinked repeatedly, shaking the dreams away. "She made the run to the creek at Dunbrier from our apartment pretty much year round. Always used to catch the sun over the trees at the park there. She'd tell me about it when she made it back for breakfast but I'd never listen. Not really. I mean I would listen; I would hear the general details, but never really noticed the way she smiled as she said them or the look in her eyes. Now all I hear her say is that there are no more."

Ruiz patted his friend's shoulder then stepped back to the door. The handle turned, clicking the lock once more. The roar of conversation filled the room. Ruiz held the door for Loren. "Get some sleep, Loren. Real sleep. You keep burning like this and there'll be nothing left of you."

"Is that you talking or Mathers?" Loren asked, seeing the concern in his former captain's face.

"Right now? Me," Ruiz said. "Come tomorrow?"

Loren nodded. Jurisdictional nonsense and a pissing contest from Ruiz's daytime counterpart meant more about one man's career than the dead people littering the streets. Mathers. He'd been after Loren's badge for years. Until Loren finally handed it over. Why bother with the fight now? Let Mathers handle the case. Let him try and figure it out. The crime scenes. The victims. The connections. There had to be some connections there.

Loren stopped in the doorway. His eyes were low, watching the remaining dregs of coffee slosh around the bottom of his cup. He felt the weight of the file tucked under his arm, the way it permeated through his skin, turning each detail over and over again in his mind. Shaking his head, Loren closed the door to the break room once more. The lock clicked in his hand. Photos and documents spread across the closest table, Loren quickly positioning each one for Ruiz. Outside, Pratchett held up an empty cup with the phrase *Fill Me Up or Else* on the side. He pointed to the doorknob eagerly and was met with the waving of Ruiz's hand and the closing of the shades to the break room. The eager look faded to disappointment as the final shade cut the two men off from the dozens of people outside the room.

"So that would be a no to the going home request?" Ruiz asked.

"There's something we're missing," replied Loren, ignoring the glare from his concerned friend. "Something he's put right in front of us and we're too blinded by everything else to see it. Is it about the signs or the trophies? Is it about the victims or the locations? They're almost too elaborate."

"Greg." Ruiz nodded, checking his watch for the time. It was more than concern that met Loren's eyes now, something the two of them hadn't spoken about since the former Portents detective stepped foot in the building but both knew might become an issue. Loren hated the look.

"Stop it," said Loren, his fist hitting the table. "Stop with the nonstop concern and worry. You asked for my help."

"I know." Ruiz raised his hands in surrender. "I know I did."

"Then stop looking at me like my wife just died and start looking at me like I know what the hell I'm doing!"

Ruiz leaned in close. He dropped the manila folder he had been carrying since retrieving the sleeping detective. It landed between them, though neither looked at its contents as they flooded out over Loren's case. "Do you?" the captain asked, quietly.

Loren felt the shadows of everyone on the floor near the door to the break room. They were all waiting for a word to pass around the water cooler.

"In the last hour I have had a lot thrown at me to suggest otherwise, Greg," Ruiz went on. "Finney's book. These notes."

The folder between them contained Loren's preliminary notes. He peered down, running his tongue along his top lip. His eyes remained on the frantic messages he had put to paper during the early morning hours after the death of Urg. He felt Ruiz's bearing down on him.

"I think it is worth looking—"

"Property records and archive reports on buildings dating back to the founding of Portents?" Ruiz interrupted, pointing to requisition paperwork never signed or authorized by him yet somehow carried his signature. "That's your only lead? And sending Pratchett without my authorization was a nice touch too."

"Did he?"

"Do you even listen to yourself?"

"I saved time, skipped a step. We've done it a hundred times before. Especially working the cases we work, Ruiz. You know—"

"Dammit, Loren." With his hands firmly entrenched against his hips to keep them from slamming against something or someone, the choice becoming less and less clear, Ruiz paced the length of the room. "Just shut the hell up for one second and listen to yourself. Yes, they are in the damn file. Yes, you saved time. No, it's not like it used to be and you know it. You're reaching for some great mystery that isn't there. Same as always. Same as Beth."

The words held there for a long moment. Loren huffed audibly through his nose, his eyes wide from hearing how things truly were between them. He understood the rest of the department. He knew the mistakes made. The lessons learned. It was the reason he left. The reason he wanted to stay gone. He came back for Ruiz against his better judgment. He came back for a friend. A friend who had lost faith in him as much as everyone else had.

Gathering up the papers before him, Loren tucked the file under his arm again. With his coffee cup in hand, he made for the door. "Nice, Ruiz. Real nice."

Ruiz followed the angry detective into the hall. Gawkers shifted to the side, pretending to be in any number of situations that didn't amount to simply wasting time. Loren refused to slow down, long strides carrying him toward the elevator and the rear stairwell. He needed air. He needed to think. The coffee was hitting him already. The thick black liquid did little but give him the adrenaline surge he needed in the morning. He hated the taste, the smell, the texture. He hated everything about it—except for the surge. As his hand reached for the door to the parking garage, Ruiz cut him off.

"Come on, Greg."

"I think we've said enough today, don't you?"

Ruiz nodded in agreement. His words were little more than a whisper. "Go home, Greg. I'll have a car take you. Sleep in a bed with a pillow instead of a damn spiral notebook for comfort."

"Sold the bed. Tossed the pillow," Loren replied. He stopped, leaning against the wall near the back stairwell leading to the parking garage. He finished off the coffee and tossed the cup in a nearby receptacle. "Nothing left there, Ruiz. Nothing left at all."

"I'll make arrangements then."

Loren rubbed his eyes and beat his head softly against the wall. "If it's not the locations, then what? The signs? The trophies? The victims? There *is* something between all of them, and the locations…"

"Are a distraction. Not the way in." Ruiz shook his head. His hand fell on Loren's shoulder. "You'll get there. We will get there. But right now? I don't see it."

"This isn't me reaching, Ruiz. Four victims now," Loren continued. Ruiz shook his head once more at the mention of the number, pointing to the notes Loren had gathered from the break room. Something else had changed, though Loren refused to let it derail his train of thought. He needed the pieces to fit. Needed to make someone else see them fall into place. "No seeming connection between them except for their bizarre—"

Ruiz interrupted with a scoff. "Bizarre barely scratches the surface with them. A wolf boy? Or how about the little old lady with the magic eyeballs? An orc with a better bowling average than me? Yeah, after all the fun we've already had today, we don't need to mention your little tip about the apartment murder last night and why I wasn't your first call to handle the scene. All of this running around this city. Bizarre doesn't touch it. Hell on Earth is more apropos."

"Is that what you really think, Ruiz?"

Both men were startled, turning quickly. Soriya Greystone stood in the stairwell, smiling.

"Or is that your pet name for things you don't fully understand?"

CHAPTER TWENTY

In the cavernous chamber hidden beneath the city, a lone figure knelt before a great, glowing orb. With his eyes closed, yet open to the mysteries before him, he sought the answer to a single question. The identity of a killer loose on the streets of Portents. He was not the only one seeking something.

He was also not the only one in the large chamber.

Tucked behind the domicile erected in the corner of the expansive room, a shadow stayed low and unseen. The man in the large trench coat with the mismatched eyes watched with great interest at the actions of the figure in the center of the chamber. When he arrived, darkness and emptiness surrounded him. The dim, green glow of the large floating orb in the center of the room was muted against his presence but came to life with the arrival of the white-haired individual with the thin beard. With the darkness as his guide, he peered around the room, taking in the languages marking the four tall columns with a wry smile on his face. At the approaching footsteps, he found the deep recesses of the cavern, allowing him to view all in the room without the threat of discovery.

The end was close now. He saw it in the glow of the orb and upon the face of the tired, old man reflected along its surface. The time was approaching when he would finally take back what was his all along. The city of Portents. Every street. Every building. Every sign was his. All his. The final piece lay before him to accomplish the long-time goal. It was something he had only seen once long ago but had never forgotten, not through the fires he endured or his return.

Rumors of the glowing orb of green light dated back longer than even his days in the city. Talk of a light that saw backward and forward in time. A light that granted its user the ability to know anything and everything with only a simple question. The shadow who had once been a man scoffed at the notion. He believed in the real world, in the power a man wielded only with his hands and his mind. The idea of a single item capable of unlocking the mysteries of the universe was absurd and he laughed in the face of every man, woman, and child that relayed its tale. Over time, the stories faded from the memories of him and the populace surrounding him. Hard times came in the first days of his city. Long winters and bitter crops. Still, he persevered. He rose beyond the qualms of his fellow man, finding his own truths in the universe through less accepted methods.

Until the Square.

It was a feast, a celebration of survival and the true founding of the city that rose around them. There were dances in the streets, ravenous and craven with lust for power. The people were enthralled. He sat above them on the third floor balcony, watching with the wry smile on his lips. For hours the cheers rang through the streets; from the textile mills of the east to the docks along the west, Portents was a city of unity the night of its true birth. Simple-minded pleasure turned to darker pursuits that matched the waning evening light, the liquor flooding the gullets of men and women alike beginning to run dry. There was something among them. A new focus for the joyous people of the city. The shadow that was once a man watched the events unfold, a silent observer to the controlled chaos he created for his citizens.

It started slowly. A cry in the darkness. Then the roars of men and the beating of drums. Then it turned ugly. A young woman was brought into the center of the Square. Only the dim light of the streetlamps guided her through the street like a runway. It was a mistake calling her a woman. Calling her young was the second mistake. As she neared the center of the Square, it became clearer. Her clothes were torn from the beating the men gave her in the darkness. Her skin was not the pale pink, white, or black of the people of Portents. It was green. Her eyes were black as the night, not even surrounded by white. Her body was bony and weak, a starving old crone looking for scraps left by the revelers during their festivities. Only she was caught in the taking.

The shadow that lorded over his people continued to revel, allowing the events to proceed. The woman screamed for mercy, pulling and scratching at the men who held tight to her. The cries of drunken fools filled the air. Cries of a witch among them. Cries of the obscene horrors hidden in the darkness of the city they had built. They would not stand for it. They would not allow the darkness to overtake their purity. The word made the shadow laugh and with him, the roar of laughter infected them all.

The woman was strapped to a large wooden stake and positioned in the center of the street. More people gathered for the viewing. Smiles clung to the faces of even the youngest of children, aroused from their sleep in the tenement housing that lined the Square by the screams of their parents. Large hay bales were brought from the east end of the city for kindling. The street lamps were dimmed further where preparations were made to bring a greater light to the city. Fervor swept through them all, their eyes bloodshot from the hours of drinking and celebration. Low murmurs turned to chants turned to screams. Women cackled, men beat their chests, but all demanded the same thing: a fire to purify their streets of the evil among them.

The bales were on their way down the street when the winds shifted. Not the actual winds, as there had been little of the cool breeze that typically struck the city when the sun went down. The winds that changed were that of a different kind. Winds that turned the loud cackles and the wry smiles of citizen and leader alike to quiet looks of confusion.

In the midst of the change, one of the two large bales of hay and the cart carrying it erupted in flames. The eruption shot fifteen feet into the air and the shockwave from its ignition threw back the half dozen men surrounding the cart. Hundreds of eyes shifted to the flames, the heat searing their senses. Even the shadow that called itself a man was taken aback by the sudden flickers of fire. It illuminated everything around them; the Square was a series of shadows along the buildings on all four corners. All but one remained in a fixed position, staring at the bright beauty of the flames. One shadowy figure shifted among them toward the large wooden stake. Eyes that flickered with the same red as the flames watched the man untie the claimed witch. She raced into the night but the man lingered, keeping a guard over her while she escaped the justice of the city. The stares of the citizens returned to life after being lost for mere moments in the distraction of the flames.

They shifted back to the empty stake, their angry focus now gone from sight.

In the corner, a single pair of eyes remained fixed on the man who had freed their prize. Eyes that pulsed with vengeance watched the man raise his hands, pointing toward the second bale of hay. The eyes never left the man as the second bale erupted into flames the same way the first had mere minutes before. No, the second bale did not pry that pair of eyes away from the man who had somehow willed the bale to explode with nothing but a glare and a small object wrapped tight within his grasp.

A stone of grey.

The stranger vanished in the darkness of the city and the man who would one day rise again as a shadow never saw him again. However, he never forgot about him or the stone. Even at the end of his days at the center of the city, he remembered that night and the stone that created flames with but a thought from its bearer.

Now it lay before him.

In the center of the room, on the floor of the large cavern it sat. As he reached into the hovering orb of light searching for the man who had become a shadow of his former self, that shadow found the object he had waited centuries to obtain. The object that foretold the end of his journey, the final chapter of his story.

In front of the man was a stone of grey.

CHAPTER TWENTY-ONE

"You shouldn't be here," Ruiz snapped, slamming the door to the rear stairwell behind him. The aggravated captain quickly shuffled Soriya and Loren out of the hallway, away from the prying eyes of the stationhouse. There had been enough drama in the department. Soriya knew it was coming the second she opened her mouth, but it needed saying anyway. Ruiz was always pushing things he failed to reconcile with to the side, forgetting the face of the city while spouting the fact that he was born and raised within the city limits. He had known the truth years ago, had even been called an ally by Mentor on rare occasions (though only while drinking alone in the darkness of the Bypass domicile when he believed none could overhear his ramblings). Still, Ruiz's inability to come to terms with the dichotomy of the city forced the ugly out of her, which in turn brought it out of him. It was a hate-hate relationship that worked for them. Even when it didn't, it was the only one they had.

"Where then, Ruiz?" she shot back, jumping up to the railing along the staircase. She took a seat on the cool metal. "Where would you feel comfortable with me being?"

"I have plenty of options for you, like straight to h...." Ruiz stopped, his eyes wide in anger. If they burned any deeper at the young woman, they would have seared two holes through her. He took a deep breath. His hands found his hips as he did so, looking away to find a new focus.

"Every time," Loren muttered, more to himself than anyone else. He glanced over at Soriya. She knew it was coming. She turned away from him on the handrail to put it off as long as possible but when he stepped down to the first floor landing below, he caught a glimpse of the large welt that covered the left side of Soriya's face. It was a deep red mostly, but around the edges of the wound, a purple and black bruise was already forming. Loren's eyebrow rose slightly. He casually sipped his coffee and looked away but the question was there for her to answer. She felt her hand softly graze against it, holding back the wince, and wondered when she would learn to just walk away from things.

Soriya and Loren had parted company outside the apartment complex before any other officers arrived. As she slipped into the shadows of the city, she realized there were little options left for her. Mentor was in the Bypass chamber digging up his own answers, and for her to walk in with another failure, to show up with tears dried on her cheeks and another friend dead, was unacceptable. He needed to see her succeed. She needed him to see she was strong, that the responsibility was meant for her. She needed validation and it was never going to come after that night.

So she ran. Alone, cold, and tired, Soriya Greystone fled deeper into the city of Portents. Her city. Despite that her vantage typically came from the ground up, she knew every rooftop, every fire escape, and every connection that kept her above it all as she traveled through the night. The cold wind bit her uncovered skin. It stung her eyes, but she never blinked. She ran faster. Urg was dead. Vlad was dead. She ran faster through the night, remembering them, trying to put them aside as Loren would during an open investigation. She needed to see past them. She needed to figure out the puzzle laid out before her. Every instinct made her want to cry out. Mentor would know. Mentor had answers to questions Loren had yet to conceive…but not her. She was stuck on the faces of two men lying on metal slabs in a morgue. So she ran through the night until the day began to creep over the city.

With daylight approaching, she found a quiet alcove, a no longer functional bell tower that sat atop Saint Sebastian's Church. There she slept for a time, fighting dreams of friends no longer with her.

Dusk was her alarm clock and she woke refreshed with only a minimal amount of deep rest. Mentor always asked where she was during the days when her room in the small domicile was not occupied. She never answered. The city was hers and hers alone when she needed it most. He stayed cooped up underground for so long it was hard to remember a time he saw the sun rise in the sky. Soriya was more of a sunset person and as she waited for the glowing orb to fall behind the horizon, she started moving once more through the city. This time with a purpose. She headed for the docks and the Town Hall Pub.

The air populating the bar was stagnant, muggy from being closed off from the world. Few people sat around; all but a handful remained dismally focused on the beverage before them. The pub was built over the remains of the city's first town hall. The citizens of Portents burned it to the ground when the mayor was discovered to be involved in a series of heinous acts in the shadows of the city. That was the story they painted for visitors, which were fewer and fewer each year. The pub was a reminder of those long lost days, a dark and depressing glimpse at the city that was and how little things had truly changed.

Soriya sat alone in the back corner of the bar. She had ducked under the police cordon that did little to assuage the customers of the establishment. The taped outline of Martin Decker remained around the last stool at the far end of the bar. It was roped off with police tape but someone had placed balloons on the tape, making it more a toast-worthy celebration for the patrons of the bar than a deterrent for what could happen there.

Decker was a shifter as far as she knew. Mentor, over the course of her years with him, did his best to prepare her for the city and that meant knowing the people within its borders. Decker was once a colleague and informant to the old man and she easily understood him.

A typical shifter could change appearances on a dime to look like anyone. Decker was not that skilled. His abilities were left to his hands. They could be the world's sharpest blades or the key to a locked door. The skills he developed with his fingers led him to an illustrious career as a petty thief for a number of gangs, but his skill was only meant for survival in his eyes. Profit equaled exposure, which was never the goal of one of his kind. People like him, hidden in plain sight within the city that Soriya did her best to protect, needed the cushion of anonymity. Of the mundane. Decker wanted a life and he was good at the one he had drawn. For a time. The deceased spent much of his final years on the stool that sat in front of Soriya, a quiet lonely spiral until the end.

His hand was the prize, the tool used to murder Vlad in the abandoned warehouse. Each victim led to the next and the next and the next. But Urg's death was meaningless. No trophy was collected. The skin of the orc was lost in the chase. A pointless death, except for the sign left behind.

Decker's sign was similar in nature to the rest, scrawled in a deep crimson barely discernable along the faded wood trim that covered the walls. Though the forensics team had collected all of the evidence and taken photos of every inch of the scene, no man was stationed on the site to watch over it. The bar was not closed; the owner had refused the order, with the help of a friendly call to the mayor. So the sign sat above piss and puke from the few disheveled patrons that resided more in the pub than their own homes.

/\

Although she recognized that she'd seen the letter before, Soriya did not recall the language the letter belonged to. She chalked her memory lapse up to exhaustion, mostly physical and emotional, but she knew it to be more. This was her job and she was failing at it, the pressure of Mentor's approval bearing down on her at every step.

Her thoughts were cut short by a hand slapping against her shoulder. He hugged tight to Soriya's shoulder, six inches taller than her, with thick black hair styled perfectly in place. He wore a smile to match his physique, big and bold, with pearly whites that reflected the overhead lights along the ceiling.

"Name's Ed." His voice rang loud enough for everyone to hear. "Buy you a drink?"

"No thanks." Her reply was curt and she was quick to remove his hand before turning back to the scene of Martin Decker's murder.

"I don't think you mean that." His breath reeked. His hands balled into fists as he fought to maintain his smile.

"Pretty sure I do, slick," she said, not looking at him but at the small puddle of dried blood beneath the stool where Decker bled out. Where Decker died and no one noticed the man's passing.

"Like I said," Ed replied, his hand coming back down on her shoulder. It slammed against her harder this time. "I don't think you do. So a drink and a game of darts. Maybe more if you're lucky."

"My dream date." She smiled back at him. The message was clear—Ed wasn't going away. He turned to see the reaction from his friends. As he did, Soriya reached up and took his hand from her shoulder. She twisted it hard and the man yelped in pain. He tried to turn to face her, his other arm flailing to grab her. Her hand snatched his wrist and sent the gripped arm up behind his back. She brought her leg up and slammed it into his backside. At the same moment, she released her grip on his arm and Ed went tumbling into a nearby table. The patrons of the bar turned but remained silent. Ed's friends quickly raced to his side but he waved them away. He spit the floor in front of him, rose to his feet, then turned back to Soriya and her widening grin.

"Do you know who I am?" he screamed at her.

"Ed, right?" she mockingly replied. "Last name, Dickhead?"

"Hilarious, lady. You have no clue. This is my bar. Hell, this is my *city*. They should have damn well changed Portents to my name!"

"I don't think Dickhead works well as a city name." She was ready to leave. There was nothing more to see here and she needed to find Loren to see if anything else had occurred while she was sleeping. She moved for the door but Ed stood in front of her. She shifted to the side and he followed suit. Soriya licked her top lip. "You should let me leave."

"Make me," he sneered.

He did not see her fist. If he had, he would have ducked, blocked, or at least closed his eyes to the impact. Instead, he did nothing but take it. It shattered bone; it bent his nose until there was a crunching sound. Her fist carried him off his feet and flat on his back with a crash. Ed did not get up.

The patrons of the bar simply watched. There was no reaction other than the occasional sip of their beverages. The brawl was a mild distraction from their evenings, nothing more. As Soriya looked over to make sure Ed was still breathing, she failed to see the fist coming at her. It slammed against her left cheek and she spun around from the impact. She did not fall, instead stumbling on her heels to regain her center of gravity.

Her focus returned and she immediately caught sight of one of Ed's friends standing before her. He held his fists high in defense.

Soriya's eyes narrowed as she stared down the unconscious man's friend. Her cheek burned from the impact but nothing was broken. She felt her chest heaving, threatening to break open and release her anger upon the man. Instead, she simply glared at him. Her hand balled into a fist once more, readying her small frame. Ed was still on the floor, unmoving except for the slow rise and fall of his chest. Slowly, his friend's hands fell to his side and he stepped back. He kept his hands in clear view, fingers wide and spread. His eyes were conciliatory and she accepted the act.

She left without a word.

Loren was still locked on her bruised cheek when her thoughts returned from the night's events. She turned away, still feeling the anger toward her attacker but now had a better focus. Ruiz.

"You keep hoping it's all a bad dream," she spat. "That I'll just fade into the shadows with the rest of the nightmares. Somewhere you don't have to hear about us or think about us. You've known about Portents for years and you still refuse to acknowledge it."

Ruiz's eyes were sullen. He looked to his watch, time slipping from him as assuredly as his temper. "How can I live with it? How? I tuck my daughters in their beds and pray to God that the beasts you let roam the streets don't take them from me? There is a monster out there right now ripping the hearts out of people, skinning them, for Christ's sake!"

Vlad's image met all of them differently but all fell silent at the thought of the young man, dead on the floor in the abandoned warehouse. There was no justice in it. There was no forgetting it either. Each of them felt some pang of guilt over the open case that sat before them. It was written before them. Loss of family. Loss of friends. Children, lovers. For Loren, it was most assuredly Beth. No matter the victim, no matter the place or the circumstance, Loren saw Beth in the dark. For Soriya, though, it was Vlad. Alone and broken. She should have called him, instead of waiting for him to come to her, as was always the case. She should have been there even if he wasn't always reliable in return. They held their images in their minds but all felt the pang of failure over his death, deserved or not.

"Tell me how I explain it to my six-year-old, who wants nothing more than a perfect score on her spelling test?" Ruiz continued. He stood at the top of the stairs looking down at Loren and Soriya. His eyes, once filled with fire, looked solemn. Loren stepped in front of Soriya before she could answer.

"Ruiz," he said plainly, and the captain nodded. There was more to say—there always would be. However, there was more to do as well, and in the end, that always had to win out.

"I have a meeting with the mayor and the commissioner. And Mathers. Latest victim today was better connected and less inclined to have flame breath or grow wings, so of course his death will be my fault. Be lucky if I'm not asked to clean out my desk...let alone your temporary one." Ruiz's words were cold in the dark of the stairwell. He pointed to Soriya and then to the small window that looked out to the neighboring park and the city streets. "You shouldn't be here. You should be out there."

Ruiz opened the door to the second floor of the Rath Building. Immediately, the sounds of the hall filled the stairwell. The conversations of dozens echoing in the dark. The aging captain stood silent, the light behind him throwing his tired frame into shadow. His eyes cut through the darkness, finding Loren's.

"This needs to be over. Now."

CHAPTER TWENTY-TWO

Loren paged through the case file Ruiz slipped between his own notes. Notes that had split them apart on the case at hand. Soriya paid him no attention, instead looking out to the city past the small ledge of the parking garage. Both remembered the conversation only three months earlier. It was meant to be a goodbye, not a "see you soon" for another case of murder and mayhem. Loren hoped that was what it would be, anyway, but he had the feeling Soriya was much happier with the current results instead.

The file was thick. New photos and evidence piled up during the day, a day he lost to nightmares. The amount of new information, including another death, took Loren by surprise. He paged through each new item quickly, unwilling to lose any more time, to see anyone else fall at the hands of the madman among them. Silently, he catalogued each new piece of information for future reference, adding them to the existing photos locked within his methodical mind.

When he looked up, Soriya was seated on the ledge just as she had been the night Loren left. This time, instead of sorrow, there was rage in her stance, evident from her balled up fists to the furrow of her brow. The bruise on her left cheek was more substantial than she let on, shifting darker and darker with each passing moment. Still, Loren saw it in her eyes. He knew that look very well. She wanted another fight. And soon.

"He's not wrong," Loren said, closing the file and placing it on the ledge next to her. He put his hand upon it to keep it from whisking away into the night. No passing child needed to see the photos contained within the thick manila folder.

"Doesn't mean he's right," Soriya answered, refusing to look at him.

"Arguing won't win him over. Especially the same argument."

She spun around on the ledge so her legs were dangling over the side of the parking garage. The city was quieter than it had been the night before. Quieter than either of them had seen it in a long time. Something was coming they needed to be ready for, not pretend it didn't exist.

"Ignorance is not bliss, Loren. You know it better than most."

Loren nodded. It was a thought that plagued him four years earlier. If he had known more about the city, if he had truly seen it for what it was and accepted every facet of the culture beneath the city lights, could he have saved his wife? He had tried to reconcile that man or beast may have committed the heinous act as far as he knew from what little evidence was found on the scene and in the apartment, but the question remained. Had he done enough?

"This was Beth's city. Not mine," he said, eyes distant, overlooking the city. "That night? The night we *truly* met? If Beth was still around, I would have asked her to pack her bags and head as far away as possible from the city and never look back. She wouldn't, of course. No way in hell. The fight would have lasted for hours and we would both still be here. For her. Not for me. Honestly, though, I expect it would be *my* reaction that almost everyone would have knowing Portents the way I do now."

Soriya's lips softened, the rage fading from her cheeks. Her hands unclenched against the concrete of the ledge and Loren saw her head lower in thought. She looked to him for the first time since entering the garage.

"How would you have ended the fight?" she asked quietly.

"Same way we always did." Loren smiled. Even the memory of his wife brought back the thin grin he always carried in her presence. "We'd run out of things to say. And a kiss."

"Guess Ruiz and I still have things to say."

"Just don't give him a kiss."

She laughed, spinning back into the parking garage. Her hands pushed off the ledge and she landed square on her heels. "Yikes. Please talk to me about the case before that mental image takes hold."

"Right." Loren opened the folder and handed it to her. She flipped through it and immediately peered back up.

"Something new. What Ruiz was mentioning about the better connected victim," she stated, holding up the image of a man buried under a mountain of garbage in a back alley. Little could be seen of the victim but what could explained the goal behind the murder.

"Found this afternoon," Loren nodded. "Fifth victim. No skin. Looks like our guy found that new suit."

"The sign?" Soriya asked, flipping through the photos without success.

"None. He didn't seem to be anything more than human too."

Soriya's eyebrow raised and she tilted her head to the right. "He's meticulous with his victims except this guy?"

"Doesn't make sense."

"Add it to the list."

"Yeah," Loren agreed. "Ruiz is pushing for a curfew and more patrols. He'll get the patrols at least, but the commissioner and the mayor won't sign off on taking people off the streets. Knowing their feeling on it, Mathers won't push for it either."

Soriya closed the file and handed it back to Loren. Her hands leaned heavily on the ledge, her shoulders slumped in frustration. "I shouldn't be here."

"What?" Loren asked, curious.

"What Ruiz said about me. That I shouldn't be here." In the moonlight, her eyes shifted rapidly. She was working through something, Loren noted. It was why they worked together so well in the past. He had questions, sure, and could even find answers to some of them. Nevertheless, she had questions that no cop could think up.

"You know he didn't..." he started but she raised her hand to wave him off. She wasn't fishing for pity or a compliment.

"He shouldn't be here, Loren." Her eyes were wide. Her hands moved before her, willing the answers out of her with thoughts moving faster than her lips. "The murderer. These trophies aren't trophies at all. Mentor was right about Anteros. The balance has tipped."

"Slow down, Soriya." He tried to follow as best he could, knowing more questions were already being raised. *If the trophies were needed, what were they needed for?*

"Loren," she continued. She crept up on the ledge of the parking garage and began to pace above him. "This killer. He shouldn't be here and he knows it. The fact that he knows more about this city than us. The placement of the murders. The signs themselves. Something or someone ripped him back but not all of him made the journey. His body was cracked and torn when he came back and he's…"

"Putting the pieces back together," Loren chimed in, following her train of thought.

"Showing Humpty Dumpty how it's done too." She jumped down and started for the far side of the parking garage and the exit. Loren hesitated for a moment, wondering what she was up to, then quickly pursued.

"What's the endgame once the pieces are back in place?" Loren asked.

"We can't figure that out yet. We need to know who he is first."

"So we find Mentor, right?" he asked, knowing the old man wanted in on the case. His last request continued to echo in his thoughts. *Keep her safe.* The question, of course, made the joy fade from her face, the two failures from the last two days playing in Technicolor behind her eyelids.

"No," she replied. She let the answer hang between them for a long moment until Loren nodded. Then she smiled widely, ever the child holding onto a secret she couldn't wait to share. "He has his methods. I have mine."

CHAPTER TWENTY-THREE

The sixth floor of the Rath Building was a different animal than the second, where Ruiz made his home in the corner office overlooking downtown. Where stained ceramic tiles, mostly cracked or mismatched with their neighbors, lined the floor in the detective bureau, the sixth floor carried lush carpet throughout. The doors were stained glass with thick cherry frames, each with the name of its occupant in the center. Turnover made this a lucrative endeavor but one always justified when it came time for budget review. Personnel be damned.

A long hallway extended from the elevator. Secretaries and aides were set up in cubicles along the left hand wall. Restrooms were to either side of the sliding doors of the lift upon entry to the floor. The right hand wall was made up of two large offices. The second was the commissioner's with the first acting as home to his personal staff, a connecting door between them to keep contact with the outside world and any unwanted appointments to a minimum. Commissioner Phillip Thorne was known for this tactic, doing his best to keep his head out of the line of fire as often as possible.

Wide double doors stood at the far end of the hall. Behind them was a large conference room, home to many weekly meetings with every department in the building but more often than not the meetings were between only two people—the mayor and Thorne. City Hall was never where Mayor Reginald Dunn wanted to end up. He fell into it over a career of quiet ineptitude, at least from what Ruiz gleaned during election season or every single time Dunn attempted to say his name with his best Spanish accent. Ruiz preferred people butcher his name rather than his heritage. Every week since taking office, Mayor Dunn found his way to the Rath for his weekly meeting with the commissioner, bringing his entourage and taking over the entire conference room for the day. The standard meeting was more to placate the masses when it came time to vote or to figure out the next best place for a catered lunch than it was about crime statistics and open cases...until five murders hit the headlines in a single week. Weekly meetings turned daily. The entourage was left at City Hall and arguments over the cheese platter turned to screams over what was being done to end the string of violence infecting the streets of Portents. As if it started and stopped as easily as that. But that was how the mayor saw it, so that was how the commissioner saw it. A simple fix without seeing the underlying problem, a problem Ruiz knew went deeper than most anyone else did in the Rath, although he was hesitant to make it known without first checking to verify his pension was secure.

There was another reason Ruiz kept quiet about Loren and Soriya's suspicion about the murders: fear. Fear that saying it out loud would make it real. Fear that no one would believe that the city contained the monsters of myth and legend that they had only read about as kids, because half the time he had trouble believing it as well. More than anything, it was fear that because they refused to believe, things would get worse. There was already that feeling with the latest rash of homicides in the city. How could there not be that feeling? Five dead in a week's span was an ungodly statistic to hear on the news or read in the paper. Ruiz knew it could be worse, though. There was a line he held close, a line that allowed people like Soriya and Mentor their own brand of justice, even though it went against everything Ruiz stood for but he could see it sliding without Loren. Without himself at the captain's desk. Especially when the next person in line for the job stood in front of him, arms folded across his chest and a scowl across his face, waiting to take over and run the ship directly into the ground.

Captain Rufus Mathers.

Mathers waited patiently outside the glass doors of the conference room, watching the two shadows within. Muffled curses flew freely and the bald, bespectacled officer of nineteen years watched silently with mild enjoyment upon his face. Ruiz met the man, ten years his junior, the first time he walked into the stationhouse. He wore the same black suit with the same upright posture that placed him higher than most of his fellow officers.

Mathers started as a simple beat cop who quickly found his place in front of the cameras. His eagerness to please his superiors assured him room for growth and when the captain's desk opened there was no discussion, though Ruiz fought tooth and nail for an officer with experience over a younger face to put before the cameras as the voice of the law in the city, which was exactly the role the commissioner wanted for the exuberant Mathers. Mostly, he was meant to be the buffer between the commissioner and the press, but even knowing that didn't slow Mathers down from snatching up his role with vigor. He loved the game and played it well. There were many occasions where Ruiz thought his time was over, mistakes made on a personal level or even with the job at hand, but Mathers always snaked his way out of the firing line and back into the hearts of his superiors.

Times were shared between them that could have been construed as moments of true friendship. Both men shared similar paths, held similar faith both in God and in the world. The differences, however, were insurmountable. Mathers was ambitious to the point of open betrayal at every opportunity. His suit was worn as a sign of his station, while the coffee-stained cuffs of Ruiz's own button-down carried the look of a man willing to dig into the job rather than sit back and wait for the report to land on his desk. Mathers was in the office at the start of his shift, no sooner, and out the door at the end. His desk was clean and organized. Ruiz never left on time, rarely showed up less than an hour early to start his night at the station, and could not say what color his desk was, as he had not seen it clearly since his first day as captain.

"I'm sure we're next," said Mathers without turning to see him. His eyes were level with the shadows pitched against the glass doors of the conference room. Muffled curses became audible though neither would acknowledge them outright.

Ruiz stopped next to his daytime counterpart. "Mathers."

"Ruiz," replied Mathers.

The handle to the doors fell within Ruiz's grasp but before he could turn it, Mathers called out without looking. "I'd let them finish."

This was where Mathers knew the game better than Ruiz, or more to the point, where Ruiz couldn't be bothered to play games. The politics of the position, the face time with the public, were all nuances that Ruiz was capable of handling when necessary but never sought out beyond that necessity. Playing to the crowd, winning the support of the press and his superiors, were the wrong motivators when it came to police work in the city of Portents. They were the obligatory evils of the system, but obligation only went so far when it came to closing cases. Mathers knew the arena. He lived it daily. He loved the games, played them very well—as evidenced by the barrage of questions and accusations thrown Ruiz's way instead of his own during meetings. Mathers wanted the spotlight and took it as often as he could, from drunk driving arrests to corner store robberies. He was hired to be the face of the department and thrived on that role.

"I don't have time for them to figure out how to run my case," Ruiz answered, though he let his hand fall from the conference room door.

"Your case?" Mathers scoffed. He turned from the conference room, allowing his wiry frame to lean against the wall behind him. He loomed over Ruiz, who could see his reflection in the younger captain's thin, round spectacles. "That's funny, Ruiz. I was under the impression Greg Loren had taken it over. I must have been mistaken, though. I mean, we wouldn't let that lunatic back in the building unless he was in cuffs. Would we?"

Ruiz's voice fell low. "I'm not going to do this with you, Rufus."

"Please, Ruiz. Let's." Mathers' hand slipped into the small portfolio that rested by his feet. The zipper snapped open, revealing a number of files. Mathers found a bright green file among the pack of manila and snatched it with his free hand. "And look. I even brought his personnel file."

Ruiz felt his eyes roll. This was the part no one understood, from his own wife to Loren, though sometimes he received more pity from his former colleague than Michelle. There were battles to be fought with each case. The officers that served with him fought theirs on the streets. Ruiz was forced to fight *his* in the Rath, and fight them with his own team. It was exhausting, and since the promotion of Mathers five years earlier, it had become much worse. More than anything, it was jealousy, an envious nature at the amount of cases handled and closed by the night shift over the day. While Ruiz saw this as simply the way the city worked, Mathers saw this as a challenge to take over the Latino's job and become the top captain at Central Precinct. Another difference to add to the joy of their working relationship.

"Hmm," remarked Mathers, flipping blindly through the file. Both men knew it by heart, Ruiz because he noted most of the events within and Mathers because Loren was one of the few officers that managed to piss him off. "Three disciplinary hearings in two years. Two cases thrown out from negligence and, oh yeah, that little bit about putting Detective Standish in the hospital."

"Dammit, Mathers. Loren's wife died."

"So he gets to John Wayne the job the rest of his life?"

Both men turned to see the stares of the men and women congregating in the sixth floor hallway. The muffled curses had also faded. Mathers cocked his head away from the doors. They took a step away, glaring at the others until they took the hint and resumed their work.

"No," Ruiz finally answered. He kept his voice to a whisper, both men positioned next to each other against the outside wall of the conference room away from the double doors. "He doesn't get to write his own rules. But he does get the benefit of the doubt. Or did you suddenly forget your buddy, Standish, was misplacing evidence to cover his gambling debts? Evidence that caused those two cases of Loren's to be thrown out." Ruiz grabbed the file away from Mathers, flipping back through the papers until he landed on a report with his own letterhead. "Why, that's strange. It says that right in this report that you seemed to skip over. Don't worry, though. When you pout and cry to the commissioner about Loren's awful behavior in order to take over the case yourself, I'll be sure to bring this up."

Mathers closed the file. A single finger slipped up to his glasses, fixing them against his face. He turned away from Ruiz. "That's not what this is about."

A small chuckle escaped from Ruiz's lips. "Of course it is. You live for high profile cases. Hell, you were probably already in there helping write their victory speeches with special thanks to the efforts of Captain Rufus Mathers, the man who solved the case of the missing prize in the Crackerjack box. Too bad that won't cut it with them. Domestics and B & E's just aren't front-page news, especially this week, and that's all our supreme overlords are able to read before flipping to the funny pages. But a murderer? A serial killer on our streets? That would set you up for quite some time."

"Quite the imagination, Ruiz," replied Mathers with a thin smile.

"Yeah, it must be the kid in me that sees the world so completely screwed up," Ruiz snapped. "Let's just get this over with. I have a murderer to put away."

Ruiz gathered up his files and started back to the conference room. The deep voice of Rufus Mathers called him back.

"Loren's a loose cannon. Standish didn't deserve what happened to him, and don't think for a second Loren won't do it again."

Ruiz stopped, thinking back to Standish bleeding on the floor of the second floor hallway outside his office. He remembered the screams and the fury of Loren, standing over him. There was nothing in his eyes but rage. It had been that way since the death of his wife, but never against his own. Charges were brought up and the record of Loren's other questionable acts came to light, leaving Ruiz little choice but to take his friend off the streets until he could work through the darkness that had infected him since Beth died. He should never have let it go so far, never let him near Standish. Internal Affairs helped ease the suspension once Standish's own actions were brought front and center, despite Mathers' attempts to back his friend and detective. Loren put in the time. Therapy. A new outlook. He came back just to quit. Ruiz remembered the smile plastered from lens to lens on Mathers' face. He held that image while he walked away from the conference room.

"Standish deserved worse than he got, and don't you think for a second I've forgotten who helped him out of his jam. Loren is on this case because he'll solve it. You want to argue about it in there, know that I'll win. Find another sandbox to piss in, Mathers, and stay the hell out of mine." His chest heaved from the anger in his words, but Ruiz managed to keep his voice calm. Finished with the game of the day with Mathers, Ruiz looked to the still-closed doors of the conference room and started for the elevator. The secretary at the end of the hall kept her head down but her eyes flitted to the wide strides of Ruiz as he passed. When he caught her gaze, he smiled. "Call me when they're ready for me. Thanks."

Ruiz stepped into the elevator, leaving Mathers and the rest behind. He hoped the toad of a captain could not see his face as the doors slid shut—or the look of worry plastered all over it.

Loren was the right choice. Ruiz knew it. He just hoped Loren knew it too.

CHAPTER TWENTY-FOUR

This was a move of desperation. That was what Mentor thought as he pierced the veil of the Bypass, his eyes closed to all but the floating green orb in the center of the cavernous chamber. There were dangers involved. He knew them well; every single one rang through his head with each passing moment. Ask the right question. Stay on the path. Focus on the task. They were motivators but also detriments, pulling him to a side of himself he rarely visited. His fears. Walking through the gateways of universal entropy that shifted within the confines of the orb was never something he dreamed of as a child. It was not something he would wish on anyone else either, which was why Soriya had never been involved in any work relating to passing the veil.

His own attempts were rare. Early in his life, the life he chose so long ago, there were moments of enthusiasm that were best left forgotten. Mistakes that cost him much. He was wiser, he thought, looking back on the mistakes made, the trials he endured. He was wiser, without a single ounce of pride mixed in for good measure. It was simply fact.

Within the void that sat buried beneath the center of the teeming city, millions of voices could be heard at a whisper. Cities, some long since destroyed and others yet to be imagined, shifted and faded as he journeyed deeper behind the curtain of the multiverse. Only the strongest voices were truly heard, the most adamant screaming out to drag him to them, hoping to pull him in and be lost to the world.

"We know you," a voice called out of the wilderness. Behind his eyelids, Mentor saw the city of Portents. The entire city, kept perfectly in view as if it were caught in a snow globe. The voice was distant yet familiar to the old man meditating before the floating orb and he moved in closer to hear more.

"Knew you," a second voice chimed in, similar to the first. They were too familiar, almost like they were voices he always heard in the back of his mind when lost in thought.

"NO!" a third screamed, and the city shattered from sight.

A woman cried out to Mentor, pleading. He barely saw her through the thick haze of the Bypass but noticed her pale green skin. Fire burned beneath her. Mentor felt the heat of the flames and turned away quickly.

No longer in view of the woman or the city, Mentor was lost between places until a temple came within view. "The third Pillar of Faith is Zakat, the paying..."

The voice continued to speak but Mentor traveled further within the veil, unable to stick to one place—or unwilling to be lost asking the wrong question to the wrong person.

The first voice called him back to the city. "You are a mentor, but you were once student."

"Greystone," the second voice confirmed.

"Christopher," said the first. The name hung in the air around Mentor. It was a name he had not heard in over twenty years. He felt his mind retreating from it, but he shook it off and continued. Once more, the city unfolded before him, only differently. It was no longer the city as it stood but as it was long ago.

"LET ME OUT!" the third voice returned. The cry shattered the city and the woman returned, encased in flames. She pounded against the air, begging for release, but Mentor looked away. He hoped to see the city surrounding him, but time was fluid within the confines of the Bypass and he overshot his mark. As his focus returned, he found himself in the center of a large theater troupe performing.

"TO LIVE! TO DIE!" the actors called out all at once in merriment.

Time slipped further and the troupe was gone as quickly as it came. The past was winning out and Mentor did all he could to remember the city to no avail. Deeper and deeper he fell into the Bypass, his thoughts and questions the only reminder that kept his mind from splintering within the green haze of the orb.

"They know not what they do...." Mentor closed his eyes before the scene finished unfolding, refusing to witness it. His eyes remained closed, his thoughts constant on Portents. On the murders. On Soriya.

In the darkness, a single voice called out.

"You cannot hear answers from without unless you face those within."

They were words he had not heard in a long time. They came from a man he once called Mentor. He also called him friend until the very end, but the words rang true no matter the speaker behind them. *Christopher.* That name was holding him back. The voice's knowledge of the man he once was kept him from finding the answers he sought. Mentor refused to allow that to happen. He refused to live in fear by the past he lost so long ago. Refusal brought with it a moment of clarity. Focus. It centered him from the path he was wandering and brought back the image of the city of Portents. A city on the verge of being born.

The first voice greeted him upon his arrival. "What do you need from us?"

Mentor stood in the center of the city, what was once known as the Square. Over time, the Square became the Rath Building and the park that stretched out over three city blocks inhabited the space then occupied by tenement housing. Hundreds filled the streets on what appeared to be an average day in the city. There were merchants peddling their wares and newsboys announcing headlines. Mentor circled the people, unseen, like a ghost in the system.

"Show me," he commanded.

The people vanished around him and the dim haze of the city shifted from the green glow of the Bypass to deep red. It filtered through the air; it ran along the buildings and streamed onto the streets of the city. He felt the red through shoes not his own, smelled the red as both luscious as a rose and acrid as blood. A pair of eyes looked over the buildings, and the cityscape, crimson as the blood that washed between his toes. They burned hotter than the flames that gave sound to the third voice. They hovered over the Square, watching over Mentor, who felt small and insignificant, the way the eyes intended for all to feel.

"Can't stop him…" the third voice sobbed in the distance but Mentor refused to look away from them.

"He is among you," the first voice answered. This Mentor already knew. Three dead bodies that he was aware of confirmed that fact and precipitated the visit beyond the veil. He needed more.

"He is aware," the second voice continued.

The red turned to black and everything was covered in shadow. Slowly, the green haze returned but the red eyes that covered the city with their glare continued to rise over him.

"HE'LL KILL YOU ALL!" the third voice screamed from within her cage of flames. Mentor did not need to look to see her, but was surprised her voice rang with truth behind every word. She knew the killer. She knew him very well.

"The valley of shadows has released him," the first voice said.

"The price was deep," the second voice continued.

"A deal was made."

In the darkness, Mentor saw another figure join him in the street. The figure kept to the shadows near an alley off of what would one day be called Evans Avenue leading toward downtown. He recognized the brick of the neighboring buildings and the trash that languished on both sides of the wide alley. The figure carried a sigil on its arm. From a distance, Mentor had trouble seeing the entire image but was able to make out one aspect of it. A small torch with gold flames rising above it. Mentor's eyes widened.

"Christopher," the second voice called him back.

Distracted for but one second, Mentor turned back to the alley and the shadowy figure was gone. *A true retelling or simply the mind's eye playing a game?* It was a question he would have to answer later. There was only one name he needed for now. All others involved would have to wait their turn.

"You won't stop him," the third voice laughed. She was lost in the final throes of death that encompassed her eternity. Still, Mentor refused to look toward her. Validation meant acceptance and he refused to accept that an enemy was incapable of defeat. Not even this far removed from the world, as he knew it, would he dare to contemplate that notion.

Around him, the city fell away and he was floating over it. Portents burned and shifted as time bent around his floating frame. Out of the chaos of its birth, the city grew beneath him. From the docks of the west to the warehouse and rail yards of the east, it stretched out before him like a puzzle coming together. Through all that time, through all that change and growth as the world turned quickly around him, there was one constant. Though it started small at first, it grew in front of him in the blink of an eye until it rested like a shining example of civil engineering and the modern age. Where it rested was of even greater importance, sitting in the very center of the city. *Watching over all.*

A black tower.

"He knows," the second voice warned. The tower loomed before Mentor but he refused to look away. There was something on the black spire that he needed. Something emblazoned along the side like a neon sign. The name.

"HE IS FREE!" the third voice cried, her laughter continuing. The name was there on the side of the building in giant, red letters.

"He can see you in the darkness," the second voice went on.

"LET ME OUT! I WANT TO SEE IT BURN!"

"His eyes carry him from the beginning."

"From our beginning," the first voice returned and through the dim haze, Mentor realized who was speaking to him. He was hearing his own voice cutting through the wilderness of the Bypass, through time itself.

The name shattered before him but not before Mentor read it upon the side of the thin, black tower looming over the center of the city. As it crumbled from view, so did the city…and Mentor could hear the dim roar of the trains overhead when he fell back to the world.

The second voice called after him with a final warning. "He is the end."

His own voice responded, but to whom he could no longer tell. "He knows. And now…"

Mentor's eyes snapped open.

"I know."

CHAPTER TWENTY-FIVE

Soriya's methods were never straightforward. They were never a clear delineation to an end goal. They were, however, revealing. Revealing of the city in which Loren had spent the majority of a decade before deciding to leave for a new start. They were also revealing of his guide and her age. It had not been long since Soriya started her task as the Greystone, a task Loren remained skeptical about despite her obvious talent and enthusiasm for it. She was only twenty-two, barely starting her adult life, and together the two of them had faced monsters in the dark, both human and otherwise. It was not something he would wish on anyone.

It was during these jaunts through Portents that he forgot about all of it—the murder, the darkness of the city, the fear he felt creeping on the periphery. There was only the two of them racing through the night, searching for more than a simple answer. They were finding themselves as well.

He volunteered to drive. She laughed at the notion. It wasn't her way.

It started with a cab ride to the east, ending at a tram station off Court. While they journeyed in the slow-moving evening tram, Soriya pointed out a street performer surrounded by the late night denizens of the area. He was a contortionist, bending and twisting his body in all manner of shapes for a crowd. Only the two of them caught sight of his blinking eyes. Horizontal instead of vertical. The thin tongue barely slipping out of his lips, forked and wiry like his body.

There was more. The city took on a strange dichotomy, blurring in the darkness between reality and fiction for the former detective. It disturbed him, made him nervous that at every turn there would be something else. Something unknown. Something dangerous. To

Soriya, it was the opposite. Her smile grew with each step, with each discovery she was able to share.

This was her world. This was her city.

The tram took them to Allure and the market within. Street vendors pedaling their wares at all hours. It was deemed a safe zone, outside the rules most of the residents of Portents obeyed, knowingly or subconsciously by vacating the streets with the sun's departure. Along Allure there was contentment. Fruit carts, jewelry, art, and more. All for sale. All the time.

Soriya stopped at a fruit cart, peering for something quickly. The crisscrossing journey through the city may have been diverting to the pain of the last few days, but both knew there was still the task ahead. Loren needed answers. He needed them soon. Ruiz was able to bring him back into things easily enough with his experience in the city. Keeping him on the case, one where the body count continued to climb without a solid lead, would not be justifiable. Not with Mathers whispering in the ears of the commissioner and the mayor, his own tongue hissing louder than the street performer.

Loren stayed back, patiently waiting for Soriya. Her selection came with ease. A golden apple, bright against her dark skin. Loren felt his lips part to ask the only question that sprang to mind but she was on her way to the bus stop at the end of the block before he could get the words out. She left him with the bill too, the vendor's open hand and furrowed brow waiting for payment.

At Ness and Lincoln, Soriya's tour ended. Neither of them said much during the trip. There were subtle attempts at conversation that never went anywhere. Both reached for something to connect them beyond the case, letting the city fill the emptiness. Answers would come when they were absolutely necessary. It was always the same. Everything was about the work and life resumed when the work was done. Loren remembered stakeouts lasting full days where nary a word was spoken. In all honesty, he needed that from Soriya especially after his earlier conversations with Ruiz. It was an unspoken trust. Neither pried further than needed; even the question of the large bruise upon her cheek fell into the chasm between them to keep the focus solely on the task at hand. No small talk needed. *Just the facts.* Loren chuckled with the thought.

Loren stopped with Soriya, curious. She moved so briskly through the city streets, it was rare to see her so still. There was anticipation in her stance. Excitement in her eyes. Loren knew the look, but not the reason behind it. Where they stood was a section of the city that few visited. It was known as the Corridor to most of the citizens of Portents, a place where residential and business separated, leaving a great void in the center. The buildings that lined the Corridor were mostly abandoned, having never truly benefited from the divide. The homes that lined the left side were in disarray from those that dwelled within them, which were few and far between. The business side to the right fared no better but the buildings looked nicer. One in particular stood out from the rest. The one Loren found himself standing before, next to the eager Soriya Greystone.

Large concrete steps, typically found on government buildings in Washington or great libraries in cities far more important than Portents, led to a pair of bronze doors. Stone railings ran along the edges of stairs, where two statues adorned their bases. One was of a tiger. Its paws were seated upon the base, but the eyes of the beast showed a hunger for whatever or whoever walked in its path. The other side was home to a woman carved in stone. Her eyes were covered but her hands extended, welcoming all to her side.

"Stay close," Soriya whispered. She positioned herself between the two ends of the concrete steps and the two statues. She looked to each for a long moment, placing her foot directly equidistant from both before stepping upon the first stair. She looked to Loren from the first step and nodded. Loren took the meaning though not the reason behind it and followed her every motion up the large steps to the double doors of bronze at the peak.

The first steps were slow. Soriya looked back at each step, keeping close watch over Loren. It made him nervous, his eyes shifting around the area. No one was around. The late hour saw to that, as well as the strange location of the building that Soriya deemed so important to their case.

What he did see was the tiger turned toward him. Subtle but definitely shifted from the base of the statue, the tiger's eyes were wide and her paws no longer resting on the base but extended, hoping to grasp the detective at the first chance she had. The woman was also turned, her hands cradled before her. Thin lines were apparent on her forehead though Loren no longer remembered them being there previously. She appeared concerned, almost pleading for his safety...or to embrace him fully.

He took a step toward the stone woman, curious. As his feet wandered from the small path Soriya left behind, the ground shifted. The hands of the statue snatched at his clothes. The thin lines of concern along her face were gone, shifting subtly to anger and anticipation. Her nails grew, scratching at his thin coat, looking for a foothold.

"Soriya!" Loren cried out, falling back. He hit the steps hard, the statue's stone hands reaching through the air for him. His sneakers skirted away quickly. But too far. He felt hot breath on his neck. His backpedaling had taken him too far from the center.

And back to the waiting maw of the tiger.

"Holy…" Loren muttered. The tiger growled, thick paws rising for the kill. Loren tried to reach for his gun, unable to move, unable to think clearly in the moment.

A foot shot past him, connecting soundly against the stone. The tiger fell back, paws missing their easy prey. Soriya's hand fell on Loren's shoulders, helping him to his feet.

"What the…?" Loren started. Soriya placed a finger to her lips.

"Stay closer, Loren," she instructed. She turned back to the stairs, finding her place along the wide steps. Carefully, she resumed her climb, Loren's hands on her shoulder. He peered back, watching the two statues on either side of him salivate, waiting for another opportunity. Loren stopped looking back.

When they reached the top of the stairs, Loren felt his pulse slow. He forced a breath, then a second, waiting for his heart to return to its slow throb instead of the loud thumping that echoed in his ears. His jacket was in one piece. He was in one piece, thankfully. Soriya was already at the door, her eyes ablaze with excitement.

"You coming or not?" she called, waving him onward.

"Are we going to talk about the statue things or not?" he asked, moving beside her. "I think we should talk about the statue things."

"No, you don't," she replied, her eyes back on the double bronze doors.

"True," he agreed. Knowing meant having to carry that information with him the rest of his days.

"There are paths we take and paths we ignore. Knowing two paths lay before us offers us a choice but it limits our perceptions to only those two options. Walking the line between gives a third choice. A true choice." Her words were distant, her eyes cold and calculating. Neither was her. When Soriya usually spoke, there was a youthful glee behind each secret revealed, a glow that circled her brown eyes. As she recited the explanation, he knew the words were not her own but those of Mentor.

Loren looked around, content enough for now to move along rather than dwell on being eaten by a concrete tiger statue or hugged to death by a blindfolded crone. The street stretched out before them, down Ness and split off in all directions in and out of the city. No traffic was visible for blocks but Loren heard the engine of the bus lines continuing their routes, even in the dead of night. He looked back to Soriya, who was studying the stone frame around the bronze doors closely.

"When you talked about this place I assumed it wasn't quite so out in the open."

She laughed, still looking forward intently. "Best place to hide something."

The doors stood fifteen feet tall and the frame extended around them was of a thick gray material that resembled stone. Embedded in the stone, carved with a fine edge, was a maze of images that ran up the sides and on top of the double doors. Signs and symbols, some recognizable to Loren from the recent murders and others completely foreign to him. More signs hidden in plain sight within the confines of the city of Portents. Signs that said more than he knew, though he kept trying to piece them together into his own narrow worldview. On each side of the great doors, centered at eye level, there was one image presented in gold, where the rest remained the gray of the material. Each one depicted a small torch with a thin flame rising into the sky.

Soriya pushed in front of Loren, her hands resting against the doorframe. She was searching for something. The curious detective could do nothing but watch as the young woman pushed one of the symbols into the wall. The sound of grating stone rang in his ears, and he watched the wall shifting before him. New symbols appeared. The motion was fluid, seemingly through gears and tracks hidden beneath the thick stonework, but Loren watched with the amazement of a child at the shifting tiles. Soriya, on the other side of the frame, located the image of a bull with a broken horn and pushed it. Once more, the frame shifted, replacing each symbol with a new one. The only two that remained constant were the two of gold on each side of the bronze doors.

Soriya's feet floated rather than walked. Symbol after symbol fell flush with the wall, then caved inward and the shifting continued until she stopped her hand over the golden torch to the right of the door. She looked back to Loren, his head nodding for her to continue. She smiled wide. He asked no questions. He had them for sure and sometimes they had to be asked. For the most part, however, there was faith between them. Faith in her.

Soriya's fingers ran along the edge of the torch image emblazoned in gold along the stone frame. Deftly she turned it clockwise until it was upside down. As it hit the mark, a loud clicking sound rang through the frame. The door, once bolted with two large handles resting in the center completely in bronze, now stood ajar. Loren stepped closer to grab the handle and Soriya jumped in front of him. Her joy was infectious and his excitement matched hers. Her fingers gripped the handles of the doors softly and threw the great double doors open before them.

"Welcome to the Courtyard, Loren," she said. He tried to find words, some form of language to express what he saw, what he felt, what he smelled in the air that rushed around him. There was only one when it came to life in the city of Portents.

"Bizarre."

Stretching out before him was the true city of Portents. Where it appeared to be a single building from its edifice, dozens of buildings sprang up, spreading out from the bronze doors in all directions. A double-wide city street paved in bronze with thick stone walkways on both sides as far as he could see. There were modern homes, mixed with medieval castles, thrown next to cave dwellings and early twentieth century tenements for good measure. Time was lost and so was Loren. He felt Soriya's hand slide into the crook of his arm, pulling him farther and farther into the unknown.

The main street of bronze was filled with people, vendors and merchants. Loren stepped closer and realized that *people* was a misnomer. They were beyond people. Angels walked with demons. Orcs sang drunken songs along the sidewalks. Elvish archery unfolded amid the chaos of the crowds, arrows splitting between pedestrians in a competition between brethren.

"All this…" Loren started. He stopped when he realized Soriya was no longer by his side. His gaze broke from the crowds of people that continued to go about their business to see Soriya close the doors. In an instant the doors shut; they no longer glowed in the bronze hue but appeared dull and worn with age. The doors were also not the end of the place but simply a midpoint. More merchants and buildings unfolded down the double-wide street. "How?"

Soriya once more grabbed the crook of his arm and pulled him along. "The Courtyard is self-sustaining and hidden in plain sight. Within the walls of the building we stepped through is the equivalent of twelve city blocks all existing in the city and slightly out of it."

The true city. She always mentioned it in passing. Loren thought she meant the insanity that surrounded them within the confines of Portents and the mysteries that presented themselves through their work. But this? To see so many different beings, to view so much life hidden from so many people by a simple pair of locked doors, brought a whole new meaning of hidden city to him. Like Urg, there was life here in the Courtyard beyond anything Loren imagined when he thought of creatures of myth and legend. Fact and fiction had no meaning in Portents. In the city and the Courtyard, they were one and the same.

Loren stopped in the center of the street. Surrounding him on all sides was a small pack of blue imps in dervish caps. They smoked cigars as large as their faces and cursed in tongues foreign to him. Above them, the sky was no longer made of the deep shadows that fell over the city with the coming of night. Instead, there was an unearthly red-purple hue to the cloudless sky. Stars littered the atmosphere, brighter than he had seen them before. Loren found a few he recognized, the Little Dipper and Orion's Belt but few others amid the dozens of constellation patterns.

"I don't recognize all of the constellations. There's so many." His words were light as the air around them. They were the musings of a dreamer instead of the lost soul he felt he had become. So much of his imagination was lost to life over the years. Cold, hard reality was the kingdom he lived within and it suited him fine for the most part. This, however, was something unique. It pulled out the boyhood spent reading Superman comic books on the back porch, watching the clouds move across the sky. A star winked out above him and two more disappeared in quick succession after that, only to be replaced by other stars of brighter intensity. The sky was brighter too, it seemed. He turned to Soriya, pointing up at the spot. "Did it just shift?"

She nodded, the weight of everything washing away at the sight of his curiosity. "Don't let the science slow you down, Loren. People, creatures, monsters, and gods all reside here. Some have been brave enough to live in the actual city. Most, though, those who have been here since before the city and those who have crossed over since the founding of Portents, typically stay here."

Loren felt something large brush past him but failed to see anyone. Between more creatures, there was the outline of a woman but she had no physical form. Light bounced off her frame as it did others but it created a transparent nature rather than reflect the natural hue of her skin. Soriya grabbed him and yanked him back before a giant foot slammed against the streets, jolting everyone in the impact. A pair of giants moved toward the bar at the far end of the Courtyard. They spoke of all you can eat wings and bottomless pitchers of beer with wide salivating grins across their faces. Safe from being caught underfoot, Loren and Soriya crossed the street to the sidewalk.

"Why would anyone want to hide in the city with this place here?" Loren asked, though he knew as soon as he did what the answer would be. Urg was the reminder that hiding was not what the true city of Portents was all about. They were about life.

"They don't hide and you know it," she said, scanning the street. "They live in the city. From street merchants to business owners. From psychics to florists. The city isn't just for mankind. It never was."

Loren stepped in front of her. The imagination from his childhood gave way to the burden of the file tucked under his arm, drawing him back to the real purpose of their visit. The wonder of it all had to wait for now. He knew it and so did she.

"So why are we here? Are you going to tell me that much or at least where we might be going?"

"Someone has escaped the Bypass," she started, her eyes falling on a large alley that split the medieval castle and the tenement housing. She pointed to it, then pulled Loren along. She walked slowly, giving him time to listen. "Someone who knows the city. We're dealing with an old soul that even freaks out Mentor."

"Mentor is not alone on that one."

"It happens every once in awhile," she continued. "Escapes, that is. Most are through sheer force of will. Some by morons on our side looking to strike bargains they can't possibly understand. But when these guys come back looking for blood, or worse…."

She trailed off, leaving the thought unspoken. She pressed on for the alley faster, until Loren stopped.

"Tell me," he asked. "How bad?"

She hesitated, moving close to him. The world of the Courtyard did not care, the lives of its inhabitants failing to even notice the two strangers in their midst. "It's never good to be out at night in the city, Loren. You know that. Most people do, though they might not realize why they feel that way. But these guys? The really bad ones? They bring down cities. Entire civilizations."

They reached the alley, Soriya continuing through the darkness. Loren called after her, her last words echoing. "How is this place going to help?"

Loren followed his companion into the thick, black shadows. Even under the red-violet sky of the Courtyard, no lights pierced the veil of the alleyway. One side was brick and mortar, reminding the aging detective of home with every edge cracked and every brick written upon in multi-color graffiti. The other side was brick and mortar as well but it was old, ancient even. The bricks were shoddily constructed and the mortar held together with the thinnest of strands. The castle wall had seen better days but when compared to the tenement by its side, its majesty still poured through.

"We're here." Soriya's hand was barely visible. Loren almost felt it graze the tip of his nose. The worn heels of his sneakers squeaked to a halt; he was a cartoon character amid drama players. Soriya glared to him and he muttered apologies, though for what exactly he wasn't completely sure.

In the back of the alley where both buildings met a third on the opposing street, there was nothing that stood out to Loren as helpful. There was no great insight into the killer that he could see through the thick black of the alley. No sprawling sign with the killer's name in giant block letters. There was no army of men to help him catch a killer capable of eviscerating a man with his bare hand or leaping twenty feet to adjacent rooftops without flinching. There was nothing in the dark, except for a broken-down dumpster. Instead of garbage inside it, the refuse was strewn around it, offering up smells best left forgotten. Beyond the centerpiece with the large piece of cardboard strapped to its lid there was only a small shelf bolted to the wall of the building that brought the alley to a close. The detective saw nothing else and the wonder faded from his eyes.

"Seriously, Soriya," he said, reaching for her shoulder. He needed to see her face. He needed her to look at him when she answered him. "How is this going to help?"

Instead, Soriya pulled away and moved for the dumpster. She removed the apple from the small bag she had wrapped on her belt. She held it out like a recovered jewel from the ocean. "I made an appointment."

"How does that...?" he started.

The sound of a knife cutting through the air silenced his question. Soriya took the small blade she always carried and dug into the side of the golden apple. Juice ran from the small incision she carved into its side. She cut away a small piece and placed it on the cardboard. The rest of the apple joined it in the center of the dumpster lid.

"Soriya," Loren called.

"You'll see." Her words were barely a whisper. Her eyes told the real story. Even in the darkness, Loren saw the deep, brown wells cutting through him deeper than her knife through the apple. "No more talking, Loren."

She bowed her head, turning back to the dumpster altar. Calling out to the darkness she said, "I offer life for wisdom. Honor my request."

Green slits cut through the darkness of the alley. On top of the small shelf hanging from the building before them, two green eyes opened to their presence. Loren and Soriya sat still for a long moment, then great black wings spread in front of them. A large raven leapt into the air, heading straight for Soriya. Loren reached for her, panic in his wide eyes. Her hand shot up the instant his feet left the ground and he stopped.

The raven landed on the cardboard altar. It circled the golden apple, curiously. Its great beak pecked at the surface of the apple with each pass. Satisfied with the small sampling his curiosity provided him, the black raven snatched the piece of the apple offered to him by Soriya and soared back to his perch upon the edifice of the building. The raven loomed over them, green glowing eyes staring in judgment of the two visitors to the dark alley. Another taste of the apple brought a look of total satisfaction on the black bird's face. Its great beak opened to greet them, but instead of caws or chirps of a bird, a deep voice fell over them like a tidal wave.

"Of course, child. I cannot resist," the great raven answered.

CHAPTER TWENTY-SIX

"Enter and be welcome." The black raven spoke with a thunderous voice. It continued to nibble on the golden apple fragment offered to him by Soriya Greystone. The rest of the offer remained on the cardboard altar atop an obsolete back alley dumpster. Darkness surrounded them, but the green glowing eyes of the raven shone clearly through the night.

Loren wanted to speak. No, truthfully, he wanted to scream. The raven being the key to solving the case was something not easy to swallow, though Loren believed it could have been much worse. The giant foot that almost crushed him into the bronze pavement of the Courtyard street may have had a magical big toe that spoke, so the raven was by far more appealing than Loren's imagination. The question remained—how could a raven locked up in an out-of-phase city within Portents have any knowledge of what occurred outside the double bronze doors at the gate? Loren was loath to ask it at the moment. Soriya's eyes never faltered from the dark raven. He needed to know what to ask, what to say, and what the hell was going on, but knew without her eyes on him that he should remain in silence. For a little longer, anyway.

The raven finished the small piece of apple and crooked its head toward the altar. Soriya nodded and retrieved her knife. The small, silver blade glistened under the red-violet sky. She delicately cut into the apple, creating a number of slivers. After she finished the task, the raven soared down on wide, black wings of fury. It snatched another piece then flew back to its perch. A small nibble was greeted by a moan of satisfaction.

"Smart girl," the shadowed creature complimented the black-haired woman before him. "Knowing the key to my heart. They do not grow apples like this anywhere else. Ask, child. Ask and be answered."

"Soriya?" Loren's voice was a whisper, but it carried through the expanse of the alley. She nodded, unable or unwilling to look back at him but understanding his need.

"He's Kok'-Kol, Loren," she started with ease. "One of the First Ones of the Miwok."

Loren understood English. He was very adept at the language, especially four-letter words. His Spanish was a little rusty and his Kryptonian was a thing of Comic-Con's past, but despite knowing all that, he still wasn't quite sure anything said by the young woman made sense.

"That makes it much clearer," he replied, a little louder. The raven crooked its head to the right, green eyes tearing through his sarcastic shell. Loren saw the smile return to the creature's beak. A smiling raven was not in the top five of his scariest mental images but it was slowly working its way up the list.

Soriya turned to him, moving by his side. Her words were soft and slow, begging the detective to follow each one without question. "The Miwok tribe believed that there were people before this incarnation of man. Some say the first ones simply died away, while others believe they became something more. Animal spirits."

Animal spirits. Older than mankind. They were the notions of children but as Loren stared deeper into the great green eyes of the raven called Kok'-Kol, the thirty-six-year-old detective with a lifetime of pain and tragedy weighing upon him saw eons more glaring back. Depth of ages long past and lives long forgotten all caught within the two long slits of green in the dark.

Soriya's hand rested on his shoulder. "Don't say anything stupid."

"Why would you assume I...?" He stopped, her head crooked to match the raven's above. Loren nodded, taking a step back. "Point taken."

Lights flared from the sides of the alley when the great raven raised its black wings. Small sconces of light flickered to life, little torches blazing along each side of the alley, causing the dark to retreat on all sides. The torches reminded Loren of the two golden markings on each side of the stone frame of the Courtyard doors, but these were rusted from age.

"You are looking for the old soul," Kok'-Kol confirmed, his voice washing over them.

"Yes," Soriya answered. She stepped closer to the altar with eyes wide. Loren took a step as well, hoping for the answers they needed to catch a killer that had claimed the lives of five people in the city.

Kok'-Kol continued, green eyes pointed directly at the young woman before him. "He is looking for you as well, but has now found another."

"Another?" The word escaped Loren's lips. It was barely audible but both raven and friend turned quickly to silence another from escaping the confines of Loren's thoughts.

"He is from the beginning," the black raven said. "He was the start, though he has been forgotten. Buried beneath the sins of his past. His return was foretold, a deal from the darkest of lights. It matches his purpose for the darkness he will bring to the city."

Silence fell over the alley. Kok'-Kol returned to the apple fragment, the raven's beak taking large bites from the golden fruit. Soriya lowered her head in thanks. Both were content with what was given. Loren, however, wanted more.

"Some specifics would be nice," he called out to the great bird.

"Loren," Soriya spat in anger, spinning on her heels. The small piece of apple fell from the raven's beak to the floor of the alleyway. The bird remained silent. Loren stepped forward, pressing the issue. Soriya's fists clenched at her sides. Loren didn't care.

"Time, place, who, what, how. Something," he demanded.

"That is not…" Soriya started. This time Loren stopped her, moving in front of her to grab a sliver of apple. He took a bite out of the golden fruit.

"We came here for answers, Soriya. We came here to find out who this killer is and put an end to him. We didn't come for fortune cookies, or fortune apples, or whatever the hell this is. Every minute, every damn second we waste living in this fantasy world is another potential death on our hands. I can come up with great narratives about dark lights and who's on first or whatever the hell the great First One over here said, but without a name, we're where we started and I am not so cool with that."

For a long moment, Loren believed Soriya would follow through on the rage that built from her brown eyes, down her dark-skinned arms to the balled-up fists on her sides. He begged for it, almost. Some reaction. Some movement that made it worthwhile to be in this place. Instead, the thundering voice of the raven called to them.

"That is not what you desire," Kok'-Kol said. "You desire to put the puzzle together."

"Not at the expense of lives lost while I wrap my head around old souls and talking birds," Loren replied sharply.

"Lives will always be lost. Yours. Hers. Beth's." The name cut through Loren. "Some are not yours to save."

"But I damn well try. I don't sit up there, watching."

"That is not my place, child of man. *This* is my place. As it has always been," the great raven replied. Black wings tucked close, small black feet inching to the edge of the perch. Green eyes looked down over Loren, curiously. "I have given all. I cannot end your search. You have the signs needed to complete the story. The pieces needed to finish the puzzle. You have the knowledge, Greg Loren."

"The signs..." Loren muttered aloud. The signs at each scene? What did they mean? What could they have to do with what the killer was after? The lights surrounding them flickered and faded, but Loren pressed forward. "Wait!"

"No," the raven replied, and the alleyway went dark. In the thick black that settled over them, Loren still saw the thin slits of green in the shadows and the great wings of the raven spread wide before them. "It has begun. The end he attempts to bring. The lights will rise. No one can stop him."

The green eyes shifted, the thunderous voice from its beak changing in the darkness. No longer was the raven looking at the shabby detective. No longer was he interested in his questions or rudeness or snark. Everything fell on Soriya Greystone in the thick black of the alleyway.

"You can't stop him," the raven spoke with a voice not his own. Soriya's eyes followed the great spirits, hearing the tone and inflection of the words and the man that spoke them through the beast. They were words she had heard dozens of times in the years of her training. They always ended the same.

"Not as you are."

Green eyes closed and all was darkness around them. Her head lowered and her eyes closed, listening to the words repeat in her mind.

You can't stop him. Not as you are.

They were not the words of the great raven before them but the words of another old man, liking nothing more than to teach a young woman about the universe. *He is looking for you but has found another.*

More words meant for her. The killer's next target.

Mentor.

CHAPTER TWENTY-SEVEN

"You cannot hide from me," Mentor roared, standing near the center of the Bypass chamber. The moment he split from the great, glowing orb, a new sense was born within the old man's tired frame. He was aware of everything, from the small glyphs that rose higher than all the others on the four great columns in the expansive chamber to the whisper of the flames crackling in the small fireplace. Mostly, though, he felt the presence of the large shadow in the corner. So much time had been lost gathering information about the killer that walked among them, only to learn that he was hunting them as well. Much more efficiently, in fact, having found his way into the secret place beneath the center of the city without so much as a hand of resistance. Still, Mentor continued to bellow against the buzzing lights above, calling out the snake in the grass. With each word they fell dimmer, as if beckoning forth the shadow through the room.

"You cannot hide in this place. Step into the light and be seen for what you are."

In the corner of the large cavern, the shadow of a man stepped forward. Under the dim lights that lined the high ceiling and ran along the four walls of the chamber, Mentor saw the shape of a man come into focus. He saw the hand of Martin Decker, larger than the left that remained the beast's own. Through the shadows, Mentor saw the soft gaze of the creature's right eye, that of Abigail Fortune's, the first victim slain by the monster. It was overtaken by the scarlet of the other, beaming rage down upon him from across the room. The skin was not one he recognized but he knew it not to be the man he had seen beyond the veil of the Bypass. Nor was it special, in regards to the other trophies the old soul had claimed during his time in the city. It covered his tall frame but was built for someone fifty pounds heavier. It sagged in the chin and the cheeks so that the flesh of his face peeked through the shadows. Mentor saw blood running along the muscle and sinew that the skin failed to conceal.

"You welcome death with open arms?" the shadow spoke, hands extended.

Mentor saw it in the beast's eyes. The bloodlust, the need for a fight. It was more than that, though. It was destiny to the creature whose name he now carried. He had seen it beyond the veil, seen the look of a power-mad tyrant among the members of the city. Through it all, the images of the black tower, the blood red tide that carried along the sky was what Mentor remembered. The old man felt the cringing of bones, the creaking of arthritic joints struggling to stand. The stone lay beside him on the floor of the Bypass chamber. If ever there was a moment to end the threat with a single blow, it was then, but Mentor hesitated. Something had drawn the old soul back—something greater hidden in the darkness and he needed to know its name. That was the lie he told himself when the truth was pure pride. For so long he had told Soriya there were more ways to battle the dark, to learn more from a foe through combat, and now his trial was before him and he was looking for the easy victory as well. *You cannot hear answers from without unless you face those within.* They were words he knew very well, but rarely thought of before that night amid the chaos of the Bypass. There was fear in asking the questions, doubt in facing the answers. He knew Soriya went through the same ordeals all the days of her life, knew he was never really there to give her his insight. There was none to give. He felt the same fear, the same doubt, but he refused to feel it any longer. Leaving the stone on the floor beside him, he turned to the shadow of a man. His fists were clenched, his teeth gritted.

"No." His voice was loud, carrying throughout the chamber. "I welcome the challenge of death."

They circled the chamber, each taking the measure of their opponent. There was nothing human about the killer. Not from his look, not from his movements, or the thin breaths he took as he shuffled around the room. Though he knew the beast's name, it did not matter. To legitimize its existence with the name meant to give credence to its purpose. He would learn that purpose before sunrise, never to reach its endgame. Mentor would see the beast fall before him, under his fist and his purity.

The shadow leapt forward, skin hanging off his arms, though contained by the overcoat he wore. His fist cut air, Mentor sidestepping the blow. It had begun. The shadow struck out again and again only to feel nothing but the cool wind of the cavern, his opponent stepping out of reach with each assault. It was a dance and the lithe figure with the thin white beard stayed out of harm's way, dodging attacks left and right as he skirted along the cold concrete slab at his feet.

"You have failed," the creature said, falling back. His hands dropped, the circling continuing. The plotting. The planning. His words cut sharper than his blows, his eyes never blinking. "You must realize this. No one can save you from me. From my vision of the city. My city."

"No one has to save me," Mentor replied. He moved deftly before the creature but already could feel it creeping up his legs and back, shooting pain that caused his jaw to clench. "Your motives are clear. Your rage uninspired. I have seen your vision and it lacks clarity, determination, and pure will."

The shadow screamed, hands extended toward Mentor. The attack was sloppy and both knew it, though Mentor was content to use the moment. The shadow slipped past Mentor, and the old man used the opportunity to cut a swift jab down into the killer's back, knocking the creature to the floor. The blow was hard but Mentor felt it through his arm. The creature's frame was solid and barely impacted by the blow. The extra folds of his borrowed skin acted as a buffer to the assault.

The shadow found his feet and was met by another strike, this time a right cross slamming against the sagging cheek of someone else's skin.

Mentor stepped forward, landing another punch. This time, his left hand slammed into the torso of the beast. The shadow reeled, fell back but never lost his footing. He raised the hand of Martin Decker and Mentor saw fingertips become sharp blades of silver steel. The old man kicked the hand away and then shot the same foot back into the side of the beast's head. He fell back against one of the four large pillars that supported the chamber.

"The power within the orb is mine to use as I will it," the shadow promised.

"It belongs to no one," Mentor yelled over the sound of his fist slamming down upon the shadow's stolen visage. "We are but servants of it."

Another strike sent the beast back, followed by another. Mentor felt blood, his own mixing with the shadow's, pouring down his knuckles. He could feel their fight coming to a close. He saw the end before him. He grasped victory, the creature continuing to falter from the pummeling of each blow. The Bypass was safe. The city was safe. Soriya, above all, was safe.

Just as quickly, that vision fell away. Shooting pain greeted Mentor's right leg when he extended his frame too far and too quickly with an inaccurate blow against his opponent. His leg screamed and he cut air with the assault. All Mentor saw was the grin of satisfaction upon the shadow's lipless face to know the truth.

The beast's fist crashed down, cutting Mentor's cheek. The old man, however, did not feel the attack land—or the dozen that followed. He was already gone, knowing the opening was too much, too soon. He knew that his pride was the one gift he was able to pass along to the only family he had held close over the last two decades—Soriya. For a moment, as his eyes looked out, passing the frenzy of assaults that shattered his tired frame, he saw her in the darkness of an alley with green eyes lording over her. She heard his words through the dark and called his name, but he could not answer.

Blood was his only response, coughing it on the floor before him. The shadow raised his weary body from its resting place on the cold concrete of the Bypass chamber. He held it up and Mentor saw him through swollen eyes, triumphant.

"I will control it," the beast bellowed before the floating orb of green light and its aged protector. "As no other before me. I will show my city the light and purify every shadow. You will give me that gift. Just as you have given this pathetic plane of existence your worthless life!"

The Greystone sat before them. The raised glyphs adorning the four columns that supported the chamber around them glowed in the fading light of his swollen eyes. Mentor saw it all, fully aware for the first time of everything that had been building over the last week. He saw the destiny he had handed the great beast in his arrogance and cried out.

"No." His voice thick with his own blood. He was wrong. He was wrong about so much and, in that moment, he felt every mistake in the fists of the shadow slamming into him, stealing what little remained of his life. He saw his pride holding back his love for Soriya. He saw more. Life once held so dear, slipping away. Mistakes no one would ever know. And more. The mismatched eyes of a killer and the name he carried. He knew it and held it in his mind. No one else knew. No one knew anything about the beast but him. He, alone, carried the knowledge and now it was lost. Failure was his reward. Instead of his vision as a protector of all he held dear, he had damned them by pushing away everyone and everything. *It was the most reckless, that was why you chose it.* His own words to Soriya bit back at him.

"No," he called out once more to deaf ears.

The shadow answered with a smile.

"Yes."

One final blow crashed against Mentor. The old man felt bones crack in his torso and a fast leak filling his insides. The shadow held his tired, broken frame for a long moment. He lorded his victory over the fallen soldier of the Bypass, then, like a cheap toy that no longer held any amusement, the creature tossed Mentor to the side. The old man crumpled in the corner of the expansive Bypass chamber. For all he had seen, for all he had known, he wanted to cry out. He wanted to stand up, grab hold of the Greystone and do what should have been done to begin with. Most of all, he wanted to live.

He felt breath slipping away from him. His heartbeat, once resounding in his ears, seemed distant and low. The glowing green orb was darker, more and more shadows creeping along its surface. Mentor tried to reach out to it, hoping against hope for a second chance. Only darkness greeted his request. As it passed over him like a wave, he called out to the only one that mattered through it all. Not the city. Not the life he once held. Not even the Bypass that stood as his only purpose and drive for the last thirty years. Only one name carried against his lips and escaped with his final breath before he closed his eyes to the world.

"Soriya."

CHAPTER TWENTY-EIGHT

The C line rushed past them before they jumped down to the rails. Loren felt a stiffness rise up his left leg from the impact but he put it aside to continue. Already, Soriya was almost out of sight, unwilling and unable to stop racing down the abandoned tracks. They had been on the move since the alleyway. Loren pressed for an answer as to why Soriya pulled him back through the Courtyard for the great bronze door back to the city. She answered with only a single word: *Mentor.*

He had heard the change in the raven's voice, the same as her, but there was nothing to indicate anything about the man who had raised her was in danger. She knew better, ending the conversation before it began and dragging him through the streets of Portents. She ran for six blocks to the subway station on Ness, the cool breeze stinging her eyes. It hooked up with the C Line at Bennett toward downtown. Loren could only follow, wishing he wore better shoes. Wishing he *had* better shoes.

"It's not too late. It's not too late." She had muttered the phrase since leaving the Courtyard. Even in the darkness of the subway tunnel, Loren saw the panic on his friend's face. He closed the gap, ignoring the dull pain that throbbed up his left leg from their running. There would always be time to sit, to heal. Something told him to listen to Soriya's intuition; the same gut feeling that led him to the Courtyard earlier that evening. Even though no concrete answers were gained, there was a part of him that knew more was given than he could understand at the moment. It was the same feeling that made them the partners they were. Trust. Beyond doubt, beyond hope, they carried that with them and never let it slow them down. Trust was all they had when the world turned against them.

Thinking of the Courtyard, Kok'-Kol's words plagued Loren. The green, glowing eyes of the black raven followed the racing detective, clouding everything around him in the dark beside the muttering Soriya Greystone. *You have the signs needed to complete the story. The pieces needed to finish the puzzle. You have the knowledge, Greg Loren.*

What knowledge? What pieces? Everything he saw before him was a jumble. There were signs left at every murder, except for the fifth, which failed to fit the pattern in victim as well. Was it a case of desperation? Was it something else entirely? The four remaining signs were dead languages as far as Soriya knew. Nothing Loren had been able to dig up brought any more light to that aspect of the case. *You are looking for the old soul.* They were still no closer to learning the soul's name let alone his endgame. After everything he had seen, Loren was still no closer to an answer.

It drove him mad. Old souls returning from the dead to enact some revenge plot against the city that spurned him. It sounded like something from a comic book. It was not the work of a cop trying to put in his twenty to take home a decent pension, like Pratchett. It wasn't the life of a man trying to find a life in the city, or raise a family, like Ruiz. Where Loren stood on that spectrum he no longer knew. Life in general, let alone his own, was not something he understood anymore. No, the only thing he did know was that it was all true. Every word of it. The threat was real and he could not bury his head in the sand. The rest of the city was on the hunt for a killer, one with a pathos leaning toward ritual. Loren was hunting a Lazarus wannabe with a vendetta.

"It's not too late," Soriya whispered. They turned down the abandoned junction and found the large door directly in the center of two emergency lights of dim red. The distance between them was great enough to leave the door completely in shadow from any subway line visitors. "It's not too late."

Loren heard the words and for a moment thought they were his own. He could leave. There was that option. Five dead and only a black raven and grizzled old curmudgeon living in the sewers as leads. Ruiz was right about not being able to share the world they knew with anyone. How could they understand? How could *he*? When he was a kid, Loren raced along the city streets, believing in the wonders of the world as anyone else. Aliens. Superheroes. The whole shebang. That slowly turned to killers and rapists during the week with monthly bills and dating on the weekends. That was life. That was the life he chose when he arrived and it was the life he chose by leaving Portents. Still, he remained. Still, he chased ghosts and threats that no one truly believed in anymore. The wonders of the world. They were around him and he was one of the few people that knew them. It scared the hell out of him.

The door slid open, Soriya grunting under the tremendous weight it bore. A large stairwell greeted them. Loren peered down, letting Soriya race ahead. A green light glowed at the other end of the stairs. The tired detective hesitated. He had never been to the chamber before. He had never seen so much of Soriya's world or so intimately, not in the four years they had worked together. *You have the knowledge, Greg Loren.* The words of the raven egged him forward, mocking his stubbornness. He was missing the connection those green eyes saw clearly, though the spirit walker was unwilling to share that tidbit with the rest of the class. For all his trepidation, for all his doubt, Loren was still that kid racing along the streets of Chicago looking for answers to things greater than him. He needed to know.

The stairs were sturdy and faded quickly behind him, shifting toward the green glow at their base. Vacating the steps, the wide expanse of the Bypass chamber stretched before him. The four great columns and the high ceilings, but above all else the floating orb that hovered in the center of the room. The Bypass. Soriya had talked about it in passing. It was never something she felt comfortable sharing with him, which surprised him considering how easily she accepted him into her world when they first met. It became the one topic that was always sidestepped, yet he knew the importance it carried for her. He knew it was her purpose for being, beyond the ghouls and ghosts of legend and myth. The Bypass was more Mentor's area, she would say. She would tell him about it from time to time, when she saw something dancing below the surface or heard a voice that made her think about what her mother might have sounded like while rocking her to sleep as a child. Those were moments they shared but even that failed to prepare Loren for the green orb that greeted him at the base of the stairs. It was larger than life. It was greater than life. It was everything.

The Bypass pulled at Loren—so much so, that he failed to hear Soriya's mutterings in the distance. Though she was only feet away from him, her voice was a million miles away, the words soft and lonely.

"I'm not too late. I can't be too late."

Pulling away from the orb, Loren turned to his friend, remembering her desperation. Finally, they saw the object of her searching. Behind one of the four large marble columns, he lay—Mentor. She raced over to him, forgetting everything around her, but Loren knew the truth with but a glance. The way the old man's body lay twisted along the cold concrete. The lack of movement in his chest and the blood that pooled in front of him. Loren knew it very clearly.

Soriya reached her teacher, her father, her friend and for a moment felt relief. A small smirk curled his lips. She remembered days of old when they played games like this with each other for a laugh. However, this was no game, she realized. The smirk was but dried blood, stretched from his lip. She knelt close, her hands shaking at the broken arm of the man she called Mentor. The man who raised her, who saved her from the orphanage and the darkness.

"I can't be too late. Not again."

She collapsed beside him, cradling his head in her lap. Tears stung her cheeks. She was too late. She was always too late.

CHAPTER TWENTY-NINE

Soriya Greystone slumped heavily against the oak table in the center of Mentor's small bedroom. It had been hours since she found her only family crumpled up on the stone of the Bypass chamber. Hours that felt longer, as if days had shifted from her memory without her knowing. The weight of the room was heavy, the air thick with grief. Every inch of her felt that weight bearing down, begging her to surrender and fall, but the table helped to keep her standing. Glossy eyes from tears kept her vision clouded. Her hands remained balled in fists. Everything in her demanded to scream but silence was their only release. Silence and the deep breaths of a young woman with nothing left to lose.

She remembered sitting in the room as a young girl, curled up in the corner of the bed as Mentor relayed the night's adventures to her. It would make her scared to no end, the descriptions of the minotaur tearing through the streets, taking whatever and whomever he wished, or the time Mentor chased out a horde of demon spawn looking to make the Northern Coves their new breeding ground. The descriptions were necessary to the story and she wanted to hear it all. For her, it was more than the story, though; it was the man telling it. Since he walked up to her in the orphanage and freed her from the darkness, there were times she was scared and alone. But never when he was there. The stories bound them, it tightened them, it made her part of his world in more ways and she refused to let fear end that part of their time together. Some nights she would fall asleep in the thin cot that served as Mentor's bed and he would lie beside her, holding her close. Other times, when fear won out, he would stand watch so that the nightmares faded from view. She missed those times. She missed Mentor.

Looking up from the scraped and dented piece of oak that served as his table, Soriya saw the outline of the old man's thin frame in the cot. Since she started taking more of a role on the streets of Portents, he had stayed below more, content to assist with the research she may need from threat to threat. He was getting older, the pain in his leg and back increasing with each passing year. More than that, she knew he preferred the solitude. Some cases she kept from him completely, when she saw his tired eyes in the darkness of their home within the cavernous Bypass chamber. She hated that part but she wanted him stronger. She wanted him happy, as she always remembered him when she closed her eyes.

He always knew, of course. Every case. Every threat.

He knew them all, even when she took care of it on her own or with the help of the connections she had made during her adventures through the streets of the city. Mentor knew everything there was to know about Portents, all while tucked in his cot. He was every bit the protector Portents needed. She was not, and it hurt to know that truth. It hurt to know that no matter the strength she carried, no matter the power she wielded, it would never be enough. It was not the same as when he was beside her or, before that, when the job was his and his alone. Mentor knew it too, making the pain that cut through her that much greater in intensity. He knew it with his looks of disapproval and with his final words, spoken not even by him but that of the black raven Kok'-Kol.

You can't stop him. Not as you are.

Soriya's elbows slammed against the table, her hands washing over her face. They wiped away the sweat and grime from the day including the fresh tears that welled in her eyes. Continuing, they pulled back her thick, black hair, letting it fall behind her shoulders. Her eyes widened from the deep massage they gave her. Mentor was gone, though his broken body remained within the confines of the Bypass chamber. She could see him from the corner of the doorframe leading to the main cavern. A blanket covered him from view, the only fragment of respect she was able to offer him. He was gone but the work remained, she told herself. The work always remained.

The cot lined the wall on the left-hand side of the room while the right consisted of four large, overstuffed bookcases. None were in any semblance of order though Mentor knew each and every single piece of literature he owned down to the shelf it could be found. Sitting before the Bypass and reading was the only guilty pleasure he sanctioned during their time together and it was also time she spent watching the man that raised her while he pondered the words of the universe in front of the nexus point floating before him. Reading was not Soriya's strong suit, though she made it through a fair number of texts littered throughout the room. It was a necessary rite of passage to leave the safety of the chamber, as well as the only way she could learn what awaited her on the streets of Portents.

In the back of the room, there was a large corkboard. Tacked into place was a map of the city. This served as Mentor's work surface. Where computers and technology replaced most of the thinking and deductive reasoning granted to man, Mentor used simpler methods to figure things out. Throughout the map, small tacks and post-it notes were put in place. They were places of violence, sites of unrest heard about through rumors and sources. Some were given by the Bypass in the late night through dreams that connected the old man with the crossroads of infinity and the words of those long dead. They were signs of Portents. Signs of distress. Signs of the job to be done.

Soriya stepped up to the map. There were three notes posted in various places throughout the city. She knew most of the events unfolding in the streets, though no one knew about the killer in their midst until it was too late, but the three notes were unknown to her. Each contained the same phrase though she was unable to decipher its meaning. It was scrawled in thin black marker and circled heavily on each note. It read:

A Circle of Shadows.

Another secret lost. Soriya could only imagine the others that were not noted and tacked to a wall. He held the entire city in his hand for decades, working tirelessly for Portents. Now it was hers to carry. The weight upon her shoulders returned, threatening to break her. Forcing it away, she continued her search through the small bedroom.

In the corner of the room, there was a pile of thick blankets used during the winter months in the dank dark of the chamber. It was a necessity, though Mentor allowed the occasional fire in the fireplace, next to the wood-burning stove in what they considered their living room within the small domicile. Underneath the blankets was a chest. Soriya peered queerly at it. In all her time in the room, in her studies and the long nights waiting for Mentor to return from his work, she had never seen the small chest. It was a dark cherry wood and hid in the shadows of the room so much so that Soriya was forced to toss the blankets to the floor to get a clear look at it. There was a small rune etched into the front of the latch.

ᚠ

Ansuz. A revealing message. Mentor was nothing if not direct about some things and obtuse about many others. Soriya felt the latch give way in her hand. It clanked loudly against the wood and she lifted the lid. It creaked from age, echoing throughout the room. Soriya failed to notice. Her eyes were wide, staring at the contents within the small chest.

Keepsakes. Mementos. All of her. Every moment of their time together trapped within the confines of the cherry chest to be pulled out on a whim. He kept it all. Her first dress, the drawn pictures of the artist she once dreamed of being as a seven-year-old, and stories written that always seemed to end with the words *To Be Continued.* All were from a childhood long since forgotten by the grieving young woman standing over them. Not by Mentor, though. He kept them all.

Yet, when he needed her the most, she had failed him.

The impact of that thought slammed into her harder than the fist of the drunken fool at the Town Hall Pub. Her throat clenched up and she fought for breath.

She failed. He died.

It was that simple.

Her failure. His death.

It spun before her eyes and she struggled to stay upright. Her chest heaved. The heat of the room was palpable. She needed out. She needed release.

Screaming, she slammed her fist down on the table in the center of the room. The thin oak shattered from the impact, collapsing the entire frame in a pile of shards. Her other fist lashed out wildly, taking with it an entire shelf of books. They poured upon the floor but she did not see them. Everything was gone. Everything was red, dead, and buried. Another swing of her fist cracked the side of the far right bookcase. It splintered under the blow and the top half of the unit heaved to the side before falling over to the floor. More books joined the piles on the floor. More screams joined the sounds of crashing and rending furniture. It happened in a flicker of seconds but the room lay in shambles when Soriya Greystone finally caught her breath and fell to her knees. Tears flowed freely, surrendering to the guilt.

It was when she stopped, when the tears took a break from shedding for a single moment, that she saw Loren. She thought he left, ever the detective working on a new lead with a new victim to throw into the mix, though he struggled to hold onto those former days and that former title. Instead, he remained. The screams and crashes did not faze him. He continued to stand in the center of the room, his eyes fixed on the orb floating off the ground in front of him. It was the same way for her when she first saw it, when she first began to understand it, if she could call it understanding. The idea that there was something more. Something after all of it.

Whether a single minute passed or an hour, Soriya could no longer tell, but Loren shifted from his position, stepping backward toward the small domicile in the corner of the room. When he reached the door he turned, one eye remaining fixed on the glowing orb in the center of the chamber. They were heavy, the thick brown of his eyes, as if he had stared at a computer screen for days without blinking.

"She's in there, isn't she?" he asked, his voice barely a whisper. "Beth. She's…"

He trailed off without finishing. Soriya held her tongue. It was a question that had to be asked. She knew that better than most. She had asked it of Mentor as it related to her parents, to her grandparents, aunts and uncles. Everyone she never had the chance to know because of a fiery crash that took her former life away from her like a dream. Answering the question, however, was more complicated and more times than not led to nothing but more pain. Still, she answered as any friend would.

"Yes." She wiped the tears from her eyes, finding her feet once more in the bedroom. "Somewhere. Some when. Some place. Some time. For all time."

Her dear friend and partner turned back to the glowing orb in the center of the chamber and fell silent once more.

In time, Loren nodded, still trying to understand but failing to fully comprehend what Soriya truly meant. To know that Beth was still alive in some way made him feel lighter on his feet, the pain receding. His shoulders straightened and a deep calm washed over him. Then, looking away from the chamber to the small living space, Loren realized the state of Mentor's room. His eyes fell low, regretting the selfish nature of his question. The time wasted, dreaming of the past. He knew he needed to be there for Soriya, knew he needed to give her time to figure out the next step. He should have done more. Should have spoken to her, comforted her, but instead found the Bypass and the mysteries it contained too enthralling to escape. He stepped into the shambles of the bedroom, his eyes scanning the wreckage, refusing to look at his friend's pain directly.

"Soriya. I'm..." he started only to see her head shake and the hair fall over her face.

"No," she begged. "No more apologies for my failures. It's over, Greg."

Soriya stepped out of the room, passing Loren without a glance. He heard deep, calming breaths, the cool air of the large room filling her. Leaving her to her grief, Loren took in the room. Mentor carried more possessions than Loren did in a fraction of the space. It was becoming a habit for the detective, viewing the life of a recent victim with pangs of envy. Loren stepped deeper into the room to the large map and the tacks littered throughout. The victims of the first three murders were marked, each one taking a different corner near the city limits. There was something there. Loren picked up a tack from the side of the board and placed it at the apartment complex where Urg was found. He leaned back for a better look at the map but nothing jumped out. There were too many tacks in place, for too many purposes. But there was something about those four. He felt it and heard the words of the great raven in the back of his mind, playing repeatedly. *You have the knowledge.* It made him feel worse. If he had the knowledge, why couldn't he see it clearly? Why were people still dying? Why did Mentor have to be one of them?

Loren turned away from the map. The cot on the right side of the room was unscathed by the destruction Soriya had rained down on the dead man's possessions. A single book lay tucked neatly next to his pillow. Why it was his chosen reading material over the rest of the books was unknown to the reaching detective, but Loren could not help but feel that if there was any way to find insight from Mentor, it was in the actions of his final hours. He took the book and held it near the dim light of the lamp in the corner of the room. Loren recognized the title immediately from the copy packed away in his apartment. *The True History of Portents.* Dozens of pages were marked. Notes lined the margins. Loren snapped the book shut, gripping it tightly, and stepped back into the large room. Soriya stood before the Bypass, her head low.

"We'll get him for this, Soriya." He tried to sound confident, knowing that every other time he's mentioned the fact, someone else has died. *No more.* He swore the oath in his head. *No more.* "You know we will."

"We can't stop him now. Kok'-Kol was right about that."

There was something else. It was in the way her eyes escaped his stare. He heard it in the words that slipped from her lips like whispers in the dark. Mentor's broken body lay between them, covered by a thick blanket. He had been her only family for the last eighteen years of her life. He meant more to her than anyone or anything and he was gone. Some part of her was gone as well. Her words were not those of the woman Loren had met four years earlier or even three months ago when he departed the city. They were the words of a fallen soldier, a broken child. And more.

"What is it, Soriya?" he asked. Time had failed to be on their side the last two days and he refused to let it rush past him again. "What are you not telling me?"

"He took it, Greg. The stone. Mentor's stone." She turned slowly, dried tears on her cheeks. "The killer has a Greystone."

CHAPTER THIRTY

Dawn broke in the city. With it came the masses, pooling out of their homes and their ratty apartments to go about their days. None were aware of the presence of a shadow amid the sunlight that rang in the new day. None knew how close he was to the end of the story he had written so long before, how much blood had been shed to get this far, and how much more would be needed from the city before the end could properly conclude. None understood the importance of the day. They simply existed. For the moment.

A thin smile cracked through the broken skin that stretched across the shadow's face. The skin peeled away, falling to the ground in a large clump. He did not care. Caring was for lesser beings, an emotion that tied the city down and anchored it rather than allowing it to rise higher than the rest of the world. It was the vision he held for Portents all those years ago and it was the same he would bring back to them. However, there was the matter of some housecleaning in the meantime. Housecleaning made all the more plausible with the instrument resting in the palm of his hand.

The Greystone.

It was the same as it had been all those years ago in the shadow of the flaming hay bales. Small and indistinct, yet raw power permeated through the stone. He felt it, just out of reach. It was just below the surface, waiting to be unlocked. He needed to learn. Time to understand and then time to wield the power.

He felt it under the shredded skin, stretched along his torso—the moving and shifting of bones. Tissue cracked and bubbled. He felt the broken things inside his tired frame. The old man had played his part, giving up the object he required to complete his task. The price, however, was higher than he was willing to admit.

The shadow that was once a man held tight to the wall of the alley, propping his body up to assess the damage. Broken ribs were his first clue as to the damage the stone bearer had inflicted upon him. He felt each punch when he rubbed his cheek and felt the pain of the old man's kick on his knees.

The pain would not last. Raising the hand of Martin Decker before him, the fingers shifted from pink to soft white. A glow emanated from the surface and he held it against the first broken rib. The pain was immeasurable. He wanted to cry out, but to announce his presence to the city was not part of the plan. No, the pain would be managed. The pain would be endured. The end was all that mattered. As the white glow burned brighter, it subsided. Under the hand of Decker, the shadow knew what was occurring as it had after his run-in with the wolfen boy. The hand of Decker was not only a proper weapon when used; it also served as a healing balm. All that was required was time.

Time to heal. Time he needed for the stone.

As the first bone was repaired, the shadow shifted from the depths of the alley for the city street. Sticking close to the shadows within, hidden from the morning light of day, the shadow watched the city waking up around him. Cars blitzed by him only to be halted by the ever-present red light on the corner. Pedestrians played with tiny toys rather than look at each other. Their world was about to change, although they didn't know it. They had no sixth sense to warn them of danger, no bad dreams that stirred them awake in the middle of the night. It would be just another day like the last. Only the shadow knew differently.

Staring past the people that roamed the streets of Portents, he saw it in the distance. His next destination. His final destination. It stood taller than the rest of the buildings surrounding it by close to a hundred feet. It stood at the center of everything in downtown Portents but was largely ignored by its populace, a fixture instead of the crux.

The black tower.

It beckoned him, waiting patiently while he knitted his wounds. He held tight to the stone in his grasp, refusing to allow it the opportunity to slip free. Time was all he needed. Then it would come to pass, as he knew it would.

The end of the story.

CHAPTER THIRTY-ONE

The chair creaked under her weight, each noise echoing down the hall. Soriya Greystone sat patiently across from the private viewing room at the morgue. Dawn broke early, dim rays filtering in through the thin slits of windows. Shades covered them as much as possible to keep passersby from seeing what Dr. Hady Ronne referred to as the catch of the day. Soriya was exhausted, stifling a deep yawn under her hand. Daylight was not her time. It was when the city slipped on its mask and pretended to be as normal as possible. It was when the world she knew, the world she protected and fought for, tucked away under a blanket until the safety of the shadows returned. Sleep was not an option, however, not after the previous night. Not after the death of Mentor.

His body lay in the room across the hall, blocked by thin, crooked blinds. She heard technicians starting their day, sipping on coffee and looking over reports and the man she called family. Her coffee was stone cold in her hands. She passed it from palm to palm to keep her body in motion. To keep her mind occupied.

The last six hours were difficult to say the least. Growing up, Mentor relayed the importance of the night she was still enduring and the events that had to follow it. Mentor's death would bring questions. Questions about who he was, where he was found, what he was doing. Too many questions that should never be answered in order to protect the Bypass and their work. She heard the concerns at a young age, never believing the day would arrive. Until it did.

His wishes were clear. She followed them to the letter, even with Loren's glares, though he was silent and accepted the situation for what it was. At first, he played the cop. It was a crime scene that needed to be analyzed. The detective in him needed to call it in, needed techs to scrub the scene for prints, leads, anything really. They both knew the outcome of that and the end of all the work Mentor had accomplished over his decades. They knew the killer had no prints, there would be no leads, and from the look in Loren's eyes, she realized it was easier to fulfill Mentor's wishes than to press the issue further. There was something else too, ever since the Courtyard and their time with the great raven Kok'-Kol, but she let it lie.

Mentor wrote down his final wishes in one of the many notepads he kept in the small bedroom. There were directions for where his body should be placed in the alley off Sirnow. It was a broken-down area of the city, barred storefronts and little in the way of street lighting. It was a place of endings. Soriya was careful about the placement of his body, the condition of his clothes, and of the alley. It needed to look legitimate to the police, though it would not truly matter. After Loren left to work on catching Mentor's killer, she created a hovel that would be recognized as his home, a cardboard box leaning against a dumpster behind a condemned restaurant. She tossed his shoes but positioned belongings from his room in the alley to make it genuine. Nothing she could stand to lose, but some books she knew could be replaced and other clothes that would do no good to her in the end. Not much could surround his broken frame. This was a theft turned ugly and could be nothing more. Mentor died a lowly bum.

The thought seared Soriya deeply but she refused to give in to the grief that permeated her every moment. It stung her eyes but she fought through the tears. It reddened her eyes, it puffed her cheeks, all necessary for the job she had been instructed to accomplish by the only family she knew. As dawn threatened to crack through the dim shadows of night, Soriya called in the death. She was careful to use a pay phone. Her own appearance was already pushing the limits of poverty, dirt, and grime caked on her skin from dried sweat in the race to find her fallen father figure. She curled up in the corner of the alley, keeping Mentor out of her line of sight, and waited until the patrol car arrived. There were always cops that cared, good-hearted souls that fought for every life lost or every victim of every crime as if they all mattered the same. However, there were also cops working for a paycheck and a pension. Cops that saw the world as clearly as it presented itself and no more. The time she called was part of Mentor's instructions. It shifted as the years passed but he always maintained that the call be made when certain individuals were working.

The pair that arrived were such individuals, each looking away from the broken body of Mentor as quickly as they could. Mentor was immediately seen as a vagrant, passing in the night from a fight over nothing more than a pair of boots or a golden shoelace for all the officers cared.

Soriya stayed, giving her statement to the officers under a false name. Another gift of Mentor, fake IDs. Fake histories. Their work was too important to let slip away, even in death. The morning shift also meant that no one would recognize her for who she was, and the work she assisted with as a consultant for Loren. Questions were few but they told the story she was asked to tell. No name was given. She had none to give and they understood. There may have been camaraderie and a sense of belonging with the people on the street but there wasn't trust. A fight over the alley or shoes or books. It didn't truly matter. She rambled enough to make it seem like it could be any number of things, but she was not there at the time. It was the only truth she was able to share. She was not there to save her friend. She was too late. The sadness that statement carried sold it to the officers, who were more than happy to sign off on the scene. The ambulance took Mentor's cool body to the morgue and Soriya followed, sitting uncomfortably next to the black body bag.

The morgue was Soriya's main concern, though she did her best to pass off her nervous energy as grief. Not a stretch for her, but the concern remained strong in her thoughts as Hady Ronne stepped into the hallway to greet the new arrival. She hadn't slept in what looked like weeks, her eyes deep caverns of darkness. Soriya's gaze fell, following the body. It had only been a day since Hady last saw her and Mentor with Loren as they looked over the remains of Vlad and the first two victims. If she recognized them, the questions would return and so would the officers, making Mentor's final wishes that much more difficult to fulfill. Twice, the stumpy woman glared at the body and the young woman accompanying him. Twice, her mouth pursed to form a thought but fell silent. She signed off on the transfer and shooed the EMTs away from her so she could do what she labeled as "actual work." Soriya was offered a cup of coffee and a small plastic chair outside the viewing room while they set to work.

Hady's work was quick and efficient. It raised questions about Mentor's death that would be investigated by the Central Precinct, questions about the wounds that led to his death as well as the time of death not quite lining up with Soriya's story. She knew their cover would not be 100% but it didn't need to be, not when she could simply slip back into the night and lose herself to the shadows. She needed him at peace. That was all. Or so she thought. Questions were one thing but what Soriya Greystone did not expect was Hady to learn something she had never known.

Mentor's name. His real name.

The tech that ran the prints and made the discovery was excited and exuberant about it, which confused the young woman holding tight to her cold cup of coffee. Christopher Eckhart. She heard it repeatedly in passing. Mentor's name was Christopher Eckhart. She never knew. She never thought about it. His role was his name, his job was the only title he carried with her and she accepted that as easily as her own name being that of the role she played in their work. She was Soriya Greystone, though she understood that until the age of four she held another name that she no longer remembered. She thought Mentor was the same as her. Lost in memory, finding a new purpose and a new role. She thought he was simply Mentor and nothing more.

Christopher Eckhart was much more, however. Whispers traveled the halls of the morgue in the early hours of the day. Eckhart was the longest open missing person's case in the city. Twenty-five years missing from public life. He was an author, some said. A teacher. Soriya tried to let it wash over her; she tried to let it pass through her so she could accept the information as it was delivered. To say it was a blow to her perception of their relationship was an understatement. To call it a secret was not enough; it was too small a word to encompass the truth. It was not, however, the final secret he carried she soon found out.

As the morning hours waned and mid-day reached the city of Portents, Soriya found her eyes had slipped closed for a few moments. In her dreams, she saw Mentor begging her to be saved, pleading with her to not be too late. When her eyes snapped open, she jumped in her seat, causing the small cup of coffee to fly from her grasp to the tiles below. She cursed, rubbing her eyes deeply. A young man in a white lab coat bent beside her to assist and the two shared a small smile, though he was quick to depart from the shabbily dressed and foul-smelling vagrant she played that morning. The dream left her more exhausted than ever, Mentor's words echoing in her every thought. Everything faded, though, when they walked into the hall.

Two women. One was in her fifties, small and resigned. The other, closer to thirty, had thinning brown hair done quickly in a ponytail. From the way they carried themselves Soriya immediately saw the family resemblance. Mother and daughter. As they neared, however, she saw something else in the daughter. It was in the thin gray of her iris and the light brown of her hair. It was in her walk, leaning more on her right side with each step and how she ran her thumb along the tips of her fingers. They were small things she saw in someone else. Mentor. Christopher Eckhart. Whoever the man was behind the thin blinds of the viewing room.

He had a family. A life. Secrets he had kept even at the beginning.

Soriya sat in the little garden enclosed between the rectory and the church. Behind her, the orphanage towered over her small body, wrapped tightly in a coat and wool hat. Winter was fading from memory but it was still bitter when the wind was caught in the small tunnel the garden provided. She waited patiently, her hand buried in her pocket, wrapped tight around the stone she found under the burning van.

Two voices approached. The ones she had been waiting for in the quiet twilight hours of the day. One of them she recognized immediately as Father Tomlin, the priest that gave services for the church and for the girls of the orphanage. The other was new, but she had been told of his arrival. He was interested in taking her home, a nun told her, to which she replied she had no home. She had no home and no name to be called. The nuns whispered about her, whispered about the wreck of the van and the flames that surrounded her. They spoke of her time at the orphanage and the strange sights that followed her through their halls. They spoke to each other but rarely to her. She preferred it that way.

Father Tomlin spoke in low whispers, the same way the nuns did though the young girl of four easily heard every word being said. The man he walked with made no effort to conceal his words, speaking normally. As they entered the small garden, she saw him for the first time. Tall and thin, a brown beard tight against his face, though she could see the first gray hairs creeping into the mix. His eyes were light gray like the winter clouds that rolled over the orphanage. They were calm and a thin smile crept along his face when he saw her. The aging priest held the man back for a moment, his words continuing to be low. His gaze kept away from the young girl when he spoke, as if by not seeing her there was little chance of her hearing him.

"I have to warn you. There have been incidents," Father Tomlin said. "Nothing violent, of course. Just a strangeness that I felt should be mentioned."

"I will take that into account," the man replied. He looked curiously over the priest and then back to the young girl he had traveled to see. "Has she mentioned these to you? Said anything about them?"

"No," the priest replied curtly. "Truth be told, she hasn't said much since it happened. The accident. As if she can't find the words."

The man nodded. "I understand. It takes time."

Father Tomlin agreed. An envelope passed between them and the priest quickly tucked it within his jacket pocket. The man beside him shook his hand and the priest left the garden as quickly as he entered. For a long moment, the man stood before her without a word. His gray eyes beamed down on her, his hands tucked deep in his pockets as a chilly wind ripped through the garden. When she peered up and caught his eyes with her own, his face lit up against the light that softly shone into the winter garden. He moved beside her and sat down on the bench. A deep sigh left him, his weight settling onto the seat. He patted his hands against his thighs, her eyes watching his every move. Finally, he turned to her.

"What do they call you?" he asked.

She seemed puzzled by the question. "I don't remember my name. From the accident."

"I know," he replied. "So what do they call you?"

She held her tongue for a moment, wondering where the question was leading. "Freak. Creepy. Weirdo. Others too. It doesn't matter."

"You are absolutely right. It doesn't matter." His smile continued to shine and brought one on her face for the briefest of moments. It slipped away and her head fell low.

"I am sorry for your loss, little one," he went on. "I was hoping I could help, if you will let me."

"How?" she asked, feeling the warm flames of the accident as if it was occurring all around her.

"Maybe to understand it more." His eyes dimmed as they stared across the garden. "What happened to your parents was a great tragedy, but more than that, it was balance. For what, we may never know nor ever feel it to be fair. But knowing this might help you begin to understand it."

She didn't understand. How could she understand? Her parents were gone. Her life was gone. Four years old and nothing to remember from her former life. Were there people who missed her? Grandparents? Aunts and uncles? No answers ever presented themselves to her when the questions started. Nothing but more questions. And never any understanding.

The man leaned closer to her. "I know what you carry. What you hide from the priests and the other girls. A small stone. Warm to the touch even on the coolest days. It is called the Greystone."

How did he know? How could he know? She was so careful with the small stone of grey, always keeping it hidden away wherever she went. There was no one she trusted with it, no one she spoke to about it in confidence. It was another mystery but one that connected her with the life she lost that day on the highway outside Portents. Nevertheless, he knew. Somehow, through all the secrecy, he knew it all.

Slowly, the girl of four removed her hand from her pocket to reveal the Greystone. Her hands wrapped it tightly before her, brown eyes watching over it the entire time.

"I keep thinking it can bring them back."

"I know," the man replied, nodding. "But it can't, little one. It can't alter the past. What it can do, if you believe, is change the future."

"How do you know so much about it?"

The man reached into his pocket. When his hand returned, he opened it to reveal another stone exactly like hers, sitting in his palm. Soriya's eyes widened in surprise. For months, she had been alone, lost in a sea of solitude that was deeper than any ocean.

Now, though, there was someone who knew about her. Who understood more about her than even she did. Moreover, he was there for her.

"I can show you more, little one. Things you could only imagine. If you'll let me."

"But—"

"Father Tomlin and I have discussed it at length," he interrupted. "Paperwork has been signed and noted and you are free to come with me. The choice is yours. Every choice is yours."

She didn't know what to say as the man stood up with a small groan. There were so many questions to ask, so much to know. She looked back at the orphanage. Some of the girls were at the windows looking down at her. Always looking down at her. They called her freak because she scared them. She was alone, but did not have to be that way any longer. Slowly, she reached up and took the man's hand. As the two headed toward the dormitories to gather the girl's belongings, she remembered the question that needed to be asked. The only question that truly mattered.

"Are you going to replace them?"

He stopped, bending down on one knee before her. He was still smiling. "Never. Consider me a mentor."

The door of the viewing room closed loudly, causing Soriya to jump slightly from her seat. The day she first met Mentor lingered in her thoughts. The sight of his brown beard and the smile he wore when she took his hand. They were memories she would never forget, unlike those of her former life. Nothing could take Mentor away from her, no matter the secrets or the name he carried before their time together.

The two women stepped back into the hallway. The older one was wiping tears from her eyes, struggling to walk. Her daughter stopped to talk to Hady, but found the work-obsessed woman already closing her office door. The woman with her father's eyes found Soriya sitting on the seat near the room. She locked onto Soriya's pain written across her face. The black-haired ward of the deceased saw the daughter of her mentor head her way. She stood, looking around for an exit, unable to find one.

"Did you know him?" the woman asked. She kept her eyes low and away from the viewing room where her father was being held.

"I'm sorry?" Soriya asked in response, unsure what to say or how to say it. They shared the same role, just at different times. She was nothing compared to his flesh and blood.

"Sorry. My name is Julie Eckhart," she replied, extending her hand. She didn't seem to mind the smell wafting from Soriya after being on the run for so long or the dirt that caked to her skin like armor. "Did you know my father?"

"Your father?" Soriya stumbled. She took a breath. "Yes. Yes, I knew him. He was a friend."

Julie turned to her mother who had found a seat down the hall, waiting for her patiently. Then the thin gray eyes Soriya had seen in Mentor for the last eighteen years flitted back to the blinds covering the viewing room window. "All these years he's been gone. My mother always knew he'd come back but I—"

"I had no idea," Soriya said. "He never said. Never mentioned and I never thought to ask. I'm sorry. I should go."

Soriya started down the hall, nodding to Julie's mother when she passed. It was quick but necessary, catching the eyes of the only woman who possibly loved Mentor more than her. This was the woman who would miss him more as well; had missed him more too from the deep lines of concern that branched from the edges of her eyes.

Soriya needed air. She needed to race along the rooftops and feel the wind in her face. She needed to feel something other than the grief that ruled her every thought, which soaked her entire being like a wet cloth. She felt angry—angry at her failings, at not being strong enough, fast enough. Angry with Mentor for the secrets she always knew he carried. Angry with herself for never questioning, never suspecting, what those secrets could possibly be or how much their discovery could hurt. Just like their first day together, there were so many questions to ask. So many things to learn about the man she had known for eighteen years. However, he was gone. She had been too late and paid the price for her failure.

Only one question remained, but it wasn't from her. Julie called her back in the hallway of the morgue. The woman with the thinning brown hair ran her fingers along the glass of the viewing room window. Although there was nothing to see but the dust on the thin blinds, Soriya watched her say goodbye to her father before she asked her question.

"Can you tell me about him?" she asked, her fingers falling back to her side. "My mother and I can only offer tea and leftovers but... Can you tell me about my father?"

CHAPTER THIRTY-TWO

Ruiz found Loren in the back of the bookstore, slumped over one of the research nooks the store provided for its student clientele. His face was firmly planted inside a large text and a sliver of drool soaked into the pages of the book while he slept. For as long as Ruiz had known Loren, he had seen the dedication to the job and to the city in every action he took. He saw the determination. He saw the drive. With Beth, he saw the joy and the balance of work and life in his day-to-day activities. Since her loss, there was no more balance. Joy was replaced by exhaustion and anger. Balance was replaced with obsession. Work was constant; even grooming fell to the wayside.

The shirt was different, which was a plus. There was a shower involved in Loren's activities at one point during the day, for which Ruiz was grateful. His breathing was low but audible in a dull snore. Sharp whiskers grew with each passing minute, covering his chin and cheeks.

It had never been Ruiz's intention to bring Loren back to the fold. He understood throughout his entire ordeal with Beth's passing that a change was needed. When they were working cases after her death, he saw the anger biting through his words, his rage and resentment slipping through his reports and arrests. Theories and conspiracies took root in every case, a bigger picture never quite captured. Loren always pushed too hard, straying closer and closer to the edge. Ruiz let him for the most part. As a friend. As a boss. Anger was a motivator to be sure.

After a time, though, it wasn't enough for Loren. Or too much, as it were. Ruiz had to step in the way. He was grateful his friend listened and listened well. Loren, for all his shortcomings, for all his drive to accomplish the job at hand, was much better than Ruiz had seen him months earlier. There was a bounce in his step. Even through their battles over the direction of the case, Loren remained committed to closing it. Still, the exhaustion was setting in quickly and Ruiz worried another slip was forthcoming.

Stepping quietly through the room, Ruiz looked over the photos and books strewn around the table. Maps of the city. Historical accounts. The property records Pratchett had dug up for Loren. All mixed together with the photos of five victims that had placed the city on high alert, whether the commissioner or the mayor wanted it to be or not. Even Mathers was hard-pressed to ignore what was occurring around him, which said something about the obtuse captain that stood as Ruiz's counterpart for the day shift. Slowly, Ruiz slipped his hands around the largest text on the table. It was a geographic guide and historical account of the Portents settlement from the 1800s to present. There were markers throughout the open pages, lists of prominent locations and the ever-expanding borders of the city to include the suburbs that had cropped up over the last century. He closed the book lightly, raising it over his head. His fingers retracted, letting the book fall. It crashed loudly in the vacant room.

"What the…?" Greg Loren started to say, eyes blinking rapidly to shake out the dreams. Cloudy visions of the room soon broke to crystal clear images. Ruiz's face greeted him. He wished he were still asleep. "Ruiz."

"Detective," the captain replied. He bent low to retrieve Loren's wake-up call.

"How did you find me?" Loren asked, checking the clock mounted on the far wall. It was late afternoon already, the hours slipping by without a single thought. Loren reached for his jacket and the pack of triple berry gum.

"Call came in about a belligerent man badgering a local bookstore owner. Kept swearing he was a cop but seemed to leave his badge at the office for some reason." Ruiz reached into his pocket and pulled out Loren's temporary badge. "Something about needing the place emptied and a large cup of coffee."

"Never did get that coffee," Loren replied, rubbing his left eye.

"You should apologize," Ruiz said, fatherly.

"You already did," said Loren, knowing the Hispanic's penchant for smoothing things over with the fine people of Portents.

"True. But you should."

"I will," Loren answered. His eyes were back on the books, scanning through texts as quickly as possible.

"You can't keep pushing yourself this way." Ruiz took a seat across from him at the table. The overhead light was bright, shining directly between them. For a moment, Loren thought he was back at the precinct being grilled in the interrogation room.

"I know," Loren said, leaning back in the chair. "My ass is asleep and my back is killing me."

Ruiz let a smirk slip as he reached for the case files scattered through the piles of books and records on the table. "You should go back to Chicago. Forget this mess."

"I look that bad, huh?" Loren knew it as well. After leaving Soriya to finish her plans with Mentor, he barely let himself enjoy his shower before heading to the bookstore. Atlas Books. Whenever anyone was looking for a hard-to-find book, Atlas Books was the place. No library in the city kept the stock they did and the owner, a frump of a man named Allen Mason, knew every single manuscript down to the page.

"Bad is putting it mildly," Ruiz finally said, finding it difficult to be tactful.

"I changed my shirt, at least," Loren smirked, pointing to the large 'S' symbol on his chest. He felt his back crack and snap when he stood. It felt unbelievably good after four hours curled up on the hard wooden chair. Relieved, he leaned on the table before him, eyes low. "He beat us, Ruiz. This thing beat us. He doesn't get to walk away from this."

Loren gathered up the books that lined the floor around him. Nothing was found in them that gave any clue about the whereabouts of their killer. He moved them over to the return rack. The manager of the store was not one to let his clientele place books back on the shelves. It also gave the wary clerk a chance to inspect the damage wrought by his visitors, to which Loren knew the man would not be pleased by the drool staining the pages of *Founders of the City*. Loren had been sure that book would have held something more, hearing Kok'-Kol's words on the beginning. It had to be more than the beginning of the murders, but the beginning of what? The city? The country? The world? Still, he tried the book and found it lined up with almost every other account of the city's beginning. William Rath, with a couple hundred settlers, founded Portents in the early 1890s. The same details, the same half dozen prominent residents of Portents were mentioned in every single one. There was something missing, though. Loren knew it from the book he had been carrying since the Bypass chamber. He knew it the second he saw the blood smear on the construction date of the warehouse where Vladimir Luchik was found.

History was wrong.

You have the signs needed to complete the story.

"Have you talked to her? I mean, actually talked to her, not the snark that I get."

"I'll let her know you're concerned," he said, not really thinking about Ruiz's words. They both knew Soriya was not one to talk no matter the pain. Loren was more focused on the book in his hands, which he slipped back on a nearby shelf out of order and upside down. He smiled, relishing the thank you he was giving Mason for his hospitality.

"Point made," Ruiz replied.

Loren grinned, returning to the table. He held out his hand and Ruiz returned the files. He opened them up, ensuring everything was still in place, his obsessive nature showing through. Satisfied, he dropped the file on the table and looked back at his friend.

"No," he said softly, thinking about Soriya's grief. Three losses in less than three days. Some were less significant to be sure, but all mattered. Especially Mentor. "No, I haven't talked to her since we moved the body."

"Christopher Eckhart," Ruiz said wistfully, still fighting to believe it was possible. "Missing persons case was opened decades ago. I was working the beat then. My first or second year. He's been here the whole time. Had a wife and daughter too."

"A whole life," Loren chimed in, remembering the small domicile in the Bypass chamber.

"She never knew? Never said anything?" Ruiz asked.

"Never said," Loren answered. "Probably never thought to ask. Why would she?"

Ruiz looked to his watch and then pointed for the door. "Come on. Dinner. My treat."

Loren shook his head, pulling back the chair. "I need to keep working. I need to finish going through these photos on the fifth scene. See what the connection could be and why there was no sign left. Just doesn't add up."

"Then why here?"

"Something someone said and then what I found at Ment— Eckhart's." Loren was trying to piece it together. He knew leaving the raven out of the mix was the best option when it came to Ruiz, who already looked him over suspiciously. The captain walked around the table and pushed the chair back under. He grabbed Loren's coat and held it out for him, pointing for the door.

"Greg."

"Wait." Loren looked back to the clock and then to his friend. "Shift doesn't start for another four hours. How did you get the call about me?"

Ruiz checked the door to make sure Mason hadn't let anyone else into the back room. "Called in for a meeting."

"Dammit," muttered Loren.

"Yeah."

"Mathers?"

Ruiz nodded. "He'll be taking point first thing tomorrow if we haven't closed it."

"He has no clue what the hell—"

"We know that, but who else does?"

"Please tell me that prick at least had the decency to pin it on my idiocy and not lay this at your doorstep?" Loren asked, concerned.

Ruiz's face was shadowed from the overhead lights, his eyes dark. "He did," he answered. "Doesn't matter either way. I handed you the case so it falls on me. Don't think for a second Mathers won't use it against me first chance he gets."

"He won't, because he has no chance of solving it."

"True."

"I screwed it up for you."

"Not your fault."

"Dammit." Loren ran his fingers against the scruff collecting on his chin. Of course he screwed it up for Ruiz. He should never have been on the case in the first place. He should have stayed in Chicago or brought all of his things months ago when he first moved. But now? After three days of running through the streets looking for an old soul, talking to ravens, and almost being trampled by a giant with a chicken wing fetish? He had the answers. The damn raven knew it and so did he, at least on some level, and to see it slipping away because of Mathers? "So we have a day."

"We do." Ruiz laughed at the thought.

"Good." Loren cracked open the book in the center of the table. A hand fell on top of it before he could pull it back to read the notes in the margin.

"Break time, Loren. I'll buy your dinner."

"One minute," replied Loren, pulling the book back.

Ruiz stood to fix his jacket. "Food first. Then murder and mayhem. Tomorrow, maybe there will be some sleep involved in the schedule."

As Ruiz backed up for the door, Loren tossed him the book he found tucked under Mentor's pillow. Ruiz looked down to see the title in bold white letters on the cover. There was a list of authors in small print. A book that extensive needed many hands to put it together. Loren waited for the look of recognition. It came almost immediately.

"Beth worked on this book," Ruiz stated plainly, staring at the name Bethany Schmidt—her maiden name.

"Looks like."

"Your wife worked on a lot of books."

"But this is the one that matters to this case." Loren snatched the book from the questioning captain and held it in front of them. "Every book in this store mentions the founding of the city as being the early 1890s. Every sign, every monument has different stonework, with a revised date to make the word of all of these books true. But they're wrong."

"How so?"

"This book talks about the first Portents. The real Portents that's still here, buried in the rubble. It goes from the founding in the 1870s until the revised dates. Maps, details, historical documents long thought lost. All from the very beginning."

"I'm not seeing the connection, Greg," Ruiz replied. He held the door for Loren. The detective gathered up his belongings on the table quickly, holding tight to the case files and the book. He moved for the door, giving a quick nod to Mason behind the front counter before exiting to the street. The minivan was parked next to the curb out front. Loren shot Ruiz a look, but the captain ushered him on without a word.

"I know, I know. It sounds crazy, but when you're dealing with people killing other people with their bare hands and old souls, this is what it comes down to, you know?"

"Old souls?" Ruiz tried to ask, but Loren refused to slow down.

"Anyway," he continued, "the same name keeps popping up throughout the book and I've seen it in a half dozen places in the last three days around the city. Tell me, Ruiz. What do you know about a guy named Nathaniel Evans?"

CHAPTER THIRTY-THREE

Life surrounded Soriya while she paced uneasily through the living room of the Eckhart home. Down the hall, she could hear the sounds of pans clattering. Julie Eckhart, the daughter of the man Soriya called Mentor, worked diligently to provide a meal to the wayward girl. Attempts were made to pass on the meal, Soriya wanting more than anything to leave, but after being allowed the use of their shower and some fresh clothes, the line in the sand had become blurred. Julie's mother rested comfortably in her bed, exhausted from the day's events. It was only awkward for the stranger in the living room, surrounded by the secret life of the man who raised her.

Photos lined every inch of the wall above a large mantel. Few were recent, most dating back what looked to be decades. Happier times. Times never forgotten. She recognized the man in a few of the images immediately as the one who showed up one spring day to free her from her life as an amnesiac orphan. He gave her purpose. He gave her a life. She thought she had done the same, but she was wrong. His life had already been lived.

How did she not know? Why did she not think to ask more questions about him? Every time she closed her eyes, she saw his face smiling down on her in the small garden outside the church. He had known so much about her. She knew nothing.

Over eighteen years they lived as a family. They shared stories of conquests and failures. She cried her eyes out when nightmares awoke her in the middle of the night, sobbing soundly into his chest as a daughter would. They shared their lives, only they didn't at all. She didn't because the memories were lost to her. He didn't by choice. That stung deeper than any revelation could.

When he called himself Mentor, when he took the title to train her and guide her in her task, she thought it was as he always said. The job came first. The title was more powerful than a name. It symbolized something greater than a simple word. She was the Greystone and he was the Mentor. That was how it was. It made sense to her that it went that way. She never questioned it.

Questions, though, were rampant in the Eckhart home. They had to know everything she could offer, needed to know it all. Soriya shared what she could while she sat at the kitchen table across from the grieving widow and her daughter. She told them about their time together, about the stories he told her and read to her from the books they found in their travels. Most of the telling was nothing more than a fiction but she spun it with enough truth to satisfy their queries. It would have been what he wanted. He would have shared what he could with them, though most of their time together went unexplained. The Eckharts were a connection Mentor severed twenty-five years earlier, the same way he had expected her to for the responsibility of the task he had given to her. She told the story with that in mind.

To the Eckharts, they were strangers passing in the night that connected as a father and daughter would for a time. Only a short time. Not the eighteen years she recalled vividly. Not the connection that caused her heart to break every instance she saw his body behind her closed eyelids. All of a sudden, the weight of the stone, buried in the pouch strapped on the right hip of her borrowed jeans, felt heavier than she had ever known it to be.

Standing in the living room of the Eckhart home, Soriya knew she should have listened to Mentor when she had the chance. She should have disconnected from the world and dedicated herself to the job. She should have measured up to the woman he always believed her to be. She should have listened while she had the chance.

He was right. He was always right. And she didn't even consider his way.

Until it was too late.

It started in her gut, deep thrumming sounds that tightened her muscles into a giant ball. It shot through her arms to her hands, forcing them into fists. Every inch of her was tense, staring at the life of her friend hanging from the wall of the Eckhart home. Grief turned to rage and she reached her breaking point. A killer was running free in the city. Loren was desperate for closure. There were no leads other than the dead man she tossed into an alley. Lives were being lost every second she stood in the living room of the Eckhart family, with soft socks balled up along fibers of carpet. Lives she should be saving, knowing that all she ever did was let them die. Some of the grief was from little to no sleep over the last three days but she knew most of it came from the truth that echoed in every thought, in every recollection. She did not belong there, among the family of her father figure. She did not belong anywhere but in the shadows of the city of Portents, tucked away from the waning hours of sunlight. Soriya's eyes fell on the living room door on the other side of the room, and then back down the hall.

When Julie Eckhart stepped out of the kitchen, she carried a small smile on her face. There was some doubt in her mind at first about asking the grime-covered woman from the morgue back to their house, but after hearing the stories about her father, she knew it had been the right choice. The closure of it all was something she had prayed for since she was eight. She dried her hands on a dishtowel as she stepped into the living room.

"It's not much, but I made some broccoli cheddar soup and…." She stopped at the sight of the empty living room. Confused, Julie turned away, wondering if the bathroom was in use. The light remained off in the half bath in the home's main hallway. In the living room, she felt a slow breeze. The front door stood ajar. The woman was gone.

Disappointed but not completely surprised, Julie Eckhart closed the door and clicked the lock. She started for the kitchen and the soup she had prepared for her guest, but stopped in the center of the room. On the wall above the mantel, there was a single space left wide open. An image was missing. She remembered it well. It was of her father before one of his lectures at the university. He wore a suede coat and a thin, brown beard to go along with a joyful smile that he rarely donned in photos.

The photo was gone along with the woman who took it.

CHAPTER THIRTY-FOUR

The neon sign buzzed brightly even in the light of the afternoon sun. Some of the letters had dimmed over the years, but the sign continued to blare *The Coffee Hut* in red. A small cup was poured out of the *t* at the end. Underneath, stenciled on the window where they sat in silence, it read, *Our specialty is in our name. (Huts not sold here.)*, which had become a running gag for the regulars that showed up for their morning coffee, asking for a side of hut.

Loren dumped a third sugar packet in the small cup of coffee, stirring it loudly to drown out Ruiz's glare on the other side of the table. When he first mentioned his restaurant of choice, the captain scoffed. There were dozens of options on the strip near the bookstore but Loren insisted on the small diner six miles away. No explanation was given beyond a simple "They make a good cup of coffee." It was true, in its own way, though Loren had never actually tasted their coffee before. He was content with the results, and took a long swig of the black liquid.

Few people were in the brightly lit restaurant, fewer still near Loren and Ruiz, which suited their needs perfectly. Loren needed the quiet. Ruiz needed to talk. Neither one was anxious about the proposition of another conversation so Loren stuck with the rule set by Ruiz at the bookstore. *Food first. Then murder and mayhem.* Ruiz regretted his choice of words, sipping water through a thin straw. From behind the counter, Loren saw their server retrieve their order and start toward the table. His raised eyes caught Ruiz's.

"So…" the captain started.

"Don't," Loren hissed before the server stopped in front of their table. In her hands were two plates. On the left, which she placed before Loren deftly, was a light breakfast of eggs and wheat toast. Breakfast served all day was what Loren loved most about the local diners of Portents. When sleep came in waves and mornings were actually needed, sometimes the only cure was a breakfast of over-easy eggs and butter-smothered toast during the dinner hour. In her right hand was a plate brimming with fries. In the center of the plate was a half-pound burger with cheddar cheese caked on the bun and three strips of bacon dripping grease on the fries that surrounded it. Loren noticed the drool collecting at the corner of Ruiz's mouth when she placed the meal in front of him.

"Can I get you anything else right now?" the server asked, disinterested. Her eyes were already turned to another pair of customers who had sat down at the counter.

"Yes. Sandy, is it?" Loren replied, noting the name clasped to the young woman's chest with a small photo of her smiling. He pointed to the greasy burger across from him. "Does his meal come with a coupon for bypass surgery?"

She looked awkwardly between the two gentlemen, unsure of how to respond.

Ruiz stepped in for her. "We're all set. Thank you."

Loren watched his new friend, Sandy, depart their table. Every few steps she would peer back at the two men. Loren smiled and waved, to which Ruiz slapped his hand down as only a father could.

"Leave her alone. And leave this burger alone," he said, picking at a fry. "You dragged me all the way out to this diner to criticize my meal selection. All the way out here instead of a dozen good choices for dinner on the strip so that you can make crappy jokes and not talk to me about it."

"Looks that way," Loren snapped. He pulled a slice of toast apart and tossed half in his mouth. Too much butter, but he didn't care. "Case is screwed for us, right? So since this is my last supper I think it deserves some silence, don't you?"

"Well then, I'm going to talk about it," Ruiz said. "I brought you into this. I understood the pressure and the memories this could have brought up but I did it anyway. You made your choice when you left and I respected it, but I still asked you to come back for this and I shouldn't have done that."

"No. You shouldn't have," replied Loren, peering outside at the fading light of the day.

"I didn't want this, Greg."

"No. But you wanted her out there. That's what you told her. So she did. She went out there, poked and prodded by you and by Mentor and sure as hell by me so that I can get back to what little life there is for me in Chicago. So we went out there like you wanted. And here we are."

Ruiz picked up his burger and put it back down. Loren continued to work on his toast diligently between breaths. The Latino's eyes were low and sullen. "I wasn't looking for this to happen. I didn't want it to happen this way. But I'm not talking about Soriya Greystone. I'm talking about you. I'm talking about Beth."

Loren stopped and wiped his mouth. He held tight to his fork in his right hand, pointing to the mammoth plate before Ruiz. "Eat your food, Captain."

Ruiz continued over the sound of Loren's chewing. "When these things happen, when someone dies on your watch, it makes you second guess some things. Hell, if Michelle weren't at home every night to bring me back to reality, I would snap in half. But you…I get why you left. I get forgetting about it. I get trying to move past everything. But you're here now. You came back and we're at it again. I know you have family out there…and I damn well know you probably haven't said word one to them about any of this, have you?"

"No," Loren replied, finishing his meal. He lifted his empty coffee cup, catching Sandy's eye with the shaking of the small cup. Slowly, she made her way over with a fresh pot. "I haven't said a word."

"Family understands. Your parents must—"

"Dad died a year ago, Ruiz," Loren said, nodding thanks to the silent server. She finished filling his cup and quickly stepped back behind the counter, her fake smile shining brighter. Loren stared at the black liquid in his cup then turned back to his friend. "He died while I was here. Mom called and called but I could barely function, much less grieve. I never answered. I never called her back. And he died. Mom hasn't talked to me since. My sister tries, she tries to bring us together every now and then, especially since I've been back in Chicago, but both of us can't bear to even make a real attempt."

"I didn't know."

"Yeah. Some life I recaptured. Keep convincing myself that my family and friends are there for me and maybe they will be but when it comes down to it, I've been here for three days and the only person calling and asking about me is you."

"Christ, that's depressing."

"I'll drink to that." Loren stirred more sugar into his cup and held it before his lips. His eyes shifted across the street to the real reason they had come to this diner above all other restaurants on the way. Across the street was the very spot the fifth victim was found, the one that showed no sign on the scene, the one that failed to line up with any of the previous victims. The signs were integral to the killings. Kok'-Kol confirmed that much for him, though every instinct told Loren to ignore the words of a raven and follow the clues laid out before him. The signs were crucial. The victims were vital. And the locations were key. All three, though, for different reasons. Loren knew it. He knew it more than he knew that no matter what happened, Ruiz would have his back and so would Soriya. He knew that it didn't matter how many mistakes he made, how many people he lost, those two would be with him through it all. Thoughts of Chicago became distant. It had been his escape plan, his final refuge away from the insanity around him, away from Beth and her unknown killer. Away from the anger and the mistakes. But he came back. He came back and stayed at the simple request of a friend in need. That meant something too, didn't it?

Loren's thin, brown eyes recaptured the scene across the street. From the position of the body in the mouth of the alley to garbage piled on the left-hand side, every inch replayed before his eyes. The man had been skinned, the trophy of the fourth victim passed to the fifth. No apparent history connecting him to the other victims. This one was blatantly desperate, yet more open than the others. It was rushed, too, where the others were meticulous in their order. But no sign. Nothing found near the body. No blood other than the victim's.

Then he saw it. Not on the brick building across the street. Not in the alley of garbage that threatened to spill out to the street. None of that held the answer he was looking for. No, what Loren saw was from the photo of the crime scene taken the day before. The photo of the victim and the clothes found at the scene of his death. On the right jacket pocket was the imprint of something missing. His eyes shifted to Sandy and the wide smile adorning her nametag.

"Son of a bitch." The words slipped from his lips. They were louder than he intended and some of the denizens of the restaurant turned toward their table. Ruiz huddled close, his first bite of burger hanging from his lips.

"What?" he asked as small flecks of bun popped loose. "What is it?"

Loren reached for his coat, slipping his arms in the sleeves. When his right arm was in place, he snagged the book he found at Mentor's bedside, tucking every piece of evidence from the case within the thick binding. "We have to go. Now."

Ruiz watched Loren stand. The detective reached back and grabbed a single fry, popping it in his mouth. He started for the door.

"Greg," Ruiz called to him. "What the…?"

"I'll be across the street," Loren answered, still moving for the door. He bumped into two of the patrons entering, backed out of their way, then held the door open to give instructions to his awestruck friend. "Call Pratchett. Tell him I need a map."

The door closed behind Loren. Ruiz sat stunned, watching his dinner companion race across the street toward the alley. Loren never wavered, never looked back, ducking into the alley and out of sight. Ruiz did not move. He did not say a word, unable to think of one to say over what had just occurred. He simply stared at the full plate in front of him then back to the alleyway.

Sandy returned. He instinctively placed his hand over his beverage, not wanting a refill. When he looked, he realized what she actually wanted. The smiling young woman placed their check on the table, all of her teeth glittering as she spoke.

"Can I get you a box for that?"

Ruiz's eyes fell to his plate, full of fries and the cooling slab of beef on a bun. The mouth to the alley was still empty with no sign of Loren coming back and the server was still standing beside his table waiting for a response. Only one came to mind.

"You've got to be fucking kidding me."

CHAPTER THIRTY-FIVE

The C line was late. Rush hour traffic out of downtown Portents had come and gone with the haze of the afternoon sun. Few remained in the city, those who worked awkward hours or were held up at the office for last-minute requests from bosses who cared little for the hands on the clock. They were the remnants, scurrying to get home, away from the black tower that loomed over the city and cast a great shadow when the moon rose. Those who sat waiting impatiently at the station occupied their time with their handheld devices. Some cursed signal losses. Some cursed the person on the other end of the line from their call. All were oblivious to their neighbors, including the lone woman standing near the yellow line at the edge of the platform. Tears were gone but her eyes were reddened from the sadness that crept over her every inch. Soriya Greystone had seen better days.

Guilt and despair were no longer words to Soriya, but the only emotions left to her. Mentor was dead. Vlad was dead. Urg was dead. The killer remained on the loose, threatening her city, though why she still felt that connection she had no idea. The city had abandoned her, betrayed her for an old soul willing to murder to achieve his ends. What was the point of trying to protect it when it was too busy protecting him over her? She felt alone, truly alone for the first time since the young man with the thin gray eyes first sat down next to her in the tiny garden outside the orphanage. Loren had tried his best, she had no doubt. He wanted to talk, to help her out of the spiral she found herself caught in, but she refused. She pushed him away. She pushed the Eckharts away. No one chased after her. No one followed. She was alone, half by choice and half by circumstance. It was deserved either way.

She waited for the line to pass. Once the train was gone, she could return to the Bypass. The case lay ahead, unwilling to diminish in her thoughts despite the myriad distractions of the day. She needed time to grieve, to feel the loss that threatened to crash down on her at any moment. But the case remained. The clues spread before her like pieces of a puzzle, the signs remnants of lost languages, the trophies tools used for the final task, but what that was eluded her still. Everything eluded her. From the ambivalence rooted in each face she saw at the station to the leads left at each murder scene. She was no detective. She felt no connection. It was all slipping away and she was letting it. She needed Mentor. She needed to hear the words of her old friend and father while he tucked her into her bed as a child or chided her while taking down Anteros. She simply wanted to hear his voice, call to her through the darkness that seemed to surround her every move.

The photo rested in her hands. She wasn't sure why she had taken it from Mentor's wife and daughter. They had done nothing to deserve petty theft from her, especially after allowing her the use of their shower and a fresh set of clothes. Still, the look Mentor gave, standing before the university where he once held the title of professor, gave her a kind of comfort she could not live without. It was in the way his eyes welcomed her when she looked at them. The rose-tinted cheeks before he carried the scar than ran along to his left ear. Before the burden of the Greystone. It was in the warmth of his stance, proud and determined, as he had always been. He was everything she wasn't, though she tried so hard to prove otherwise.

Eighteen years. They had been through so much, seen so many things. He showed her the wonders of the city and the nightmares that hid in the darkness of Portents. So many memories threatened to overcome her, waiting in the shadows of the platform.

In the small domicile of the Bypass chamber, five-year-old Soriya stood in awe before the mountainous bookshelves littered with texts. The girl's eyes were large, soaking in each spine and the letters they bore, though most of the words were beyond her. Mentor sat at the far end of the room, the proud parent. He found her this way daily, staring in silence at the world that surrounded them. Usually it was the Bypass where she kept her distance but never averted her gaze. More and more, it was the books. She recently discovered reading, something the orphanage attempted but kept a tight leash on rather than let the children decide what they might enjoy learning. Mentor made no boundaries; he simply waited patiently for his ward to make the first move.

One evening in the coolness of an autumn night, when the chamber turned frigid against the coming winter, she asked, "These are all yours?"

He let out a small chuckle at the question. She had been with him for weeks and seen no one else in the chamber, so the answer was obvious. Still, she asked and the question brought joy to his lips. Soriya saw thin lines running from his eyes toward his temples, but the smile made him younger by years. She wondered why the question was so entertaining, what it stirred in his memory, but she stood silent, waiting for his answer.

"They are," he answered. Making his way to the bookshelves, he slowly retrieved a text from one of the top shelves and held it out to her. "Now they are also yours. Experience. Wisdom. Faith. All within these books."

The cover was soft, its corners bent and torn from use. The title was in large letters, with small words that she knew but did not understand how they worked together. It read *The Rights of Man*. She clutched it tightly, afraid to let it fall in front of the man who had given it to her. She wanted it to be perfect. She quietly flipped through it, never reading it or skimming it, just taking in the moment of the gift. He knelt in front of her.

"Use these books, Soriya." His voice was soft, his hand firm on her shoulder. "Listen to them, for they will not lead you astray."

She nodded slowly, cautious about the book in her hands and the man before her.

"What is it, little one?" he asked at her quiet stare.

"Do you have any about dragons?"

His smile made her laugh.

A cry cut through the air of the platform. Soriya lost the sight of Mentor's smile, longing for it to return, but the cry won out. It was high and shrill from the far end of the long station underneath Evans Avenue.

No one moved. No one made any gesture at all. One young man slipped his hand into his pocket and retrieved a set of headphones, which he promptly inserted in his ears to drone out the echoes of the single scream. It was not their concern. Soriya knew that better than most. She saw the way the people of the city turned their heads at the sight of crime, both human and otherwise. She saw it in their faces, the knowing act of their obliviousness.

Soriya acted alone. No matter the pain that shook her tired frame, no matter the guilt from her losses, action was all she had left. She started in a slow walk, slipping the photo of her fallen family into her pocket. The walk turned into a trot and then into a full run, down the platform when a second scream rang out. It sounded like a bell ringing, a bell she had not heard in a long time.

Mentor set up a classroom in the corner of the Bypass chamber. Soriya asked about public school a few times in those early years. The classroom was Mentor's solution to the question. He even set up a bell that rang when class began, usually with an eager young nine-year-old sitting at attention. There were no other desks set up besides her own. Mentor stood in front of the wall of the cavernous room, using colored chalk to illustrate his teachings on the wall. Books surrounded Soriya, none containing the dragons of her five-year-old dreams but those that held deeper meaning for the job she was eventually meant to inherit from the man who had adopted her. From the Torah to the King James Bible, from *The Origin of the Species* to *The Great Gatsby*, everything was discussed with Mentor; everything was analyzed in a larger scope without the threat of curriculums and standardized testing to gauge her knowledge base. It made the learning fun, making it that much easier to excel at retaining the information discussed.

"I don't get it," she said, stopping Mentor's discussion. The quiet innocence of her youth was already fading behind the morbid curiosity of a teenager, almost as quickly as the brown of Mentor's hair faded to white. "If God created free will, then why smack down the tower before—"

"Faith," Mentor interjected. They had gone back and forth on the topic of Babel for hours. His voice bordered on irritated, but the thin smirk of contentment that kept her warm and safe in the confines of the Bypass chamber still shone brightly. "Faith is more than understanding something or someone. It is about belief. It is the ultimate tool. The ultimate weapon. One sect's belief is another's restriction. We need to know them all."

"I would have rebuilt it," Soriya answered defiantly, flipping the page in the book.

Mentor knelt beside her, turning the page back. "So would I."

Soriya circled around the winding stairs that led to the streets and the waning hours of daylight. Mentor's smile was caught in her vision and she almost raced past the voice that called to her at the far end of the platform.

A young woman, no older than her, was held tight at the forearm by a man twice her size. He sported a wide build, with short legs. His arms, uncovered by clothes or jacket, showed off his proud musculature. Tattoos lined his biceps with images of blood, tears, and broken women. His worldview was as much on display as his body. The man tore at her clothes, keeping her wrist bent back to keep her from running off.

Soriya did nothing but watch. This was the city she protected. These were the people she kept safe from the things they refused to believe, the shadows that circled them in their nightmares. Mentor was dead but the man with the tattooed muscles kept breathing. She wanted to walk away. She wanted to forget she heard the cry of the woman. She wanted to be alone, to let the city fall away when Mentor's killer finally had his way with it. Wants were all she had left, but none of them ever mattered. Need won out more often than not and her need to pummel the brute before her was vital to her survival after the events of the last few days. Saving the girl was an added bonus to be sure, but blood on her knuckles gave her life the only meaning she ever knew.

Finally, the decision was made for her. The woman's pleading eyes called to her and the man saw the look, and followed her gaze to Soriya. Her fists were clenched tighter than her jaw, her thumbnail digging into her ring finger. At first, he made no motion toward her, simply continuing to tear at the woman's blouse. Her free hand clawed at him, but he swatted it away. His eyes flitted back to Soriya, who continued to stand there watching.

"Nothing to see here, lady," he said through gritted teeth. They were chipped and yellow. "Unless you want what she does."

"Help," the girl cried out. In her eyes, Soriya saw the eyes of a child where there should have been the fire of a woman fending off an attack. In her heart, she saw herself without Mentor. Thinking of him brought it all back. She felt the stone on her hip and the ribbons wrapped down her left arm. She thought of a hundred scenarios, a thousand attacks, all ending the same way—with blood.

"You don't need any help from what I can see," the man taunted. The blouse pulled away under his tearing. The woman's bra did its job to cover her but the view from above appealed greatly to the brute. His eyes were focused completely on the woman, on his prize, and not on the observer.

A hand reached out and grabbed his wrist. He spun his head, saw the flames burning in Soriya's eyes, then heard the snap of his wrist breaking in a single motion.

His screams carried her back to a quieter time.

In Mentor's small domicile, Soriya watched the aging man jotting notes on the large map tacked to the back wall of the room. A thin black circle surrounded the note, but she failed to make out what it said from the other side of the room. Mentor remained secretive about some of the work he did, leaving the twelve-year-old teen to imagine what occurred when he stepped out for the night. She did not mind the secrets, or the solitude that came with his absence, only the loneliness that tended to remain when he was around. She did her best to engage her wayward sponsor with questions and comments, hoping to draw him into conversation. Most ended with a muted grunt, while he dug through texts littered with images of creatures she only read about but knew he had seen roaming the streets of Portents.

On the table in the center of the room was a stone of grey. Mentor's own. She always kept her own at her side in a small woven pouch she worked on when she was eight, which looped snugly on her belt. Its presence was always felt, a constant reminder of the work she would one day fulfill. Slowly, she removed the Greystone from its casing and placed it next to its twin. The air thickened around the two objects as if they were drawn to each other. Wonder sparked her eyes, small flickers of light dancing between them from opposite ends of the table.

"What are they? I mean, really? Can you tell me?" she asked, lost in the lights.

Mentor placed a small tack into the map, then turned to her. He lifted his stone and tucked it in his pocket, ending the dance. "Balance. Balance moves through us into the world. The Bypass is one half. The Greystone is the other. Balance is the key."

"That's not an answer."

"Have faith, little one. As I do in you," Mentor smiled, rubbing his chin. "In time, the stone will be the one to tell you. If you will listen."

"I'm ready to listen," she begged, the high-pitched squeal of a teenager coming through more and more, despite that she tried to curb it.

"Not yet. Not until you learn," Mentor replied, moving for the large cavern. She followed close behind after grabbing her Greystone and slipping it back into the pouch on her right hip.

"More books?" she asked, dismally. He smiled at the tone, understanding it completely. He continued to walk until he reached the stairs leading to the tunnels above.

"More than that." Her eyes were wary at first. She had wanted to visit the city on many occasions but they were rare, only used when Mentor required her presence or knew he was going to be gone for long periods and needed a second pair of eyes to watch over her. Those were the times the Courtyard became her home, though she felt ill at ease with being surrounded by the wonders of her childhood imagination, especially without the comfort of the man who had become the only family she knew. Mentor stepped to the side of the entranceway, his hands ushering her onward to the stairs, welcoming her to the next step. When she looked to him, skeptically, he nodded. "The world lies before you, little one. Take it."

Her laughter carried her up the stairs to the city above.

The man with the tattooed muscles screamed. His wrist wobbled on the single bone that still supported it. Soriya squeezed it tighter. His screams echoed louder than his victim's but no one came. The C line arrived, drowning out much of the noise generated by the thuggish brute, not that Soriya cared. Her mind was decades away, her eyes empty to the world in front of her. Instinct and training were all that remained of her senses.

The woman, her own wrist free from the attack, gathered her torn blouse and covered her chest from view. She picked up her purse and her scattered belongings, looking for a way out. She wanted to leave, but Soriya blocked her freedom, forcing the young woman into the corner of the platform, cowering in the shadows. Had Soriya been in the moment, she would have opened up the way for her to run. In the back of her mind, she knew that was what she had intended to do. Save the girl, teach the man a lesson in pain, and go home. A simple night, one that she was fond of taking advantage of during her time in the city. This was different. There was no simple plan beyond the pain she wanted the man to feel. Her pain.

The man flailed, his free arm trying to connect with her. She danced around it, maintaining her grip on the wrist. She pinched his bloodied wrist tighter, causing more screams. Then as quickly as it began, it stopped. The man's wrist slipped free. He was down on one knee when the pain suddenly ended. He curled the hand tight against his chest, cradling it. Her shadow loomed over him. His right fist, unbroken, balled up tight. He turned, winding up to strike.

"You crazy..." he started, struggling to face Soriya. Only, she wasn't waiting for the rest. Her fist crashed down on his cheek when he turned, her dead eyes lost to the moment.

It was a moment she knew she wanted but did not understand why until it occurred. One of the rites of passage Mentor spoke about when she was a child, explaining that they were what defined their lives. She laughed, thinking a single moment was just that—an instant, never to have the impact he believed.

She was wrong.

Sitting on the cushioned bench, she suddenly understood everything Mentor had said to her over the years. It surrounded her world, changed it and twisted it so that it was perfect in every conceivable way. That was how Soriya felt about her first ice cream sundae.

The decision was a difficult one but the sundae was the right choice. It had everything in it. Peanuts, hot fudge, caramel sauce covering large scoops of vanilla, chocolate, and strawberry ice cream. Mentor ordered a small custard, plain vanilla. *Just the way he liked it. Simple.* She couldn't settle for simple. Not for her first. Not when she wasn't sure if it would be her last.

Chocolate dripped down her chin. Mentor laughed. It was the perfect moment, the perfect day. She knew it would never be forgotten just as surely as she knew she never wanted it to end.

Bones snapped under her punch and the man fell back. Each time she connected, he flew back and each time she collected him, dragging him away from the corner under the stairs of the platform. The third time, the man's left eye closed and did not open again. The lid was swollen shut from the pummeling. She did not care. She did not stop. Her eyes were dead to the world, her ears deaf to his cries.

"Please! Please," he pleaded. Her fist rained down on him again and again.

Soriya felt a crunching sound and knew it was her elbow shattering against the concrete wall she had been thrown against. Fifteen minutes of pounding led to that. The minotaur paced at the far end of the room, waiting for his opponent to rise again. There was bellowing and monologuing as only a villain could, with threats made against everyone and everything in the city of Portents. He was ambitious to say the least, but standing at over eight feet with nine-inch horns extending from his temples, he had every reason to be that way.

Blood trickled from her lips as easily as the ice cream had three years earlier. This was another moment, she realized. Another rite. Mentor stood in the corner, encased in shadow and unseen by the great beast's black eyes. He nodded to her, understanding her own realizations and making his known in the process. This was the way it would always be for them. This was the job.

Her eyes thinned, her sore frame struggled to stand. The corner of her lip rose slightly. One foot fell before the other and soon she was in a run for the minotaur that looked astonished at her perseverance. She raced for her destiny. Mentor smiled from the shadows, always watching her back. Always there for her.

There was no feeling left in her hands. They pounded against dented and torn flesh. Soriya's blood mixed with the man's in each connection. His cries were silenced. His eyes were closed. Still, she continued. Even as another cry, quiet at first, rang out under the stairs of the subway platform.

"Stop," the girl said softly. Through dead eyes, Soriya saw the girl's fear. "Stop."

Soriya turned back to the man and continued her assault.

Sitting before the Bypass, Mentor held out the Greystone. Soriya did the same, following his every motion. He kept his eyes on the stone while he spoke with words that cut through her.

"The Greystone is pure. It is all of the faith and spirit one can procure in a lifetime and more, channeled through a greater source."

The Bypass shimmered in green, floating in front of them like an emerald orb.

"A source we may never fully understand."

There was nothing more to understand. There was nothing more to know about the world she inhabited. It was cold, it was ugly, and she felt the grime of it clinging to her like a second skin. There was nothing but rage left to her. Mentor's words rang in her ears but she forced them out, her fist rising and falling on top of the man. He was no longer conscious from the pounding she delivered, not that it mattered to her. She lifted him by the collar, screaming in his face for more.

"Come on!"

In the corner of the platform, the woman with the torn blouse found her footing and inched her way toward Soriya.

"Please stop."

Still in front of the Bypass, Mentor continued. The stone glowed against the dim green light from the floating orb. Soriya's eyes were wide, wondering if the awe she felt would ever fade, hoping against hope it never would.

"When all is darkness, little one, the stone is the light that will guide you back to the day. You only have to believe in it, and in yourself. As I believe in you."

His hand rested on her shoulder, his pride filling her.

A small hand rested on Soriya's shoulder. Her fist was raised for another round but the touch of the hand, the way it pressed into her flesh, jarred her back to the moment. That was what it was, a moment, one that pulled in both directions and all directions at the same time. If she let it.

"Please stop." The words were barely a whisper but she finally heard them.

Her fist fell. The man slipped from her grasp and collapsed in a heap on the cold concrete of the platform. The young woman she had saved backed away, letting her hand slip from Soriya's shoulder. Her eyes were wary, flinching every instance they connected with the deep brown wells of her savior.

"I..." Soriya began, but the words were not there. *The Greystone is pure.* She barely registered where she was or what had happened, the words of her lost father figure rattling around her every thought. *As I believe in you.*

The girl did not wait to hear the rest of the sentence. With the way cleared, she raced for the stairs and the street above. Soriya watched her depart, ashamed of her actions. Kneeling close to the man in the heap on the floor, she heard the small hiss of breathing. The train was already gone and she needed to follow suit. Footsteps fluttered down the steps toward the platform, voices in a hurry. The young girl must have found some officers to investigate.

Soriya left the whimpering moans of the broken man and ran for the tracks. She jumped off the platform into the shadows of the rails, letting the darkness consume her as she made her way back home.

CHAPTER THIRTY-SIX

Loren was knee-deep in filth when Ruiz arrived at the back alley. The scattered detective was oblivious to his commanding officer's presence as well as the doggie bag he carried. He was focused on the pavement beneath the overturned dumpsters that lined the wall. Ruiz stepped back as a bag of trash went flying by. The captain grimaced and munched on a lukewarm fry. It wasn't until Loren reached under his arm to retrieve the book he had been carrying since the Bypass chamber that he noticed Ruiz's discontented face.

"It's here, Ruiz," he said, flipping through pages rapidly. "It's been right here the whole time."

Ruiz pointed toward the street. Traffic raced by in droves. The evening rush hour was starting in earnest and soon the speeding traffic would begin to crawl until the sun completely faded. "Loren, the body was found—"

"I know where the body was found," Loren snapped, silencing the captain, who was more than happy to listen and munch on his dinner. "There was something about this one that didn't add up. The body wasn't anyone with a secret like the others. It wasn't hidden. It was out in the open. Away from this alley. It didn't fit."

"He was rushed. He was lazy. It was more for the thrill of the kill than the ritual." Even Ruiz found the last option hard to believe, but there were still dozens of explanations that poked a hole in Loren's assumptions.

"No. If there's one thing I know, it's that this guy isn't lazy enough to let something as intricate as the ritual slip away from him." Loren paced the alley, his hands in front of him working out each thought. "This one was different from the rest because it had to be different. Because he needed something different from him."

"What?" Ruiz nearly choked on a large hunk of burger. A slice of bacon dangled from his lip and he felt the rest slipping back up. He forced it down, coughing loudly.

"The fifth victim. Accountant, right? What was his name again? Pruett. Jackson Pruett. Wife said he walked the same route every day for ten years. Up Evans Avenue for the black tower after taking the A train at 7:45 AM. Every day."

"What does it matter?" asked a confused Ruiz. "He was skinned, Greg! He took his trophy same as every other victim. No different. You're looking for things that aren't there, exactly why Mathers is taking—"

"But he was supposed to be all set with the skin from Urg," interrupted the pacing detective. "It was our waitress. Don't bother to give me the patented Ruiz glare. I'm not saying Sandy over there is our killer. She probably is a killer the way she eyes up her customers like meatbags, but today she's just an inspiration."

"I'm lost. Beyond lost."

"I know." Loren flipped violently through the files in his grasp. Photos fell to the trash below without regard until he found the one of Jackson Pruett's skinned remains from the previous day. He shoved the image in front of Ruiz, causing the bewildered captain to drop a handful of fries to the ground with a loud curse.

"Look! The jacket. See?"

"What?" Ruiz asked, looking at the image of the deceased. He tried to concentrate, drowning out Loren for a long moment. On the right front pocket of his jacket there were small indentations along the lip.

"He had something there." Loren's finger poked the image in front of Ruiz's face. "You can see the imprint. Probably from wearing it there for years. Our killer took his ID badge."

"Loren…"

"Just follow me here." His hands waved in front of him. He knew how it sounded. He knew how all of it sounded, especially when spouted by a man who hadn't had a restful sleep in days. He knew all of that but he also knew something else. He was right about it all. "This is not about the body. Any of the bodies. They are necessary to what he is doing. What he is becoming. I'm sure of that after talking with Soriya. But it was the signs that were staring us right in the face the entire time."

"The glyphs. The dead languages." Ruiz wanted him to slow down almost as much as he wanted him to speed through to the ending. This had been a long time coming. The city was panicked. The mayor and the commissioner wanted their heads for it. If Mathers had his way, he would bring the axe to help out. Both men needed the win and only had hours left to bring it home.

"No. Not even those." Loren pointed proudly to the floor of the alley, carved out of the mountain of garbage surrounding it in a circle. "Just a regular sign, hiding in plain sight. Our killer had Pruett's entire route to choose from but he picked this spot. He's been trying to tell us who he is the entire damn time. Trying to bring back the past, the city buried with him. Tell me what's special about right here of all places in the city."

Ruiz stepped over and saw the manhole cover. It bore the seal of the city of Portents along the top. On the bottom, it read in small, white letters: *Evans Line. Commissioned – 1873.* He looked at the detective, confused and weary. "It's a sewer line, Greg. There are thousands of miles of crap flowing beneath us. It's just a sewer line."

"It was the *first* sewer line, Ruiz. Look at the date. 1873. Yet everything we keep in the archives, everything in Mason's famed bookstore, tells me the city wasn't even conceived of until the 1890s. It's like the damn raven said. He was here at the beginning.

"I thought it was related to previous murders at first," he went on. "I checked every record I could find but nothing backed that theory because it wasn't the murders at all. He was talking about *before* that. The beginning of Portents."

"Raven?" It was the first question of many that slipped through Ruiz's lips. He let it pass when no response was forthcoming, and pointed to the book in Loren's hands instead. "Is that why you've been carrying around Beth's book like a security blanket?"

Loren knew how he sounded. There were so many wheels turning inside his head he wasn't sure which way to pivot next. There were the rituals to explain but all the pieces that lined up before him only brought him back to the signs and the locations of the murders. Each aspect held significance. Any decent cop could tell that much, but even Loren was stumped as to what each piece meant to the grand scheme. Soriya had alluded that the trophies were pieces of the killer being rebuilt and used for other murders but the question of how an old soul, dead over a hundred years, would know Abigail Fortune or Martin Decker enough to be able to use them to further his own goals. And the fifth murder victim, the accountant dumped in the alley where they stood? How would he have known about him at all? *A deal made with the darkest of lights.* More of the raven's wisdom seeping through the darkness. What it meant, though, was beyond Loren, so he let it go, hoping Ruiz would stay with him on what he thought was next. As he opened his lips to begin, a call rang out from the street.

"Detective?" Pratchett's voice filled the alley, head peering around large piles of trash. "Captain?"

"Perfect." Loren smiled at the reprieve with Pratchett's arrival. He needed the officer's help and the map he hopefully carried to pull off any chance of convincing Ruiz as to what was really going on and where they needed to head next. "Pratchett! Back here!"

Pratchett kicked aside a small path in the heaps of garbage bags, scurrying his way into the depth of the alley. His large hands carried the map Loren had requested. He looked between the two men, then back to the captain's cold leftovers, curiously. "What are we doing back here?"

"Don't ask," Ruiz replied, popping another piece of burger in his mouth.

Loren snatched the map from Pratchett, who shrugged his shoulders, stepping out of the excited detective's way. The map unfolded on top of the dumpster, nearly knocking over the remaining fries that made up Ruiz's disappointing dinner. The aging captain, while slower than he had been when he was on the streets, was fast enough to keep the Styrofoam box from falling to the trash-ridden alley.

Both men watched Loren's frantic search over the map. His eyes flipped between the large scale rendering of Portents and the book in his grasp. Finally, he found the correlation he had been looking for, matching it to the records Pratchett had given him early on in the case when the signs were merely a hunch, an itch to be scratched when time allowed. Now his eyes sparked with excitement at the pieces falling into place.

"Look...look," he exclaimed. The two men circled him, all three standing over the map. "The third murder. Vlad's. Where was it?"

"Warehouse District. On Beckett," Ruiz replied, curiously.

Loren marked it on the map. "And the first?"

"Hob's Lane on the Upper West Side," Pratchett answered. "Some old farmstead."

Another mark made its way to the map. Loren turned the small marker to the west of the city. "The second was down here at the Town Hall Pub. Near the docks."

Pratchett felt Loren's excitement, letting it carry him like a wave. He pointed eagerly toward another site. "The apartment complex on Glenview and Forest was the fourth."

"Exactly."

Ruiz squinted at the four large dots on the map and shook his head. "I don't see anything."

"Wait for it," Loren replied. His eyes were on their other companion. "Pratchett. Can you tell me the name from the apartment complex? The building's name?"

"Started with an E." The giant of an officer thought for a long moment. "Evans."

Loren saw the flickering of lights in Ruiz's eyes at the sound of the name. He quickly flipped open the book to an image of an old tenement building sharing the same view of the lakeshore as the complex. "This is what was there before it. Look at the date as well."

Both men saw it read 1876 with the name *Evans* adorning the front of the building. Loren flipped to another page, this time showing an old homestead that matched the crime scene of Abigail Fortune.

"The old farmstead was his. There was an old stone in the landscaping with the date March 11, 1873 carved into it, though I have no way of knowing if that stone is still on the property." He quickly flashed the image before moving to another. Mentor had had all of the pages noted. He knew, on some level at least, that the scenes related to Evans. He simply never had time to confirm it before the end. An image of the first shipyard opened for Ruiz and Pratchett to view. "The docks were commissioned by him at that time too. It was the gateway for people to come and build Portents from the ground up. And this sewer line?"

He paused. He had spent so long trying to understand the city, trying to see it from Beth's perspective and from Soriya's only to come up short. Now, the city lay before him, a puzzle waiting to be pieced together and every benchmark, every sign, pointed to a single man in the frame.

"This sewer line was where he stood when an angry mob ripped him to pieces."

Ruiz waved his hands in front of Loren. A single finger rose for a moment to process everything. Pratchett simply listened, feigning understanding through eyes of bewilderment. "You're talking about the guy you asked me about earlier? Nathaniel Evans?"

"Nathaniel Evans." Loren nodded. "Pissed off and back for more."

"Seriously?" Ruiz asked. Loren knew how it sounded. Knew all of them were hoping there would be another answer. That there had to be a better answer than the one that was being laid out in front of them. Serial killers were part of the job. Lunatics of all colors and stripes were par for any city. However, a man who founded the city, then was erased from any mentioning by every historical account, only to return over a century later for some kind of sick revenge? That was beyond science fiction. That was "throw your ass in the loony bin and tie your own straight jacket" crazy.

It was also the truth.

Loren took the marker and began connecting the small dots on the map. Four dots in different corners of the city. They did not line up with the current borders of the city—there had been a number of additions with suburbs and expansion after the Second World War—but even the skeptic in Ruiz saw what Loren was drawing.

"There," he said when he finished. A large box in black marker covered the map.

"A square," Ruiz said, plainly. "Come on, Loren. It's a square."

"It's a box, Ruiz," Loren replied.

"I've always felt rhombuses were scarier," Pratchett chimed in at the sight of the two men staring each other down. Both turned to the obtuse officer, who quickly waved his hands in retreat. "Just me on that one then."

"There's the fifth victim too, Loren," Ruiz said, struggling to understand. Old souls. Talking ravens. Ruiz wanted nothing to do with it. "Shouldn't this be some weird pentagram shit or something?"

"Like I said, this one was about something else."

"The ID badge."

"Right."

"Okay. To where? And what does a box have to do with Evans? With Portents?" Ruiz asked, begging for an answer he could relay to the station. One that didn't end with laughter on the other end and a trip to a mental ward.

Loren picked up the map and moved for the street. The two men eagerly followed through the thin clearing Pratchett had left in the garbage heap. They almost collided with the back of Loren when he halted on the sidewalk. His eyes were off to the east of their position, but more importantly, they were looking up. Past the dim light of the waning sun, they all followed his gaze.

"Because, Ruiz. Because of what lies in the center of the box," Loren finally answered. "And the family that built it."

Standing like a dark beacon was the black tower in the center of the city. It stood taller than all buildings around it, obsidian over shadow in color except for a single word that ran along the side of it in large, embossed red letters. A single name all of them had heard too many times in the last few days to ignore as coincidence or happenstance.

Evans.

CHAPTER THIRTY-SEVEN

The black tower emblazoned with the name of Evans on its side stood eighty-six stories tall. Most of the floors were controlled by Evans Industries, but a number of smaller concerns had taken up residence in the tower over the last decade, some partners of multi-million dollar enterprises, some separate entities with enough capital to cover the cost of rent at the city center. Most believed it was pride that built the tower, some stubbornness, while others knew that only true will built great things.

Evans was a name associated with a number of different industries but all came together at the central hub of the obsidian tower. Food production, textiles, banking. From the mundane to the obscure, Evans was part of the city's life in multiple facets even if the people that passed the stone archway leading to the lobby had no idea. Diversity was the key to survival in the business world. Where some businesses made their name in a single field, they lived or died by that field. Evans was about survival and to survive adaptation was the key. The loss of a limb meant nothing to a hydra with a hundred arms in a hundred pools. That was the business model that kept the lights bright behind the shadowed tower's tinted glass.

The lobby consisted of two staircases and a series of elevators beyond a single marble desk where two receptionist stations were manned. A security station was at the top of the staircases as well as a small historical attraction for those interested in learning more about the business or for those with cash burning their pockets hoping to pick up a magnet with the image of the black tower to post on their fridge at home. That was what the tower became on the surface—an attraction. It was one of a kind in the city and even the state. Where engineers came and went, believing the task to be impossible, the Evans family refused to accept defeat. It made the news across the world; it brought more people to Portents than when the first port was commissioned. The black tower was the beacon of the skyline, controlled and operated by the Evans lineage.

Three elevators took visitors and employees to the floor of their choice, all of them open except for the penthouse level of the tower and the roof above. Evans employees retained ownership of the first twenty floors and the top twenty floors, coordinating with a hundred offices around the world. All of them funneled their way to the top—the penthouse office.

The penthouse office took up most of the eighty-sixth floor of the building. The executive elevator located beyond the security office on the second floor landing was gold-plated around the frame. Arriving at its destination atop the large obsidian tower, the elevator opened to a small hall that quickly flowed into the greater room of the office. The wall extending to the right of the entrance and down the width of the building was covered by large pictures in heavy, silver frames. They ranged from oldest to newest and each held the image of a member of the Evans line. Father to son and on and on for over 140 years of history in Portents. At the end of the line, with the oldest image next to the door, was a large private washroom. A full bath, shower, and sauna were installed within the wide expanse of the restroom. The tinted windows that lined the entirety of the outside of the building gave an exquisite view from the whirlpool tub.

Leisure was part of the charm of power, but everything that came to the tower came because of the power of the office on the penthouse level. The office was sparse in decoration aside from the large images of Evans throughout the history of the city. A fully stocked bar took up the back wall and a conference table was positioned in the open floor space in the corner of the room. Aside from that was a large oak executive office desk. It extended eight feet across with a four-foot width. Wide drawers supported the two sides, three on the right and two on the left. Full leather lined the chair positioned behind the desk with enough cushioning to melt into the fabric for comfort. At least, that was how the man behind the chair appeared. His photo was closest to the elevator, a passing reminder of his ascension each time he went home for the night.

Gabriel Evans.

"I want to make sure we set something up with Pruett tomorrow, Lori," he said into his speakerphone, his fingers curling up the corner of the report he had spent the better part of the afternoon reading. The sun was fading quickly, deflected by the ring of windows surrounding the large tower. Up on top of the world during the daylight was a thrill, but he always hated it at night. The entire floor seemed suspended in the sky. The overhead lights assisted but when they clicked off on his way to the elevator, there was always a brief moment of terror that filled him, as if the floor would simply open up and he would fall to the street hundreds of feet below.

"Pruett? But I thought he was already..." his receptionist started to reply. He could hear the rustling of paper under her long, plastic fingernails. She hated to disappoint him and she rarely did.

"Lori," he said softly, comforting her. She knew better on the other end, the rustling continuing for the schedule of their project managers. "This launch has to go right and I want the projections to be spot on. If I look like a jackass again for the media, someone is going to take a hard fall."

Laughter echoed in the dark of the room. Soft, rhythmic guffaws from the far side of the large office. It cut through Gabriel like a chill breeze, his eyes attempting to peer through the thick black that seemed to spread from the doorway.

"Is someone there?" he called, nervously. There were no meetings on the docket and no advance warning of visitors. Stockholders be damned for their random visits to placate their unease at some of the more recent failings from the company's initiatives. Gabriel turned back to the phone. The red light was dimming. "Lori?"

"Mr. Evans?" Lori called, distantly. "Is every—"

The light faded completely from the phone, leaving only a dial tone then nothing at all. Gabriel lifted the receiver. "Lori? Lori! Are you kidding me here?"

More laughter boomed, closer now. Gabriel slammed the receiver down. He saw the thin figure of a shadow in the distance.

"All right, enough," Gabriel shouted. "Who's there?"

A figure drenched in black stepped out of the shadows. He staggered forward, hunched. When the man grinned, all Gabriel saw were teeth. His lips and cheeks sagged too low, out of place, as if belonging to someone else. Small scraps of flesh fell in his wake.

"Pruett?" Gabriel asked. The shadowy figure looked like the senior level accountant. The same look. The same hair. But the figure was taller, skinnier than Jackson Pruett.

"Mr. Pruett had another appointment," the voice boomed in the wide office.

"Then who—"

"Call me the Ghost of Christmas Past."

The sight of the intruder sickened Gabriel. He wanted to wretch from the torn flesh that peeled when he smiled and from the wide patches missing from his open abdomen. Reaching for the phone, Gabriel kept his eyes fixed on the approaching man…if he could refer to him as that.

"I don't know what kind of sick joke this is but I'm calling security. They—"

"Will not come." The sagging lips of the man before him finished the sentence without hesitation. Gabriel heard nothing on the line as before. It was dead. He glanced at the security cameras throughout the office. No lights were recording. Everything was dead. "No one can hear us. No one will see us as long as I wish it. I want my time with you to be free from any and all interruptions."

Gabriel watched the shadow step toward the windows. He wore a torn overcoat to conceal the patchwork of skin that sagged and broke loose from his body. Reflected in the dark glass, Gabriel saw a pair of lights cutting through him. One eye of sky blue and another he recognized from his own reflection. Crimson. A genetic anomaly his family had been gifted with every few generations. Quickly, Gabriel looked to the exit but the shadow blocked the path. Could he reach it faster than him? If not, could he fight? Too many variables. Too much fear was more the case. He stood silent, watching the man at the windows, sweat beginning to rise under his hair.

"You set yourself above it all," the shadow continued, staring out over the city. His city. "Watching the fleas below. Judging them. As it should have always been. I did the same. At this very spot. Only not so high up."

He smiled, turning back to Gabriel. His chin sagged down to his chest but the smile remained in place, lipless and bloody. As the shadow started back to the desk in the center of the room, his eyes caught sight of something else and his direction shifted once more, this time for the long line of photos.

"You don't look well, sir," Gabriel called out. Slowly, while the shadow stepped away from him, the twenty-eight year old chief executive officer inched his way to the corner of the desk. Once free from the confines of the desk there was nothing to block his path for the elevator. He needed only five seconds to reach it at a full run. He could do it. He had to do it. "Why don't we talk about whatever it is you want? Just talk."

The mismatched eyes of his late-night visitor greeted Gabriel at the end of his desk. Even at their distance, he felt them reach into him and take away all confidence in his plan of escape. The moment was gone. "Sit down, Gabriel."

Down the line of photos the shadow of a man walked. At each one, he stopped for a moment, eyes shifting up and down, from Gabriel's own image to his father's to his grandfather's, on and on down the decades of history.

"You sit up here over them, the eternal victor," the voice thundered. Each word a cannon, full of fury. "But you should have taken it to the next step. The degenerates. The freaks. Every day some new catastrophe on two legs, pretending to be a man. Infecting this city with their presence. Dragging it down from the heavens. Bringing all of us down with them. I tried. Lord knows, I tried to end them at the beginning. They saw it as murder. Those peasants. They saw it as a crime against humanity, when they weren't even human. You should have continued. Gotten rid of them all. Been stronger than I ever was. All towers fall. They came for me in mine. Those people, walking around like ants under our feet…they showed me that all towers fall when you let them.

"But you? You wasted your power, your prestige, on drugs, sex, and money."

The shadow stopped at the final image. The image of the first Evans in Portents. Gabriel had heard stories of the man, tales told on his father's lap when visiting the office as a kid. They always said he shared his ancestor's eyes.

Everyone tried to forget the face of the man in the image; for a time they even removed the portrait and locked it into storage. Gabriel's father retrieved it and placed it back on the wall with the rest. The past was meant to be known, to be honed and fine-tuned for the future. That was his message.

Gabriel never gave it a second thought—until now. The shadow was transfixed by the image, his hand reaching up to comb back thin patches of brown hair that had yet to fall from his scalp.

"This was our city, Gabriel. My city." The shadow turned back to Gabriel, who fell back into the desk chair. "You wasted the future."

"Who are you?" Gabriel asked, desperately. He needed an answer. He needed to know.

The shadow smiled next to the final image of the Evans line. The first Evans of Portents, the one Gabriel heard about in whispers and ghost stories but never pushed for more for fear of the answers that would come. The image of the man he knew to have truly been the inspiration of the city around them. The image of the man that almost destroyed the city in its infancy. Nathaniel Evans. The shadow's hand lifted his chin back into place. "Can't you see the resemblance?"

"What are you...?" Gabriel tried to understand. He tried to make sense of the shadow, the man, the creature in front of him, but nothing came.

"I'm family, Gabriel," Nathaniel Evans said. His hands extended closer and closer to his descendant. A speck of blue and another of blood red cut through the darkness of the room when the light went out above them. Gabriel felt his heart leap in his chest. His body was weightless and he knew it was finally happening. The floor was gone from under him. He was falling.

All towers fall.

The shadow had known all along somehow. This was the price he paid for the life he led. The floor was gone and the fall remained. Instead of the street below, though, there was nothing but two flitting lights in the shadows of the office moving closer and closer. They called to him one last time and then all was darkness.

"Now how about a hug, Gabe?"

CHAPTER THIRTY-EIGHT

So much had changed. Three days earlier, there was joy in Soriya's world and now, standing before the Bypass, there was nothing but darkness. Mentor was gone. Urg and Vlad had joined him beyond the veil, to whatever time and place chosen by the great floating orb in the center of the chamber. Whether it be paradise or damnation, it was not for her to know, but knowing was the one thing she needed at that moment.

Soriya knelt, her head low. She gripped tightly to the Greystone, the one piece of light that remained in her world. *The Greystone is pure.* They were Mentor's words. They were uttered to tell of a balance between bearer and stone where both parts made the whole greater, yet remained altogether pure. She knew that. She knew what she was supposed to be, how she was supposed to be, and how she failed to meet that standard time and time again. She knew all that, but still she tried to pierce the veil the way Mentor had so many times before.

Even with her eyes closed, she could feel the heat from the stone, light pouring out of it. Nothing flashed before her. There was nothing but shadow and darkness. *Show me. Show them to me.* She begged the Bypass for entrance. She had the question in her mind. *Where are they?* She held it out for the glowing orb to snatch from her mind but it hung between them. Her eyes opened then closed tighter. *SHOW ME.* Still, nothing entered her mind. No images of great cities long gone. No fields of flowers where Mentor skipped along waiting for his real family to join him. There was nothing because of the real question she wanted to ask.

When can they come back?

Asking questions was always dangerous with the Bypass. She realized that from the stories Mentor relayed to her at a young age, tales about the man who once trained Mentor and how their time together ended due to the ominous orb in the center of the chamber. Nightmares barely covered it for Soriya after learning the man's fate, promising her teacher it would not be repeated. The Bypass kept her promise for her this time by locking her out. There were no answers to seek. She knew them already. They were gone. She had failed and now she was alone with the job laid before her. A job she was not ready for in the slightest.

Three days. That was all it took to change her world. There was a time when she understood the world she inhabited. The city of Portents. The people of the Courtyard. She understood it all. She knew her role. She loved her role. Three days was all it took to take that away…to take everything away. She failed.

"No more."

It started with a whisper, slipping from her tongue. Her head remained low, her eyes closed and she squeezed the stone within her grasp. *The Greystone is pure.* She wanted it to remain that way. She wanted to feel that way. About herself. About her role. The broken man above in the tunnels disagreed with that assessment. So did the young woman she saved from his hands. Her fear stung Soriya deeper than any failure she had endured over the last three days. It was the one circumstance Soriya had full control over, though control was the one thing she forgot to bring to the party.

"No more."

It was louder this time. She felt it echo off the four large columns supporting the chamber. With her eyes closed, she imagined it was written on all four, each with their own language but all saying the two-word phrase over and over again. Tears stung her eyes, her heart threatening to leap from her chest.

"NO MORE!" Soriya screamed. Her eyes snapped open. The Greystone left her hand in a rage, soaring through the air until it slammed against the nearest pillar. It fell to the floor, skipping along the cool concrete until it finally stopped a few feet away from her. Through the tears that flooded her eyes, she could see it, the flat surface looking through her. She heard Mentor's voice.

"It is a great responsibility. What we give up pales compared to what we gain. A gift to change things for the better." His voice was soft, calling to her to pick it back up, to carry on. *"It is your responsibility now, little one."*

Soriya tried to stand. She tried to fight through the grief and the rage and the failures. They weighed her down; they prevented her from finding her balance. There was nothing she could do. She was not enough for the job at hand. She would never be enough. The Bypass floated before her, glowing in judgment of her, the deep shadows taking over the green glow. She turned away from the glow and the Greystone before it. More tears fell, and she closed her eyes so the world went dark around her.

"No more."

CHAPTER THIRTY-NINE

It took over an hour for Ruiz to go through proper channels. Loren waited patiently outside Evans Tower as Ruiz made call after call for the appropriate response team for the situation. Loren saw the necessity in the act but his pacing told a different tune. He wanted to move. He wanted to race into the building and end this just as Ruiz had requested two nights earlier. Backup was needed, however. Even in Loren's anxious steps, he realized there was no way to tackle Evans without manpower. Ruiz returned with six officers to back them up, which included the ever-present Pratchett. Loren wasn't confident the number lined up. Thoughts of Vlad's eviscerated frame or Urg's skinned body made those doubts very apparent. Still, it would have to be enough.

When the patrol cars approached, Loren made a beeline for the door under the large stone archway. Ruiz tried to stop him, but was forced to wait while the newly recruited officers joined him and Pratchett on the sidewalk for instructions.

Loren heard their footsteps behind him. He kept going, his own steps clacking loudly against the lobby's tiled floor. Above him the lights flickered and faded, as if recovering from a power outage. The reception desk held two chairs but only one was occupied at the moment. The woman behind the desk tilted her head around her computer screen at the sight of Loren. She saw the sidearm tucked under his jacket, exposed when he reached for the badge in his pocket. Then she noticed the other men and women in uniform making their way toward her.

"I'm sorry, can I...?" the receptionist started. Loren waved the badge in front of her, looking everywhere else in the room. He saw the security station above them and two guards watching him intently. He saw the elevators on the first floor, open and waiting to receive fresh occupants. None of it looked right to him.

"Executive elevator?" Loren asked, still browsing the scenery. The two guards stood a foot taller than him. The guard on the left carried a scar down his chin, while the man on the right covered his with a thick, black beard. Both wore ID badges on their chests. "Or do any of these take us to the top?"

"Mr. Evans' elevator is only to be used for…." The woman's voice was mousy over the footsteps of the other officers. Ruiz was by Loren's side, trying his best to calm the confused receptionist with his patented political smile. Loren was grateful to have him there. Tact was never his strong suit when it came to saving lives or closing cases. Tact was more red tape that Loren never understood. He let Ruiz wine and dine her with his soft stare and disarming grin. He was busy, looking. He stepped back from the desk, the woman continuing to lecture him on the policy of an elevator. From the center of the lobby, he was able to see the entirety of the security office on the second floor landing. In the back, there was another elevator, this one framed in gold. Jackpot.

"I see it. Thanks," Loren said, not caring if the woman was still in midsentence. Ruiz tried to grab him but the eager detective was already taking stairs two at a time to the landing. "You should look into these lights though."

The woman called after him. "I have to page him to let him know but I don't think he's taking—"

"He won't care," Loren bellowed back, stopping in front of the security office. He looked down at her with a smile of his own, one that did not give comfort to the young woman at the receptionist desk. "Thanks!"

"Loren," Ruiz shouted, trying to slow him down. Ruiz finally caught up with him, after passing along instructions to the officers at the front door as he made his way up the staircase. "Two by the front door. The rest with me."

They were easy enough to remember and Pratchett was the first to volunteer. Crowd control or last resorts were Pratchett's bread and butter. They kept him and everyone else safe from any command decision made by him. Patricia Brennan, a relative rookie to the squad who only met Loren in passing before he left three months earlier, followed suit to join the towering officer by the large double doors under the archway.

The two guards that looked like prison wardens blocked Loren's path to the executive elevator. Loren tried to pass and they shifted in front of him. The one with the scarred chin opened his suit jacket to show off his sidearm.

"Your boss is going to want to see us," Loren said, plainly. There was a monitor station to the right of him. Twenty monitors shifted from floor to floor, each time using a different camera angle. A single chair was stationed there and the man in control refused to budge to join his compatriots.

"Doubtful," the bearded guard replied.

Loren didn't care about approvals or invitations. An hour had been lost so far and he refused to wait any longer. Finally, the monitors shifted and Loren saw the executive penthouse office of Gabriel Evans. A lone figure sat, talking into a phone, though no sound could be heard over the monitor as far as Loren was concerned. In the corner of the monitor, something caught his eye.

"Hold it," he yelled at the man watching the monitors.

"Sir, you can't." An enormous hand grabbed Loren's arm and held him back.

"Go back to the penthouse feed."

"We have to ask you to leave, sir."

"Just go back to the penthouse feed and look at it."

"Sir, all of our monitors are real time. We don't need to—"

"Except for that brief outage you had earlier, right?" Loren pointed to the flickering lights. The guard in the monitor room looked queerly to the detective.

"It was only for a minute."

"Do it and we'll leave," Loren insisted.

The guard released him and nodded to his colleague in front of the monitors. The man switched the feed to the penthouse office. Where all the feeds displayed the darkness outside the tower, night settling over the city, the penthouse feed still held the remnants of the fading sun.

"Oh, hell," the man muttered. "It's from over an hour ago."

"He's already here," Loren said to Ruiz.

"Son of a bitch," the bearded guard muttered. Both men stepped aside, drawing their weapons. Loren led them, Ruiz, and the rest of the officers to the elevator doors. One released the clasp holding his ID badge in place and swiped it in the keypad next to the elevator doors. A loud click greeted them and the twin doors slid open. All of them stepped inside, the doors closed, and they headed up to the eighty-sixth floor of the black tower.

There was silence for a long moment. Loren took a deep breath, tucking his badge away. They were climbing and he was in a tiny little box heading to the tallest point of the city. Deep breaths were only going to go so far, but Evans was up there. It was time to close the case. That's what the job was and that was what he needed to focus on.

The numbers continued to ascend. He released the clip to his holster, letting his sidearm slip into his palm. He focused on the cool metal in his grip over the weightless shifting of the boxcar under his feet. He focused on the five victims and bringing their killer to justice over the image of his dead wife stepping off the ledge of their apartment building. *No more sunrises, Greg.*

"Just him up there?" Loren asked the two security guards.

"Pruett," the scarred one replied. Loren threw Ruiz a thin glare at the name. They knew it very well from the autopsy report.

"Mr. Evans' accountant. He didn't look good but he has access."

"Right." Loren nodded. He knew Mr. Pruett's fate and who had taken his place.

"Tell us again," said Ruiz, retrieving his pistol and nodding for the others to do the same.

Loren was thankful for the distraction. He looked over each and every face in the elevator, trying to relay the importance of what they were about to do. His eyes made it clear that the time for questions was at an end. This was it.

"Nathaniel Evans helped found this city. His business brought people in by the droves and created one of the fastest growing settlements west of the Mississippi during the Reconstruction era. He was a hero to the people until they found out what he did when the sun went down. Murders, sacrifices, rituals. It forced the people of Portents to turn on him. They killed him for it. Beat him to death with the brick and mortar he made available to them and then burned his body to ash. The town was so mortified, the stigma of his heinous acts so great, that they hid their history with him, razing the city to the ground. Then they started over. That's where we get stories of William Rath founding the city, but that was all they were. Stories. Twenty years Evans controlled the city and the people within it and they buried it so that future generations didn't have to carry the burden of remembering it."

No one replied. Confused looks followed Loren's gaze. He wondered if they heard more than a simple ghost story, if some actually believed what he said. If it was even possible to believe such a thing could happen. Ruiz made it simple enough for everyone.

"Lone man up there. He's armed and dangerous. Do not get close to him. Shoot to wound if necessary. We want him alive." To Ruiz, it was always about keeping it simple. He looked back to Loren as the others in the elevator nodded in agreement. "Why here, Loren?"

"This was where he stood when he was at his height. When he owned the city and the people around him. He wants that back."

The guards behind Loren were nervous, small beads of sweat on their brow.

"Gentlemen." Ruiz addressed them, his voice slow and calm. The elevator reached floor 80 and continued to climb. "We'll take it from here. Go back to the lobby and shut down the elevator to keep anyone from leaving this floor. We will call with the all clear when it's done."

A sigh of relief exhaled from both of them. The elevator chimed. All eight passengers turned to the doors when they slowly slid open. Loren and Ruiz led the way. Silence fell over them. Ruiz positioned Merrill and Daniels at the elevator and the small stairwell beside it. The elevator closed with the relieved guards. Loren wondered how much they would regret not having that as an exit strategy, the answer painfully clear in his mind.

Jankowitz and Naeger followed Loren into the wide room, each step mere inches in front of the last to maintain the quiet of their approach. Above them, the lights flickered worse than those in the lobby. Most were out completely, though the cause was more than the simple outage explained to them below. The bulbs to the overhead lights were shattered, resting on the panels that enclosed them in the ceiling. Another popped and darkened in the far corner. Jankowitz spun on her heels, gun at the ready. Loren rested his hand on her forearms, slowly bringing her weapon down. She nodded nervously, which Loren understood completely.

To Loren's right, he saw the line of photos. The Evans line stretched back through time. The recent photo of Gabriel Evans was that of a twenty-eight year old man-child on top of the world. His smile swallowed up countries as easily as the amount of money at his disposal, and he was well aware of it. He sported auburn hair slightly darker than the red tint to his eyes, lighting up his facial features. A strong face but a young one. Too young for the job on his shoulders, though Loren was sure he didn't mind pretending to fill the big shoes of a multi-million dollar mogul.

All around them, the city stretched out in every direction. Glass covered the walls from floor to ceiling, tinted to keep anyone from looking in and to keep the full light of day out. It was awkward to say the least. Loren refused to look at the walls, keeping his gaze on his feet or the ceiling above. He sent Jankowitz and Naeger in opposite directions to scan the perimeter of the room. The center was his. He may have made the journey up, focused on the task at hand, but no matter what else he knew, heights were not his friend. Had he truly forgotten that during the elevator's climb? Had his drive curbed all rational thought? He hoped it would again. For a little while at least. Just enough so he could breathe again.

Ruiz stepped ahead of them during their sweep, inching toward the desk in the center of the room. A small pool of blood extended from behind the desk. The large, leather chair that rested in the center of the expansive executive desk was turned away from them but Ruiz saw a silhouette on the armrest. He looked to Loren, pointing out the shadow ahead of them. Loren nodded and followed, their weapons raised.

Loren stopped on the far side of the desk, covering the chair with his weapon. Ruiz continued forward, each step carefully taken in silence around the desk.

The soft popping of light bulbs continued in the distance. Ruiz ignored them, inching for the chair and the waiting shadow in its grasp. He took the left-hand side of the desk to avoid the pool of blood on the other. His right hand left the safety of his sidearm and extended out for the chair.

Ever so gently, Ruiz felt the soft leather of the top cushion. He gripped tighter and felt the weight in the chair shift. He spun the chair around to greet the shadow.

Ruiz's face dropped at the sight. Loren saw it happen so fast. The chair turned and his friend's face went white.

Ruiz did not fall back. He did not wretch at the sight of the shadow in the chair. However, Loren knew he wanted to because it was either that or shriek in terror.

A body greeted them in the large leather executive chair. Loren knew it was Gabriel Evans' body from the start, but the tattered clothing that attempted to cover the decaying frame confirmed it with *G.E.* embroidered on a single cufflink. Another victim of Nathaniel Evans.

This one was worse, though. Gabriel was skinned, just as the last two victims had been, but the trophies taken did not end there. Sockets where crimson eyes had been were empty. His hands were gone as well. Ribs were cracked open and what organs not harvested lay at his feet in the growing pool of blood on the floor. Gabriel was picked clean for parts.

"Dear God," Ruiz muttered under his breath. Loren stepped over to his friend and pulled him away from the corpse of the most powerful businessman in Portents.

"Not here, Ruiz," Loren replied.

A toilet flushed from the far side of the room. All of them turned, listening to water run in the washroom located at the far end of the long line of photos and painted profiles. The sound was replaced by approaching footsteps. They clicked with the sound of expensive shoes, the kind that demanded their presence be known well before their wearer was in the room. The door opened with a slight click and a man stepped into the room.

He wore a three-piece suit, black as the windows that surrounded him. His hair, auburn and thick, flowed to the right side of his head. Red eyes greeted them, his youthful smile belonging to the scavenged corpse behind the desk.

Nathaniel Evans dried his hands on a washroom towel when he stepped into the room. He wore the skin of his descendant proudly, revealing a wide, toothy grin he had been saving for over a century.

"Welcome, Officers," he greeted them, his voice booming in the large penthouse office at the height of the black tower. "Welcome to the end."

CHAPTER FORTY

It started small. The thump of a heartbeat amid the cascading sounds of the world above. So small, it was hardly noticeable to the languishing woman kneeling before the floating orb of the Bypass. Her failure overshadowed the small crackling in the distance, her grief overpowering the spasms running along the sides and up the ceiling of the chamber.

Until it was too much to ignore.

The quakes began soon after. Tremors that shook the ground under her. In the center of the room, the shimmer of green and shadow droned louder but inconsistent. The floor screamed in agony, causing Soriya to jump to her feet. Her eyes widened when the room shook with the intensity of a large-scale earthquake, yet remained confined to the chamber of the Bypass. The world did not break through the widening cracks in the ceiling. Trains did not crash down the large stairwell. Everything centered on the chamber itself.

Finding her footing, Soriya instinctively grabbed the Greystone she had so callously tossed away in a fit of anger. The petulant child was gone. With her, the anger and grief over the events of the last three days faded behind the wave of tremors that cracked the earth around her feet. The columns remained intact, for the moment, keeping the ceiling from falling, but fissures were visible along the corners of the room.

The stone was warm in her hand. Through her fingers, which gripped the stone so tightly they paled in color, Soriya saw the bright light of the rune on its surface.

ᛉ

Without a thought, without an inclination, the stone was in use and not by its bearer. Had she caused the tremors? Subconsciously, had she willed her entire world to collapse even more than it already had?

This was something else, she knew. The rune was not constant. It shifted between five different configurations, glowing brighter with each one. She did not recognize their meanings in the quick changes passing before her eyes. The only thing she did know in that moment was that this was not her doing.

"It's starting."

This was his doing. The man who killed Mentor. The old soul's final reckoning had come to pass on the city of Portents. The moment was finally here and she was bearing witness to it.

Tremors forced her further back. In the void of the Bypass, screams were heard even without attempting to pierce the veil between worlds. Screams of delight. Screams of pain. Screams of terror. The orb was shifting, darkening in color, growing in size. That was not the only thing it was doing, Soriya realized. The Bypass was rising. Small shards of color flitted off the floating orb. The embers of the once perfect sphere rose, slipping through the mounting fissures in the ceiling. Through the darkness of the cracks surrounding her, Soriya saw lights rising out into the city above. The Bypass was not only rising. It was escaping.

Light beamed from the four columns surrounding the floating mass of energy. On each one, a single symbol glowed brightly. They matched the signs written on the face of the stone that continued to shift, faster and faster, with each passing moment. They also matched something else, Soriya realized—pieces locked into place.

The world went from chaos to order in her mind at last. Each symbol sparked on the pillar was from a different crime scene. Four signs, symbols of dead languages, one for each of the pillars guarding the great, glowing orb hidden in the center of the city. Loren believed they were a message, but for so long Soriya saw nothing to indicate what that message could have been. Each letter, from Gothic to Vincan, stood alone. None strung to the next to form a linear thought. Because there was no linear thought behind them—only the endgame.

It was right before her eyes the entire time. The Vincan sign under Vlad. The Cyrillic symbol on the wall at Urg's apartment. Their deaths were selected for multiple reasons. The trophies to carry out the other murders were the first step. The locations were the second, though why they were selected still escaped the young woman's fast-moving thoughts. Neither one mattered compared to the third reason. The reason behind the signs. The reason behind the deaths that had plagued the city and haunted Soriya's fading life. Each death, each sign unlocked the pillars containing the energy of the Bypass. For over one hundred years, the orb was contained and hidden but in a single week the door had been opened and the waves of glowing, green light filtered through the fissures in the ceiling, escaping into the city streets above. Four deaths for four pillars. The fifth in the alley had been used as a cover, a distraction, to retrieve the trophy lost at the fourth scene. She knew that now as clearly as she knew everything else around her.

Including the death of Mentor.

His death was the final key. Where the four columns safeguarded the floating orb, containing it within the confines of the chamber, there was another piece needed to temper the energy locked in the Bypass. A Greystone. The fifth sign, the one marking the front of her stone in order with the rest, was the final key to unlock the chamber. It was a code hidden within the chamber, a passkey unknown to her and possibly even Mentor to free the Bypass from its sanctuary.

The Bypass rose, tendrils of energy flickering and fading through the cracking ceiling. The light faded from the chamber around Soriya. Everything was fading, out into the darkness of the city of Portents. The old soul's plan came together before her eyes, the energy of the Bypass the last step toward his return. She gripped the stone tighter in her grasp. She begged for it to stop, pleading with the stone's power to force the symbols to fade back into nothing, to return everything to the way it was only days earlier.

No answer came. No answer was expected. The stone would not be her saving grace. There was no reset button, no timeout to call, through the mysterious forces behind the Greystone. There was only her. Soriya Greystone. There was a time that name meant more to her than life itself. There was a time that responsibility meant more as well. It was her job. It was her lot in life no matter the pain, no matter the loss, no matter the sacrifice required.

It was time to remember that.

CHAPTER FORTY-ONE

The Night of the Lights.
That was how it was to be remembered. Some had their own ideas of the name, to be sure. There was the *Night the Lights Filled the Sky*, but most thought it wasn't punchy enough. The *Portents Chronicle* actually held tight to that one for a week before realizing it was the underdog in the naming war between every major news outlet in the city. Some were more dramatic about the night in question, believing it to be more of a sign of the end times than anything else. They were not far off the mark in that regard but no one wanted to see that lining the television screen or in black, bold letters on every newsstand in the county. When it came down to it, the consensus held that it was *The Night of the Lights* in Portents.

It was the night things changed.

In the first minutes, most believed it to be an elaborate display—fireworks and sparklers dazzling the skyline for an unscheduled celebration. Smiles lined the faces of pedestrians. They infected the shop owners closing up for the night and the lovers hailing a cab to head home from a romantic meal downtown. Green streams carried their joyous wonder up into the sky, their gaze enthralled by the magic that surrounded them. Parents called children from their beds to look out windows, while others tucked deeper into the shadows, afraid to face the rising lights.

Those moments of wonder did not last. The lights, starting slow and sparse, became brighter and denser. They were no longer small streams against the black sky but waves of glowing green swirling up from the ground through the city streets. Delight turned to worry to outright concern as the waves grew wider and brighter. They swam the breadth of eight city blocks of business and residential neighborhoods in the center of downtown Portents. The lights raced along corridors and wind tunnels, faster and faster through the streets. Parents pulled their children away, lovers returned to their restaurants, and shop owners to their shops.

The speed of the spinning lights brought with it the wail of the wind. So fierce it shattered the glass that ran along the front of homes and businesses. Concern became terror, as the citizens witnessing the moment where the lights took back their city understood the wailing that filled the streets was not the wind at all.

They were screams.

For every person it was different. Some heard screams of joy whirling around them, though joy was the last emotion to enter their own hearts. The people of Portents felt nothing but fear over the shrill laughter that cut through the glowing green wave that stretched over downtown. It rose higher and higher with each pass, becoming louder and louder. From the warehouse district to the docks, it could be heard. The laughter. The joy. But most of all, the screams.

When the visions began was when the death toll started to climb. Flickers of emerald left the wave, falling back to the street while the main fleet of lights continued their ascent into the black sky. The glowing embers of the wave that fell passed through homes and people like wraiths. Elderly saw their lost children, taken unjustly before them. Widows saw husbands and wives return, judging the decisions that followed their demise.

More and more the lights took form, some unrecognizable in the darkness of the city. Three women strode the downtown strip of restaurants and bars, on the hunt for men willing to shower them with gifts and what they perceived to be a form of love. Little did they know, the gifts were just the appetizer to murder once the men had satisfied their desires. Sirens, they had been called, once upon a time in distant lands. A myth long forgotten, now present among the living in Portents.

Other people saw strange things as well in the light that poured over them. Chariots raced through the streets. The cheers of battle rang out as they raced. The firing of muskets and cannons. The world was lost in time, the city washed over in the light of the Bypass. More light rose and with it more form, more beings finding their place in the present. Not all were concrete, some as ghostly as phantasms, slowly pulled back into the light as quickly as they fell.

Some refused the gift completely, knowing their time had passed while others welcomed it. Like the Sirens of old, they saw their return as a second chance but unlike the three women strutting the streets, they waited patiently, slipping into the shadows for another day.

If another day came.

Outside the eight-block radius of the lights, the rest of the city felt the change. From the docks of the west to the warehouses and rail yards of the east, all of Portents looked to the skies watching the green glow rise higher and higher. Although there were no visitations, no visions, no wailing and no death outside the epicenter of the strangeness, there were four points within the city that glowed with the same intensity as the rising tide above the city. Four points of light emanated from four signs, smeared in blood. From the Town Hall Pub to Evans Apartments, all four crime scenes dropped their mysterious pretense at the same moment the lights cracked through the streets for the skies above. Through warehouse and ranch home, the light that started with the symbol scrawled along walls and upon floors beamed up in a straight line for the heavens. Four points marking the borders of the city.

The lights washed over the city for what felt like ages but passed in a matter of minutes. Each witness heard and felt something so unique it would never truly be forgotten. Those who watched, even through the shattering of glass and the screams that cried out of the glowing wave, saw the light pass over the skyline in a great circle. Higher and higher, over building and skyscrapers it climbed. Eight city blocks it encompassed but as it reached the cloudless sky, it contracted and thickened. It spun faster and faster until it surrounded only a single structure.

All eyes—from the lovers to the shop owners to the parents—turned toward the center of the city, each wondering if the end had come at last. All eyes, including the brown orbs of Soriya Greystone looked up from the city streets at the giant wheel of light floating above them. To everyone else, it was every emotion locked in one from wonder to terror. To Soriya, it was nothing more than a giant billboard begging her to follow. The lights rose and rose until only a single structure lay within its wake, turning all eyes to the single tower of black in the center of the city.

Evans Tower.

CHAPTER FORTY-TWO

"Hopeless. That is what they call the situation you're in."
Loren and Ruiz stood silent, listening to the gravel behind each word spat by Nathaniel Evans. Leather shoes tapped lightly against the tile as the refurbished man, in the skin of his descendant, walked farther into the room. The towel in his hands wiped them clean of the last flakes of blood caught under the well-manicured fingernails. He dropped it to his side, his head turning to survey the entirety of his company. Naeger was closest, near the wall of photos depicting two centuries of the Evans line. Jankowitz was on the far side of the room near the bar. Her terror was palpable, with eyes flitting toward the elevator and the two men stationed there.

"Can't you feel it?" Evans asked. The skin molded to his body remained fixed but a wide grin stretched behind it. In the stillness of the evening, the darkness that surrounded the black tower with tinted windows on all sides, Loren saw lights. Dim at first, spinning along his periphery while maintaining a cool look at the man before him, Loren watched the green glow rising to greet them. Stillness shattered with glass, the lights spinning faster and faster below them. The earth around them quaked but no one budged, though Jankowitz and Naeger were ready to call it a day, sweat beading along their brows. Loren did not know what was happening. He did not know that the city was caught in the grip of Evans' smile. All he knew was that it had to end.

"The futility of it all."
Evans' hands rose slowly, his palms free of any instruments. He was the definition of calm and collected. There was no worry in his eyes, his new eyes taken from the corpse behind Loren. There was nothing but a confidence that shook Loren to the core. It gave him pause, made him question everything he had seen and learned over

the course of the last few days. Questions that had no bearing any longer, not with the murderer he had sought now in front of him. He did not want to hear another word. He did not want to see another grin. Ruiz told the same story, his hand inching toward his sidearm. Still, they waited, wondering what was behind the musings of the killer before them.

"Humanity's inability to extend itself past its own basic instincts. I achieved where mankind simply took those achievements and abused them. I created a paradise for you and you let it rot around you like a disease." Spit flew through his gritted teeth. "This place was pure. I made it pure. And the fools I was surrounded by, your ancestors, murdered me for it. I was trying to save them! From freaks and terrors that none of them knew of, that none had the capacity to understand! Sacrifices were required, to be sure. Not the least of which was my own. Did they care? No! They beat me and burned me as easily as the witches of old. Like the freaks I protected them from all that time. I created a paradise that none deserved."

He believed it. It was in the fury of his words. In the anger on his lips. In the burning of his eyes staring through Loren. He believed every word, every moment, every bit of his wretched life and turned it to the role of savior. Loren knew the account in the book he left with Pratchett in the lobby. When so-called freaks and monsters were not an option, women and children were the sacrifices of choice. Sacrifices for good harvests. Sacrifices for mild winters. Sacrifices for anything and everything that gave Nathaniel Evans the feeling of power over his city. Portents was a plaything to him, not a paradise. He was a tin god ruling over no one but his own ego, though his view may have written a different tale.

The lights, once dim and low on the periphery, now surrounded them on all sides. Through the wailing winds that spun faster and faster outside the glass prison in which they were enclosed, screams were heard. Screams of the victims of Evans' dreams. Screams of the innocents left in his wake. Loren heard Urg, Vlad, Mentor, and the others. He heard them crying for him to act, now, before it was too late. But what could he do? What could a simple man with a pistol do against someone who could raise the light of the Bypass above the city? More important to Loren at the moment was the final player in their drama, missing from the scene: Soriya Greystone. He needed her more than ever.

"Now," the man in the suit continued, "with the energy I wield I will raze this city to the ground and all within it. I will burn it back to its purest form and start anew in the flesh of my descendant. I will be a hero, the lone survivor of a great tragedy. You deserve this end. And I am more than happy to bring it to you."

All of them saw it coming. They saw it in the pure look of pleasure that refused to wane across his stolen face. They saw it in the slow drop of Evans' hands and the glint in his eyes. Loren wanted to yell but found no voice.

"Keep your hands in the air," Ruiz demanded.

"You hesitate. Captain, is it? Unsure how to stop me. Unsure *if* you can stop me. You can't."

Ruiz stepped forward, his weapon raised. They all saw it but none of them could do anything about it. Naeger was too close. He was simply too close.

"Let me make the decision for you then, Captain." Evans' left arm shot out like a bullet and snagged the unsuspecting arm of Officer Naeger. The surprised officer was jerked forward in front of Evans. The others were unable to get a shot off. Evans' cold eyes stayed on Ruiz the entire time, the killer's hands catching the falling officer's head before snapping it to the side.

Naeger's body collapsed to the floor, still twitching but dead all the same.

There was nothing left in Ruiz. No doubts. No fears. Just anger.

"Put him down. Now."

Shots rang out, mixed with screams from Ruiz and Jankowitz. They unloaded their clips in an instant. None hit their target, who raced down the wall of photos, allowing the Evans line to take each bullet in stride. The shots marked the second mistake on their part, the first lying dead before them in the crumpled heap of what was once Officer Thomas Naeger.

The shots were nothing but a call for Merrill and Daniels, both of whom ran into the room, service weapons drawn. Daniels was faster on his feet but slower to act. He barely made it three steps into the room before he saw the approaching Nathaniel Evans.

The man in the suit threw an uppercut that caught Daniels square in the chin. It drove him off his feet, his body suspending in midair for a moment before crashing down. When he fell, his weapon let loose three rounds in rapid fire. His aim was wide due to his arms flailing to right his falling body. All three connected, but not with their intended target. Merrill went down hard. The first bullet shattered his knee. Each bullet impacted higher and higher until the third met his left temple.

"No," Daniels muttered before the breath left him on impact with the tile floor. Merrill wasn't moving. Daniels couldn't look away, wouldn't, even as Evans slipped behind him. He held tight to the sides of Daniels' head. A slight snap was the last thing heard before Daniels fell lifeless next to his partner.

More shots broke the discord of the room. Ruiz and Jankowitz had reloaded in the few seconds it took Evans to dispatch their two colleagues. Two more deaths to add to the toll of the last week. Their shots met Daniels' chest, a lifeless shield for the grinning murderer. Gradually he moved closer toward Ruiz and Loren. Jankowitz shifted for a better angle but Evans kept their dead friend between them.

"No putting me down, Captain," Evans laughed, the sound of his leather shoes on the tile floor becoming louder, each one bringing him closer and closer to Ruiz. "Nothing will stop me. Nothing will stop *this*. I survived Hell's eternal flame. I stripped the flesh from my bones and transcended to this place. For this task."

Loren watched everything unfold. Just watched. From the death of Naeger to the fall of Daniels and Merrill. He never fired a shot. He simply observed the craven beast before them take three lives in the matter of a minute. With his hands. Yet not the same as before. No one else noticed. No one else saw it. Evans had eviscerated Vladimir Luchik with the hand of Martin Decker. A hand that could be turned into a deadly weapon. However, he had not used any such talents on the men lying on the floor of the penthouse office. Evans used no gifts or trophies taken from his previous victims.

Loren peered to the broken corpse of Gabriel Evans. He saw the missing eyes and the vacant hands. The skin of his descendant had not been enough for Evans. He needed the other pieces, forsaking the previous trophies. Why? Soriya would know right off. There was something about it, something that had changed the game Evans was playing.

It no longer mattered. Evans lifted Daniels' lifeless frame and tossed it aside. The body flew through the air, connecting squarely with Jankowitz. The force of the impact, the sudden connection of 200 pounds against her 130 was enough to send her crashing across the room. The force of the throw smacked her side and her body twisted enough to slam face first against the tinted glass windows of the office. Her body slid down the glass, settling against the floor.

Loren's eyes weren't on that, though. They were on the object that Evans removed from his pocket. He kept it tight in his grip, the ever-present confidence worn on his lips and in his words. "With this," Evans remarked, "it is far too late for any of you. With this, there is nothing to stop me."

He held it out before him, a white light shining on the face of the smooth surface. Loren knew what it was instantly. It had been missing since they found Mentor's body in the Bypass chamber. He knew it wasn't truly missing, just taken. Dammit, how could he forget about it so completely? Loren raced for Ruiz, knowing it was too late.

"Greystone," he said in a distant voice. The captain turned suddenly, taken aback by the scream from behind. An arm shot out to grab his friend. "Ruiz! Down!"

Too late. He knew it as soon as he reached out but was surprised at the speed with which Evans was able to channel the Greystone to his will. For a brief moment, Loren was able to make out a fresh rune on the face of the stone, one he had not seen before in his time with Soriya.

ᚱ

Though he did not know the meaning behind it, one became perfectly clear. The floor began to rumble around them. Loren fell back on his heels, stumbling farther away from Ruiz, who was caught in the center of the room. Water burst from all sides. Pipes shattered like glass within the floor under the bar and throughout the large executive washroom. With a mind of its own, the water floated in the air like jet streams until they all congealed into a single, focused tidal wave.

"No!" Loren cried. He attempted one last leap toward his friend but was thrust back from the onslaught of water rushing past him. His head slammed hard against the corner of the oak desk, his body somersaulting over the desk until it landed hard in the pool of blood that ran from the leather chair.

Ruiz was not as lucky. The wave of water, suspended in air, was directed solely at him. It slammed into the captain, a sledgehammer of liquid, driving him off his feet. It carried him until he felt the glass of the tinted windows crash into his back. Breath left him, the water shifting from his chest to cover his face. Ruiz let the gun slip from his grasp, desperately reaching into the water, hoping to block it for a moment of air. The frothy liquid poured down his throat, threatening to drown him in the tallest building in the city. His hands fought through the constant pressure of the water, unable to penetrate deep enough for a second of relief. The world was darkening quickly.

But that was not the end of it for Ruiz. It started with a simple snapping sound that quickly branched out in deep cracks. The glass behind him was breaking from the pressure of the river blasting against him. Louder now, the cracks deepened until finally the window shattered, sending Ruiz out into the brightening sky that circled Portents. Sweet relief swam through Ruiz's lungs. There was nothing around him but a sense of weightlessness. When the window shattered, the water suddenly fell away, no longer needed to carry out the execution of one without the ability to soar like a bird. The smallest of respites to the middle-aged man before he felt the floor slip away from him.

Ruiz felt the city close around him, but as the moment of weightlessness ended and the falling began, a hand shot out of the dark and grabbed his wrist. Deep breaths filled Ruiz's lungs. He was going to live. He was going to make it. Then he saw the hand holding him outside the window. He saw the man holding his life within his grasp.

Nathaniel Evans.

Evans pulled him close. In his other hand, the man held the Greystone. The rune adorning its side was no longer what it had been, shifting to something new. Ruiz barely made it out through the thin fingers of the man holding his life over the edge of the building but it looked like a cross between the letter P and the top of a medieval axe.

Þ

It glowed brighter and with it so did the arm of Evans. Heat channeled through his body, down his other arm, until it expelled on Ruiz's flesh like the deepest flames of Hell. Ruiz screamed, indistinguishable and indescribable cries of pain as the flesh seared along his wrist. The flames shot down his arm to his elbow. His skin bubbled under the heat.

Evans pulled him closer. The smile still pursed his lips. There was no pain in his eyes. The stone channeled the heat through him but away from him at all times, leaving him cool to the touch. Ruiz felt Evans' hot breath on his face.

"Taste it," Evans said, holding Ruiz higher within the frame of the window. "Smell the death it brings. And welcome it with open arms."

"Enough," a voice called from the far side of the room. Deep and booming, it cut through the gravel spewed from Evans. The heat fell away from Ruiz when Evans lost his concentration on the stone and turned to the sound of the voice.

Soriya Greystone stood waiting, thin ribbons running down her left side and her own Greystone tight in the palm of her right hand. Fire burned hotter in her eyes than any the stone was able to produce.

"You want an ending so badly?" she called to Evans. "Come and get it."

CHAPTER FORTY-THREE

The great circle of light surrounded the obsidian tower at the height of Portents. It spun clockwise around the beacon in the sky, gaining mass and speed from the flashing lights of the Bypass, slowly vacating the underground chamber. As the size of the wave grew to its maximum width, the speed declined until it stopped completely. Then it began to stretch out over the city, heading in all directions. The green cloud brought with it a storm that shattered the silence of the clear night that had settled over the city mere minutes before.

Time was running out.

Inside the penthouse, no one knew this more than Soriya Greystone. She had raced through the subway tunnels, up to the city streets, making her way quickly to the epicenter of the great tide of light that flowed over the citizens of Portents. The tower made sense. It brought everything together. From the old soul behind the killings, his name written in red letters streaking across the obsidian building, to the final chapter of his plan.

She bounded into the building, finding the staircase to the executive elevator as if a sixth sense had tied her to the call of Mentor's Greystone. Two guards were in the process of shutting down the golden-framed elevator when she approached. They wheeled toward her, surprised by the fierce look in her eyes.

"Leave it running," she commanded. They stepped aside, letting her enter the elevator. They did not try to stop her. They did not believe for a second that they could.

Chaos surrounded her arrival to the penthouse office that once belonged to Gabriel Evans. The windows were shattered. Bodies of men and women she did not recognize decorated the floor like area rugs. Loren's worn shoes were the only visible sign of him from his position behind the desk. When she called out to Evans, he tossed Ruiz aside with glee. The middle-aged Latino crumpled against the floor, unconscious from his struggle with the suited beast.

"The prodigal child. The stone bearer," Evans taunted.

Soriya stood her ground, feeling the thin coils of ribbon down her left side whip around her with the wind.

"Tired of hiding? Tired of running away? Of watching everyone and everything burn around you? Go home, child. Sleep the sleep of the damned with the rest of the city."

"No," Soriya replied. The ribbons flew forward when her left arm extended out toward Evans. The pink folds snapped around Evans' head. "No more running."

With a tug, the man flew forward. His hands moved the ribbons from his line of sight too late, feeling them sear the skin he had taken great pains to acquire in pristine condition. With his vision cleared from the ribbon, he was greeted by Soriya's right fist. It slammed against his cheek while the ribbons retracted. The combination sent him reeling back but Soriya pressed forward, allowing herself a slight smile as the feeling of the punch reverberated through her like a shot of ecstasy.

Loren moaned back into consciousness. His head felt like it had spent the better part of a week in a blender filled with rocks. Carefully, he lifted his weary body to his hands and knees. His left side slipped, causing him to crash back against the tile. A second attempt with a slow turn to his back helped him sit up behind the large oak desk, keeping him out of sight. There was blood on his hands. Fearful, they shot up to his forehead. A slow trickle had dried to the gash above his left temple where he had collided with the desk. There was nothing to indicate the streams that dripped from his fingertips. Then he peered down and realized where he had landed. The blood of Gabriel Evans washed over his body like a second skin. Pushing off the desk to his right, Loren spun around and kicked free of the pool underneath him. He blinked rapidly, attempting to shake loose the moments prior to his unwanted nap.

Soriya was there, Loren noticed while taking stock of the room around him. She looked different, more alert than he had seen her over the last few days since learning about the death of Vladimir Luchik. He was glad someone was still on their feet to confront

Evans. Merrill and Daniels were dead. It was still unbelievable to think it. Naeger as well. God only knew about Jankowitz, remembering the crunching sound of her impact with not only Daniels' body but also the tinted window. Only one person remained unaccounted for and Loren spun on his backside for a clear line of sight to find his friend and captain.

Ruiz lay in the middle of the room on his stomach, turned away from Loren. He wasn't moving. Loren focused, his head cursing each squint of his eyes. Small shifts as Ruiz's back lifted and fell indicated the unconscious man was still breathing. Loren sighed with relief, hugging tight to the floor, scurrying along to grab Ruiz without attracting unwanted attention. He could hear the wails of the lights surrounding the tower. The lights above were all but out but the green glow from outside kept the room well lit.

"Ruiz?" Loren grabbed hold of his left arm and dragged him back to the safety of the executive desk. There was screaming around him—the cries of the fight between Soriya and Evans. They were fighting for an entire city and Loren was worried about a single man. Who had their priorities straight? Not that it mattered to the bloodied detective, who shuffled back to the relative safety of the desk.

Ruiz did not stir. He did not groan from his face rubbing against the tile from Loren's pulling. He did not curse in the Spanish-American hybrid that wasn't an actual dialect of either language, though no one would admit it to Ruiz. There was nothing.

"Come on, Ruiz," Loren whispered, begging the man who stood next to him at his wedding to wake up. "This is not the time to take a bow."

Slowly, Loren turned the unconscious body of Ruiz. He needed to check his pulse, needed to see for himself what had happened while he was out of the fight. He reached over, lifting the right arm and pulling it around. It was hot to the touch. The green glow illuminated the burned flesh that ran down the length of Ruiz's wrist and arm. Large bubbles of skin and deep red welts covered his forearm.

"No." Loren almost dropped his friend from the sight. He felt the heat of the wounds, saw the pain in the shaking brow of Ruiz. He was breathing—that was the saving grace. The wounds, however, were extensive.

Loren knelt close to his friend. He should have forced him to stay with Pratchett downstairs. He should have asked for more men from the start. Dammit, he should have done more.

Suddenly, he knew what Soriya had lived through over the last three days. The sense of loss. The sense of failure. Thinking of her reminded him of the struggle spanning the length of the room around them. He found his sidearm amid the pool of blood left in the wake of Gabriel Evans' demise. Loren felt the grip of the revolver slip into his palm.

Soriya's heel smashed into Evans' side, but the man did not fall. She went at him with everything she had left. There had been little sleep, little food, and little time for her over the last three days, but with each breath, she found a little more to give the suited man. He responded in kind but she kept her distance, waiting for openings when they came. His fist extended and she sidestepped it, using his reach against him to grab his arm. She lifted up her small frame, rolling over his arm and allowing her legs to kick out. Her feet connected squarely with his nose. A loud crunch resounded through the large office. She let loose his arm, allowing him to fall to the ground.

As he fell, she found her feet and pressed forward once more. "No more doubt. No more questioning. I am the Greystone."

Her fist struck solidly across his lips. Skin sheared off his face and she felt blood cling to her knuckles. From the force of the blow, Evans wheeled around so that his back was to her. He lay on his hands and knees, his breath erratic from the assault.

"This is my city. Not yours," Soriya's voice boomed.

Soriya loomed over the broken and beaten form of Nathaniel Evans. The winds flowing through the shattered windows surrounding the floor carried the long ribbons through the air. They snapped with each brisk wave of air, circling Soriya like a thin, pink shield. Her fists were clenched tight, small dribbles of blood falling from them. She failed to notice. It did not matter. All that mattered was that Mentor's killer stayed down.

Reaching into the pouch secured to her hip, Soriya once more retrieved the Greystone and held it before her.

When she turned, Evans made his move. He spun around quickly, his newly acquired stone tight in his palm. He extended it before him, the rune on its face glowing brighter with each second. Soriya fumbled with her own weapon at the sound of the rumbling outside the walls. Lightning cut through the glowing green cloud. It struck down then cut across the skyline of the city directly for the tower. She held tight to the stone, readying herself for the blow. It struck her straight on, sending her soaring across the floor away from Evans.

Crashing to the floor, she felt the impact of the first blow and the sizzle that left her blouse singed at the edges, her skin burned from the intensity. Evans stood tall, rubbing the dirt off his freshly pressed pants and jacket.

"This city is mine," he screamed over the lightning strikes that snapped past him. They kept her isolated in the center of the floor, unsure which way to turn. She cradled the Greystone, hoping for a moment to repay his kindness while he inched closer and closer. "This city has always been mine."

She saw the rune dim, shift to Thurisaz, and glow once more.

þ

Fire burst from the floor, pipes bursting around her. She felt the heat reach toward her, slowly collapsing in on her, causing a scream to escape her lips.

"It is mine to create or destroy." He laughed over her anguish, the stone extended before him. "Its fate is mine to determine. Learn that lesson well."

Fighting through the heat of the flames that nipped at her body, Soriya forced her arm up. The stone in her grip illuminated, and water pummeled against the onslaught of the flames. Steam separated them but Evans continued to step closer and closer, his leather shoes clicking along the tiles.

"Your teacher had to learn that lesson," Evans continued. The flames stretched farther, forcing the water back. The steam stung his eyes. It burned his flesh. Still he approached, his taunts filling the air. "I believe he finally understood just as I snapped the life out of his broken body."

"You bastard," Soriya shouted, hoarse from the vapors rising from their attacks. She was losing. She could feel it in her voice, in her stance, in the way the air constricted and the flames glowed brighter than the red eyes of her assailant. She found her feet, determined not to let another failure occur.

Loren watched in silent desperation as Evans inched toward Soriya. There was no doubt she was weakening. He had seen the onslaught of water slam against Ruiz with the force of a train. Her stream was a leaky faucet compared to that.

The flames slammed forward.

Loren found his feet, his sidearm in hand. Ruiz's breathing was shallow but continued. Loren let his friend rest on the tiles and moved for Evans.

"You can't stop the freeing of the Bypass," Evans continued. "You barely understand the power contained within. All yearning to be free to rain death over this world."

The water stopped and the flames erupted in Soriya's face, causing her to fall to her knees. Evans slammed her stone away with the swat of his hand. The Greystone flew through the room, skittering across the tiles. His fist returned with a backhand, hitting her cheek. Blood filled the inside of her mouth. She spat it out defiantly.

"You resist the inevitable. You fight things you can never understand."

Soriya understood plenty. She understood the threat the rising lights truly were for the city, watching them continue to amass and spread out over the skyline. She understood the power her attacker had accrued with the stone in his grasp. She watched the light under his fingertips glow, another rune activated. This one was not for her but for him, his cuts and seared flesh beginning to close and heal. She understood how defeated she was and how unlikely victory would be for her alone.

Evans leaned in. Soriya wound up and let a right cross connect with his cheek. He followed suit, pummeling her with his fist. Three quick blasts slammed into her with the force of an anvil. Her left eye swelled shut. Her cheek puffed. Blood soaked her hair, down her shoulders. All that and she still felt the smile creep across her face.

"I understand enough." She coughed, and blood spattered to the tile floor. "Like how human you've become to pull this off."

Evans right hand shot to his lip. Blood slipped to his fingertips and ran down to his palm. His empty palm. His eyes widened at the Greystone in Soriya's grasp.

She smiled. "And when a distraction is needed."

Evans heard the click of the gun near his temple, catching sight of an extremely pissed off Loren in the corner of his eye.

"Understand this, asshole."

The gun snapped back in Loren's grasp when the bullet ripped through Evans' head and out the other side. For a moment, the killer stood, carrying a look of shock in his red eyes. The shock dimmed, and his body—complete with his descendant's looks and clothing—fell to the floor of the penthouse office. Eyes once wide with victory and triumph closed and never reopened.

"Soriya." Loren rushed to her side. He helped her find her footing, sticking with the right side of her body to stay in sight, the left completely swelled over in a giant, purple bruise.

"I'm okay. I'm...."

Leaning heavily on Loren, the two waited over the body of Nathaniel Evans. They stood in silence, hoping, praying that the body remained fixed in place.

Satisfied with the results after what seemed to be an eternity, the two continued toward the shattered windows. As they inched closer to the edge, Soriya's hand clasped against Loren's chest to hold him back.

He shook his head. "I'll be fine."

Around them, the lights continued to spread outward. They glowed brighter and brighter, screamed louder and louder, slowly covering Portents from above. The shifting runes that covered the stone no longer glowed across its cool surface. Yet the lights continued.

There was fear in her eyes.

"What is it? Soriya, tell me."

Her voice was soft. A whisper against the wind.

"It's not over."

CHAPTER FORTY-FOUR

"What do you mean?" Loren yelled over the rushing wind. He took a step back from the ledge, turning Soriya so that she faced him. "How can it not be over?"

"Take a look, Loren. Do you see it ending?"

Around them, the lights spanned as far as they could see. There was nothing but the glowing green cloud, the city lost beneath it. The rushing wind pounded against them along the edge of the building. The wind continued to howl, forcing them to yell over it.

"We beat the bad guy, Soriya," Loren replied. After three days of running around looking for answers, the nightmare was supposed to be over. Evans was dead. It should have been over. "That's the rule. You beat the bad guy and everything goes back to normal. No freak storms. No quakes. Done and done. I'm talking fifth dimension rules here."

"Loren." Soriya smiled. "Sometimes I have no idea if you're speaking English or not."

"Good," replied her friend. "Tell me what we're facing."

Soriya looked out over the storm cloud of green light. "The energy is still bursting from the Bypass chamber."

"Causing the quakes and this."

She nodded. "There is a point where this ends. Where the cloud will reach maximum distance and then…"

"The box." Loren thought of the map and the four points he had drawn for Ruiz and Pratchett. "The scenes of the first four murders. They formed a box."

Of course, thought Soriya. Where she had spent her time unraveling the signs and the trophies, Loren figured out the location aspect of each scene. "If the chamber falls, if the energy stored within the Bypass spreads to those end points, the box as you called it, the cascade effect will level the city."

"Exactly what Evans wanted." Loren looked to the unmoving body of the mastermind. He wrote a story he wasn't able to see the end of after all. "How do we stop it?"

Soriya felt Mentor's Greystone within her grasp. From the far end of the room, she glimpsed her stone between the fallen bodies of Loren's colleagues. She turned to Loren, worry and doubt vanishing, her mind running through solution after solution to no avail. "We can't. I have to do this."

She left Loren, hobbling on weary limbs and burned flesh. She grabbed the stone in her free hand and held both before her. This was bigger than her. She knew it would take more than she had ever done, more than she had ever imagined. Looking at Mentor's stone, she felt him by her side. She needed him and he was there. That was the way it had always been. One last time, that was how it would be.

In the center of the room, she stopped. She looked in every direction. The cloud was moving faster, spreading wider. There was no more time for thought, no more time for planning when there was no plan to make.

She knelt on the floor, holding the two stones in front of her. She took a deep breath. Channeling energy into the stone was never something she had contemplated before, and never with two stones at the same time. There were so many unknowns. So much could go wrong. She refused to allow it.

Loren called out to her.

"Soriya."

She glanced at him, his ruffled hair and uneven beard. He looked better than he had in years, even soaked in blood. She smiled at him. "I am glad, you know. Glad you came back. Even now."

"So am I. Even now." He nodded. There was concern on his face. He needed answers to a question he was afraid to ask, knowing she wouldn't reply. "You don't have to be the one to do this."

She took a deep breath. "Yes, I do. It's my job."

"But—"

"Greg," she said, closing her eye and holding the two Greystones before her, letting them rest on open palms. "No more talking."

"Right." Loren stepped back toward Ruiz, pulling the unconscious man further under the desk.

Soriya lifted the two stones to eye level. Every ounce of will, every shred of concentration poured from her mind through her body to the waiting stones. Every hope, every dream, every single moment of pure joy fed into the Greystones. Slowly, they began to glow.

She pictured in her mind the five symbols scrawled throughout the city. Five symbols that unlocked the secret of the Bypass for the entire population of Portents to see for the first time. Each one lay before her mind's eye and she fed them into the Greystones. She started with the final one—Mentor's sign—and worked her way back to Abigail Fortune. Each one, from Vincan to Gothic, fed into the stone in reverse. The stones began to hum within her grasp. She inched them closer together, the light of each sign illuminating the surface of the stones. Faster and faster they scanned atop each slab, causing the two stones to vibrate as they closed in on one another. Her two hands pushed together and so did the stones, folding into the same space while the light of the rotating signs glowed brighter and brighter on their surface. All shadows in the enormous office faded before the light of the Greystones.

"Balance is the key," she heard Mentor say, his stone and hers working together as they always had. He was with her, the teacher watching over his student. She believed that more than ever, no matter the name he carried and no matter the past. He was with her when she needed him most. She was never alone.

"Balance moves through us into the world. The Bypass is one half. The Greystone is the other. Have faith, little one. As I do in you."

Light exploded outward from the stones in all directions. The eighty-sixth floor of the obsidian tower lit up like a Christmas tree, everything turning white before cracking along the heavens.

The light spread out from the tower, riding the wave of the glowing green cloud stretching over the city's skyline. Melding with the energy of the Bypass, it became a giant spotlight in the sky. Below in the city streets, the quakes dissipated. The cracks along the pavement folded. The city healed from the combined efforts of the Bypass and the Greystone.

The light washed over the city, taking with it everything Evans had set forth, and put it back where it belonged. The energies of the Bypass folded into the light and faded when the bright white of the Greystones spread out faster and faster.

As it passed the limits of Portents, it faded, leaving behind only the clear night sky. Darkness returned over the city. The streets were no longer cracked, no longer exposing the sewers and tunnels below.

The city was safe. The threat was over.

Loren stood up from the safety of the desk. Ruiz did not budge. Loren watched his chest rise and fall with each breath. He stepped to the side of the floor, the cool night breeze cutting through him. The shadows of the evening sprawled out over the city like a blanket. His feet did not shake beneath him. There was silence in the air. No wails of pain or screams of joy riding the wave. Silence filled him with peace.

"Fifth dimension rules. That's what I was talking about." His laughter echoed out over the city he never called home, yet felt more in tune with every second he stayed. "No more quakes. No more lights. Tell me we won, Soriya."

Her body lay in the center of the room. It convulsed wildly in the darkness. Loren raced over to her, pulling her bruised and broken body close to keep her from shaking. She fought his hold, her eyes refusing to open. Her body wanted to shake itself loose along the floor but he refused to let go.

"No," Loren whispered, holding her against him. "Dammit, Soriya. Come on now. Stay with me."

As suddenly as it started, it stopped. Soriya's body simply stopped. Her eyes refused to open. Her lungs refused to breathe. Her heart refused to beat. Loren called out to her in the darkness.

"Stay…"

CHAPTER FORTY-FIVE

Mercy Hospital saw a surge in traffic during the two weeks that followed *The Night of the Lights*. The initial waves of patients brought lacerations and concussions from the shattering of glass throughout the eight-block radius engulfed in chaos that night. The hospital was always a hotbed for this type of activity and several others, with its position downtown in the shadow of the obsidian tower. Most patients arrived from drunken arguments from the downtown bar scene, or were escorted by police from failed attempts down the diamond strip. Never had there been so many people from a single incident that seemed to stretch the boundaries of the services offered at Mercy.

There were side effects from *The Night of the Lights*. Headaches. Nightmares. The Children's Ward was maxed out with youngsters carrying fevers of 103 and higher. The Suicide Hotline carried double shifts for its employees with every line occupied. When one call was completed, successfully pulling someone back from the ledge, sometimes literally, another call would break through seconds later. There was no end to it during the fourteen-day period after that night.

No one on the staff spoke about it. They were too busy, too focused on the patients at hand. Looks were the only thing exchanged between them, cold and fearful stares at what would come next. Every nurse, every doctor, every intern and resident on staff fought through the fear to get the job done. The city of Portents came together to work through that night at Mercy Hospital. Volunteers lined the halls, helping talk patients through what was seen, what was felt, to try to heal the wounds created by the singular event.

A wall was started. A single nurse came up with the idea, late in her shift. She had finished checking the vitals of a young boy. His fever broke in the middle of the day and a youthful glow was slowly returning to his face. She sat with him listening about the night he saw his grandparents walking the halls of his home. He was scared of them, but he didn't know why. The nurse held him close, whispering repeatedly. *"You survived."* She took out a flyer, one they used during charity drives, and wrote the boy's name on it. She placed it on the wall leading to the emergency ward of the hospital. Soon, other names joined the wall and a large banner hung above them reading, *Survival Makes Us Stronger.*

As the second week rolled on, every patient filled out a flyer and posted it on the wall when they were discharged from Mercy Hospital's care. Hundreds of names hung on the wall. From the young to the old. From the scared to the wounded to the sick. It was an affirmation. It was a point of pride. Surviving in Portents. There was much discussion, through the news, about what occurred. Speculation. Theories. Each one that arose made the night seem less real to the people, until finally they stopped. The night was still there, held around their memories like a fly buzzing near an ear. It was real for the patients of Mercy Hospital. The names of every patient hanging on the wall confirmed that much. Every name with every face as doctors and nurses rushed back and forth to the dozen emergencies that lined the halls and filled the rooms.

Only one patient remained nameless—a young woman in her early twenties. Brown skinned with long, dark hair that covered her shoulders. The purple had faded to yellows and greens but the bruise that made up the left side of her face remained. Small burns covered her arms and legs. Her knuckles were broken on her right hand. Dozens of monitors and machines surrounded her bedside on the third floor of the ICU. Heart monitors. Breathing tubes. Everything to keep her body functioning while it attempted to knit itself back together. She was one of the few with serious injuries from that night, as if she had been in the fight of her life. To the staff, she was the only Jane Doe in the building. To the detective that visited her room nightly, she carried a different name.

When Loren brought Soriya to the hospital that night, he was sure he was too late. There was no pulse. There was no sign of life. Her face faded before him as he carried her down a city block to the hospital from the base of the black tower. In the swarm of people that had taken refuge at the facility, he was a lone man screaming for help. It took Pratchett's calming presence to slow the panic in Loren's heart. The tall officer held tight to Ruiz's body, his badge shining on his uniform like a beacon for the doctors passing in the hall. They rushed over and took Ruiz and Soriya. Ruiz would be fine, Loren knew. There was breath in his body, though Evans' brutal attack would never truly leave his friend.

Soriya, though, was another matter. Pratchett asked no questions. He made no comments, the two of them waiting that night in the shadow of the dark tower. Jankowitz had joined her colleagues on the eighty-sixth floor; the crushing blow of Daniels' body in combination with the tinted window had killed her as easily as the other three officers. Loren and Ruiz were the sole survivors.

It took hours but eventually someone returned with news. Soriya, her name not given by Loren or Pratchett for her safety, was alive. Barely. She was in a coma and that was where she remained two weeks later.

Loren sipped his coffee by her bedside. The small Styrofoam cup crinkled in his hand, distracting him from the beeping of the machines that surrounded the bed. He had been stopping by the room every night since the tower. He sat, mostly in silence, watching the breathing tubes keep air in Soriya's lungs and listening to the slow beeping of her heart monitor. The first week had been split between her room and Ruiz's down the hall. Most of the time he stayed away as Michelle and Ruiz's three daughters showered the lucky man with love. After seven days of Jell-O and daytime television, Ruiz had had enough. As he always did, he discharged himself rather than wait for a doctor to give approval.

Loren spent much of the second week by Soriya's bedside. When the nurses came by asking if he needed anything, he waved them off. He held his coffee cup up and claimed that was all he could possibly want. It wasn't true. He wanted—he *needed*—her to wake up. It took that night in the shadow of the tower to see that he needed her by his side as much as she needed him. Through loss, through failure and darkness, they found each other.

As the stares continued, as the questions mounted from the staff of the hospital, Loren realized from their eyes how bad he truly looked. His beard was completely overgrown. His button-down shirt was missing two buttons, one on the cufflinks where his sleeve was torn. Showers were staggered. Sleep was even less periodic. It was as if the night atop the tower had never ended, would never end until he saw the wide glow of her eyes again. Some sign that they would make it.

The coffee made him jittery, his leg beating a tune against the floor. It was drowned out by the sound of the monitors. His eyes refused to watch her struggle to live. He took another sip, his eyes on the floor and the small bag he brought with him.

"The newspapers have stopped fishing for stories about what happened," he said aloud, trying to keep his eyes from closing. "They know they'd never understand what we would tell them anyway. Understand or believe. Keeping the public in the dark makes more sense than informing them that a corrupt soul from Hell just tried to destroy the city with a mystical energy source that no one can comprehend."

He imagined her anger rising at another secret kept from the city. Soriya believed that Portents could handle the truth, no matter how extreme. She, however, did not see the fear that ran through the people in the hospital or the despair of the calls that rang through looking for someone to explain why the screams of the dead wouldn't go away. Some truths came with too high a price. The sanity of a city was such a cost and Loren refused to pay it.

"Ruiz is back on his feet," he continued, finishing the cold cup of coffee in his hands. "I've only been to see him twice since he escaped his tormentors here but he looked like…well, he looked like Ruiz, I guess. He wouldn't talk about what happened or the scars it left him down his right arm. He wouldn't talk about much, actually. I've known him a long time. We've been through a lot, seen a lot, and I don't think I've ever seen him look so tired. He'll bounce back. He has to bounce back. Just like you."

His hand reached out and covered hers. He squeezed it gently. They were all more tired than they had been weeks before. Before Evans. So much had changed.

"This is my city." He felt a smirk creep on the corner of his lips. "I can't believe you said that to him. But it's true, isn't it? It is your city. Just like it was Beth's. Did I ever tell you what she used to call me? The world's worst date. Married me anyway, so what does that say about her, but it was true. I was. I went to the same restaurants, ate the same food. Take me out of my comfort zone and I was a wreck. I knew everything I liked in a three-block radius around our apartment, and that was it. Everything else was foreign and I wanted nothing to do with it. She owned this city, knew every corner, every deli, every store. I was too wrapped up in comparing Portents to Chicago that I never saw it the way she did. The joy and the wonder she saw and wrote about in her work. The joy that you see."

Loren leaned in close. The bruise that covered her left side blocked the right side from view. It shone in the dim overhead lights of the room.

"She knew, didn't she?" Loren picked at the cup in his hands, tearing little pieces of foam from the lip. "The way she knew about the city, the true city. It wasn't just something in a book. Some research she had done. Somehow she knew the truth about the city, the truth you shared with me after she was gone. She knew about it the whole time and never said a word. Never told me."

The weary detective sat back, letting it sink in. He had thought about it since he found the book sitting on Mentor's bed in the Bypass chamber. Since cracking it open for the first time at Atlas Books and learning about the existence of Nathaniel Evans. Beth was more in tune with the city than anyone he had ever met. The true city.

Even Soriya Greystone.

"I called my sister after that night. After Evans. She didn't understand, at first. Thought I needed to be back in Chicago, thought it was the right move so I could forget Beth. I thought the same thing for so long, convinced myself of it every day I was here because without her, even those three blocks became shadows. I convinced myself that my family was there, but that wasn't true either. It was here. In Portents, of all places. With Ruiz. With you." His voice was soft, little more than a whisper in her ear. "Dammit, Soriya. I won't do this without you."

Leaning back, he reached for the bag by the chair. He set it on his lap, letting a hand slip in to retrieve the single item within. The Greystone. He held it in front of her closed eyes, then placed it on the bedside table. It was bigger than it had been, no longer a small pebble resting on a single palm but a hefty weight that clanged when it came to rest on the table.

"I brought this for you. I was hoping to bring it sooner but if Ruiz knew I took it from the scene, he would have flipped. I don't know how or why but there was only one. Like the two stones melded, if that even makes sense. Hell, nothing ever makes sense when it comes to this stuff." Loren stared at the stone, little more than a paperweight when carried by anyone else. "I don't know what it can do. After that night, I don't think I ever want to find out. But it helped you stop Evans. It stopped the lights. I'm hoping it can help you too."

"I'm out of fuel." Loren held up the empty cup with a smile. The stone sat silent on the bedside table. No light glowed. No change occurred. Slowly, he stood up. His knees ached from sitting. His head rang every time he took to his feet from the small gash above his temple. The door clicked open. He waited in the frame, looking back once more, hoping for open eyes in return. When the machines continued to beep and buzz around her as her response, his head lowered. "I'll be right back."

The door closed behind him, leaving nothing but the sound of the machines keeping Soriya Greystone alive. It began moments later with a whisper and a glimmer. Soft light lit the surface of the stone on the bedside table. Gradually, it turned to a white glow, its surface marked by a single rune.

𐌔

The white light expanded, spreading across the room. Monitors buzzed and beeped louder and louder. The light beamed out of the half window of the doorway into the hall. A sharp cry for air echoed in the room as lungs fought to breathe on their own.

For the first time in two weeks, brown eyes burst open.

Down the hall, Loren watched the cup of coffee fill up slowly. It came out thick and black. He stopped halfway to give him space for the powdered creamer and the three packets of sugar he needed to block the awful taste of the black ooze. Coffee was a means to an end but never an enjoyable one. It served a function for him.

When he looked back at the room where Soriya lay, light greeted him. It showered the hall in a bright haze, spreading farther and farther. Loren dropped the coffee on the floor of the hospital hall and raced into the light. *Was it the stone? Was it something more?* He didn't know. All he knew was that he needed to see her, see that she was safe. To know she would always be safe.

The light faded before he reached the door. His hand fumbled with the lever until he heard a heavy click and the door flew open into the room. No surprise covered his face. No shock at the sight before him. All that remained was a grin that grew wider upon entering the room. An empty bed greeted him with the sound of flat-lining monitors and sensors from the machines. The stone was missing from the bedside table. The third floor window was open, blowing the shade back and forth with the night air circling the room.

Soriya Greystone was gone.

Loren stepped toward the window, peering out into the warm summer night that had settled over the city of Portents. His smile refused to fade and he called out into the night.

"I guess I'll see you at the office."

CHAPTER FORTY-SIX

Ruiz stood in the dim light of his office, looking out the window at the streets below. The desk lamp cast a long shadow over him. He was decorated in his dress uniform, his badge shining on his left with twin medals adorning the right side of the jacket. All of the flags that lined the Rath Building stood at half-mast. They had for over two weeks, ever since *The Night of the Lights* and the black tower. Four officers fell in the line of duty that night at the hands of a monster that threatened to take Portents with them. Merrill and Daniels. Jankowitz and Naeger—gone. The thought of their names brought back the night, the sight of their bodies on the tiled floor and the heat from the wound that covered his right arm from wrist to elbow.

The memorial service was earlier that day. It rained, of course. A fitting tribute for a city in mourning. A warm summer rain that brought an array of colors to the field where his fellow officers now rested. Michelle and the girls joined him on the podium when he offered a final tribute to his fallen friends. It had been a long time since he had to go through that, a long time since a man had fallen under his command. He hoped it would never be necessary again, though the sting in his arm assured him it was inevitable.

Everyone was there. The mayor and the commissioner used the opportunity to return hope to the people, while also remembering there was an election only a year away. Even Mathers kept a low head and a somber tone, sharing thoughts on the tragedy that befell the Central Precinct. Ruiz hoped it meant a truce between them, at least a holding off of hostilities, but as the day shift captain stepped away from the podium, a look shot Ruiz's way let him know there would be no end.

Of all the people gathered in the crowd, Ruiz was glad to see Loren among them. He wore a dark blue shirt with a red tie under a black leather jacket. Though his eyes were deep shadows from lack of sleep, the thick beard that had covered his face was gone. The long threads of hair were trimmed and combed. He looked like a new man to the aging captain.

Loren stood in the dim light of the office, his leather jacket slung over his arm. He played with his tie, threatening to rip the clip free from his collar. Ruiz kept his back to him, maintaining a long silence. Both men carried the burden of that night. They would never forget the four fallen colleagues that could have easily been them lying on the tiled floor of the black tower. The right arm of Ruiz was tucked in front of him, out of sight from Loren, though Ruiz noted the concern in his friend's eyes every time he grazed his forearm.

Neither one wanted to speak. The precinct was running quietly all around them, the memorial service carrying over into the hearts and minds of everyone wearing a badge. Heads were low, voices muted. The men and women of the Central Precinct went about their work to keep nights like that from occurring ever again. All discussion of the night in question had fallen away. It happened. Something happened.

Ruiz kept the official report as clean as possible. A madman had taken the lives of six people, including the head of the city's largest corporation, Gabriel Evans. The madman had no name, Hady Ronne coming up empty on any identifying markers on the corpse. Turning away from the endless questions and making it about the dead officers was a clear sign of what truly mattered when all was said and done.

The lights. The Greystone. Nathaniel Evans. None of that entered into the matter. There were inquiries, there were debates, but all were agreed that the lives of their four colleagues outweighed everything else. Loren agreed as well, surprising Ruiz. There was a calm in him, one that settled the issue that had been hanging over the weary captain since recruiting the man for the case.

Sitting in the center of the desk, amid the mountain of reports and paperwork put off during Ruiz's hospital stay, was a badge. Gold plated metal shined under the dim light of the lamp. Across the top, it read *P.P.D.* with the word *Detective* underneath the shield in the middle.

It sat before Loren, daring him to act. It drew him close. He felt the weight of it even from a distance. He had come so far. He had lost so much. Yet the badge was clear, polished, as if the history they shared was erased and this was a new beginning. His call with Chicago went badly; he would be lucky if his sister picked up the phone again if he needed her. His shot with the Chicago P.D. was blown as well, having used up every excuse to stay on in Portents to watch over his friends. And now the badge.

Loren lifted it up, letting it rest across his palm. Ruiz remained silent at the back of the office. His left hand ran up the length of his right arm. Each touch sent a visible chill through his body.

"Are you sure?" Loren asked. His finger ran across the embossed lettering on the shield.

Ruiz turned his head slowly, keeping his right arm out of sight. "I don't need another counseling session from you. Michelle pushes me enough."

"You're making important decisions, Ruiz," Loren replied softly, turning to close the door to the office. "If they're coming from a personal place instead of a professional one, we should talk about it."

"I can still feel it, you know." Ruiz turned. Slowly, he removed the glove covering his right hand. It fell flat against the desk, the light washing over his scarred appendage. He rolled the sleeve gently up his arm. The scars ran along his forearm in no distinctive pattern except for at the wrist. There, the fingers of Evans were still visible from their point of contact. "Even though the nerve endings are shot to hell, I can still feel his hand burning into my flesh. I'm warm all the time to the point of sweating even with the air conditioner blasting down on me. The feeling wakes me in the middle of the night and I swear I'm going to see those red eyes staring at me from the end of the bed. Worse, that I won't see Michelle or the kids ever again. Doctors say I'll be lucky to lift a coffee cup much less my sidearm, so the department softball team is off the table for me this season."

Neither laughed at the joke. The scars were too deep between them.

"I know where I'm coming from on this, Loren. The commissioner signed off on it, despite Mathers pitching a fit. There was no denying your role in the Evans case, no matter the result. You saved lives, Loren. Hell, you probably saved the damn city." Ruiz's eyes locked on the badge in Loren's grip. "You know it, same as I do. The real question is, are *you* sure?"

It was a question he had been asking for days. He debated it for hours on end in the hospital room where Soriya lay sleeping. Beth was here, the memory of her death and the absent feeling of closure in solving her murder. The anger and the mistakes. The feeling that took most of the last four years away from him, years lost trying to solve her case. To understand her death.

It had been a downward spiral. He lost his last chance to reconcile with his father, and unwittingly lost his mother in the process because of his obsession. He was afraid it would happen again. He was afraid he was not strong enough to fight the urge to spin out of control again. There had been moments in those four years when he closed his eyes, where he was fine with never opening them again. There were moments of true depression mixed with rage and anger over the pain of her death. His own inability to see past her deep blue eyes when they closed before him on the pavement in front of their apartment made it impossible to breathe during those years.

But here he was. Here he remained, even after all of it. All of the struggle. All of the grief. Here he was in Portents. Always Portents. He tried for so long to pass the city off as not his own. Now, he wore it as clearly as the badge he held in his hand. Like the signs littering the wall of Mercy Hospital, he survived. This was his city as much as anyone else. There was no more denying that.

Ruiz watched his friend's sullen eyes, carefully studying the badge before him. "The city is changing, Loren. Evans showed us that and I can no longer stand idly by. I'll never see it the way Soriya does, never understand it the way she always has or allow the city to see that way either no matter the cost, but we have to hold the line. Us. You'll be completely independent in operational status, answerable only to me. You will, however, follow the procedures and guidelines laid out to the rest of the department. There will be questions. Especially from Mathers who will be watching like a hawk. People will not understand so you'll have to handle a regular caseload on top of the...let's call them *special circumstances* that arise. The job is yours...if you want it."

The corner of Loren's lip rose slightly. His finger ran along the badge one last time. Then he slipped the cool metal shield into his right pocket. "You knew my answer the second you called me for the Evans case."

"Yeah, I did." Ruiz nodded.

From the darkness that washed over him, Loren saw the calmness settle over Ruiz and the slight twitch of his lips into what passed for a smile. Few of those were visible over the last two weeks. He hoped that was changing.

Loren turned for the door. Reaching for the handle, he could hear the slow buzz of the floor. People scattered from place to place. He smelled the thick odor of black coffee in the air and heard the clattering of reports being typed. It felt right. It felt like home.

Ruiz called him back as he stood before the open door. "You can't do it alone, you know."

"I know," Loren admitted. A stick of gum slipped between his lips. *Filthy habit.* Ruiz returned to the window and the city streets below. Night was covering Portents like a blanket.

"You think she's out there?" Ruiz asked. Loren's tall reflection gleamed in the window. Ruiz heard the deep confidence in the voice of his friend echoing through the office before Greg Loren stepped out to start his shift.

"I'm sure of it."

CHAPTER FORTY-SEVEN

She unlocked the door to the apartment, her lips inviting, her name unknown. She was quick to leave the bar where Francis McKay had been having a bite to eat and a lemon-lime soda with some colleagues. Beer never agreed with him and liquor made weeks fade from memory. Caffeine was also an irritant that caused his bladder to shrink to the size of a walnut so the flat lemon lime soda was the beverage of choice when among friends. At least, Francis thought they were friends. He never really knew. Half his life spent in a lab, the other reliving the first half in his own mind, so sitting with other people and listening to conversations was a nice change of pace.

A nicer change was her arrival. Tall, with long legs barely covered by a tight red dress. She approached quickly and efficiently, never letting his mumbling or stuttering slow her down. She wanted him, though he had never seen her before. His mother told him never to talk to strangers—but truthfully, everyone was a stranger. The woman in the red dress was no exception. She pulled him away from his colleagues, away from everything in the bar, and he never stopped her. Never wanted to stop her.

Dating had been a trial and error process with Francis at a young age, in the fact that he tried and failed to land a date his entire life. Women that surrounded him walked the line between too attractive or too self-involved, much like Francis was when it came to his work. The fact became apparently clear that the choice between work and women was relatively simple for a man who went to three proms without a date. His little black book contained more formulas for fusion reactors than it did telephone numbers of women.

Saying he was happy for the change of pace was an understatement.

He tried to speak during the trip to her apartment. He managed a few mumblings that were lost to the summer wind that whipped through the streets of Portents. Mutterings that would never outstrip the rush he felt at her advances, forcing him down streets he never knew to buildings he had never seen before. Her place was in a large ten-story building near Fulcrum by the expressway running north to Venture Cove. She had a corner apartment on the seventh floor. Unlocking the door, Francis kept his hands busy, fumbling with his tie. He tried not to think of the three lemon-lime sodas he drank or the square root of 1,232,100, hoping to keep everything perfect.

"Come on in," she beckoned. Her hand, with thick red fingernails, ran along his back, pressing him forward through the opened door.

A fixed grin ran from ear to ear along his face. His feet carried him through the living room of the apartment, but his eyes failed to see what was around him. All he saw was the red of her dress while she closed the door and locked it. He wanted to say something clever. He wanted to be charming and funny, with a "you sure don't waste time," but the only sounds that exited his lips ended up being more nonsensical gibberish that only an infant would find entertaining.

"Enough talk," she said, her hand gripping his tie. She pulled him deeper into the apartment. She let the tie slip away, stepping into the darkness of the bedroom at the far end of the hall. Francis stayed in place, unsure of what to do. He loosened his tie. It felt natural to do that for some reason. The collar of his shirt opened up. Two buttons. *That was enough*, he thought, *right? Two—wait, three. That works.* He wasn't sure how much time had passed during his scientific deliberations on buttons, but when a hand reached out of the shadows and a single finger rose, begging his entrance to the room, he was sure it had been too long.

Francis McKay entered the bedroom. He was greeted by a thin stream of moonlight through thick curtains. They blew casually, the wind carrying them through the open window on the far side of the room. From the light, he saw the large bed in the center of the room, stripped down to the sheet. He walked over to it and sat on the edge, waiting patiently. He looked around for his host, confused.

"Hello?" he called into the dark. He played with another button on his shirt then slapped his hand away. Instead, his palms slapped against his thighs with a distracting melody. He did not know where he was. He did not know whom he was with. What the hell was he doing?

He scanned the room until he caught sight of a single leg. He followed it up until the shape of the woman came into view through the darkness.

"I didn't see you there," he managed to stammer out between deep breaths that reminded him of bad asthma days and gym class.

She stepped out of the shadows, the woman with the red dress and the long legs. The moonlight greeted her, only she was not the same as she had been when she first approached him at the bar. Her brow was creased. Her eyes were tinged with a dark yellow. When she opened her mouth, Francis McKay saw nothing but fangs and heard his mother cursing him from beyond the grave for not listening to her sage advice.

He screamed in a high-pitched squeal, though he pretended that the fear brought out a deeper quality to his voice. He leapt to his feet, racing for the door, only to find her barring the way.

She laughed, her sharp teeth glinting in the light of the moon. He fell back against the bed, her long slender legs carrying her closer and closer to him. She bared her teeth.

Francis McKay was not happy with the current change of pace, wishing the last would have endured a little longer. He whimpered, his hands folded in prayer.

"God, no..."

He felt a hand wrap around his chin and hot breath on his neck. "Shhh. No praying. It sours the taste."

"We wouldn't want that, would we?" a voice called out of the darkness. Both turned to the young woman stepping out of the shadows of the room. She wore a tight bodice and torn jeans. Ribbons ran down the length of her left arm, whipping around her body with the night wind. Behind her, the moon shone brightly in a cloudless sky though the rumble of thunder rang out in the distance.

"Who the hell are you?" the woman roared, fangs dripping with saliva. Francis McKay felt his attacker's grip loosen. He slipped away from her, stumbling backward for the hall and his freedom.

"Call me the welcome wagon," the dark-skinned woman answered, her wry smirk escaping the shadows on her face. In her hands, she held a large stone. Adorning its surface was a symbol.

ᚺ

The rumbling of thunder outside grew louder. The symbol burned brightly, illuminating every corner of the room around them. The woman smiled widely. "Hope you enjoyed your stay."

Out of the clear night sky, a single bolt of lightning snapped from the heavens. It split the skyline, turned down over the city and shot through the seventh floor window of an inconspicuous apartment building.

Life continued in the city of Portents.

ABOUT THE AUTHOR

Lou Paduano is the author of the Greystone series of novels including the upcoming collection, *Tales from Portents*. He lives in Buffalo, New York with his wife and two daughters. Sign up for his e-mail list for free content as well as updates on future releases at www.loupaduano.com.

GREYSTONE CONTINUES IN…

Six tales of monsters, the dead rising, and the terrors of Portents.

The beasts Detective Loren and Soriya Greystone battled in *Signs of Portents* were just a hint of what lurks in the city. *Tales from Portents* explores the city's immersive history, including stories of Loren's descent after his wife's death—and his opportunity to have her rise from the grave.

Among the pages, Soriya battles gremlins, navigates lessons with Mentor, and meets the werewolf Luchik. Follow new characters with expansive histories as they come face to face with the horrors of Portents—both human and otherwise.

From the Greystone Collection, *Tales from Portents* navigates the cases that make even Detective Loren lie awake at night.

Made in the USA
Middletown, DE
29 March 2023